In LIEU

Barry Dean

IN L.I.E.U.

Copyright 2019 Hague Publishing

Hague Publishing
PO Box 451
Bassendean Western Australia 6934

Email: contact@haguepublishing.com
Web: www.haguepublishing.com

ISBN 978-0-6480503-8-4

Cover Art: *In LIEU* by Jade Zivanovic
https://www.steampowerstudios.com.au/

Typeset Garamond 12/13

Acknowledgement

Many thanks to my wife Theresa for her patience and indulgence, and my friend Colleen for her sensibility.

Preramble

THERE are some who believe in destiny and for them life follows a fixed line with the future preordained. Others believe that life meanders toward crossroads and decisions made at those times determine the pathway to the next sliding door. Holly Penworthy believed in the latter, but she was wrong. Her destiny was decided by others when she was chosen to participate in a physics experiment involving time and motion. Not the archaic practice that allowed management to harass workers, but an experiment infinitely larger and, to most humans, mind-bogglingly complicated. This experiment concerned the manipulation of time and the relative movement of Earth within a minor outer arm of the spiral galaxy we humans call the Milky Way.

Holly had no idea about her selection. In fact, she had no knowledge that there are two schools of thought on the relative movement of Earth. The first is that Earth moves around our sun in a roughly circular orbit. It covers this route at a speed of around 30 kilometres per second. In addition, our solar system whirls around the centre of its galaxy at some 220 kilometres per second. With such speeds, it seems that Earth must be in a hurry to get somewhere. The question is: 'where?' It matters little to most of the planet's inhabitants but we are actually hurtling through space toward a structure called the Great Attractor. This thing is in a region of space about 150 million light-years from Earth. Accordingly, it's a waste of time keeping an eye out for it. The second school of thought is that you may become just as confused by listening to Monty Python's Galaxy song. The bottom line is that Earth hurtles through space while its inhabitants sit on their collective arses and go along for the ride.

You may well ask what this has to do with Holly Penworthy. The answer is simple. The movement of Earth leads to science, science leads to scientists, and scientists can be genii. In AD 2253, one such genius worked out how to harness the dark matter of the Great Attractor and created a machine capable of travelling backward through time. This created paperwork, paperwork created the need for a library and every library must have a librarian. Holly Penworthy was trained as a librarian.

First Encounter — 1940

HOLLY Penworthy's first encounter with her future occurred on the twenty-ninth of September 1940. Her parents had sent her to the small village of Agarle in southern Kent to keep her safe from the London bombings. She caught the train from London to Ashford and then the bus to Agarle. During the journey she tried to understand why her parents would send her to a place between the coast and London but fourteen year olds have no say in family decisions.

She was picked up at the bus stop by her Uncle Ben who was a man in his late fifties with the stoop of a peasant farmer and ginger hairs growing from his enormous ears. He probably had a face but Holly couldn't see it under the matted red beard that hung from his eyes to his chest and made his face look like the back end of a tailless wolfhound. Aunt Edith, on the other hand, had a face that Holly could not help but notice. Unfortunately, it was hard to tell whether it was the cankerous mole on the side of her nose or the beagle eyes that won the most prominent feature race. To Holly, they shared the honours.

Despite looks that would scare a ghost from a house, both Ben and Edith were kind-souled individuals who, as part of the civil defence league, were on duty that fateful night.

It was just after eight, and Holly was alone in the house. She was brushing out her long, blonde hair before bed when the light of her bedroom lamp was suddenly overwhelmed by a powerful light shining through the blackout curtains. She froze. It was impossible. She stared at the curtains, not knowing what to think or what to do. If only Uncle Ben and Aunt Edith were home they would guide her. But they weren't, so she had to make her own decisions.

Pinpricks ran the length of her spine and goosebumps covered her arms as she pulled the curtains aside. Outside was another impossibility;

a small patch of daylight in the night sky. A perfect circle of blue and cloudless visibility stretched up to the outer reaches of space. She closed her eyes and shook her head, trying to deny what she saw. When she reopened them, the patch of daylight was still there. Elsewhere, the night sky pervaded everything with an eerie blackness, broken only by the searchlights that created a curtain of light along the coast.

Holly couldn't understand what she was seeing. She stepped back from the window and reclosed the curtains. It made no difference to the light; some unknown force was holding the darkness at bay. She flung open the window, stuck her head out and looked left and right. The houses on either side were shrouded in darkness. Daylight shone only on her window. Something was very wrong.

Holly reclosed the window, pulled the curtain across, changed from pyjamas to her floral cotton dress, and then pulled on her school socks and shoes. She ran downstairs and out of the back door of the house. Once outside, she looked again at the sky. The daylight circle had followed her.

At that same instant, six thousand feet above her, the pilot of a German Heinkel He-111 cursed as his second engine spluttered and died. He wrestled with the controls, trying to angle the crippled plane slightly upward, but to no avail.

Holly first saw the Heinkel as it entered her patch of daylight and knew immediately that something was wrong. The plane's only sound was the rushing of the air past its wings as it plunged toward her. She stood, transfixed, gawping at the falling aircraft. Her brain screamed at her to move but there was concrete in her feet.

It was at the moment she turned to run that she saw the door in the wall. Given time she would have wondered why, despite staying with her aunt and uncle for a week, she had never noticed the two storey granite brick wall that now consumed the backyard. But she didn't have time, so ran toward the beaten copper door that stood inside a narrow Corinthian columned portico. She reached the door and grabbed at its huge brass handle, shaped like a musical F clef. It didn't budge. She looked over her shoulder at the plane. It was much closer and seemed to be hurtling directly toward her. For some reason she read the name above the door *Li . . . In . . . A . .* The rest of the name was covered in bracken and dead leaves.

She pounded the door, frantically pushed down on the handle. Her small wrists strained against the pressure of exertion. After what seemed like years but was, in fact, milliseconds, the handle moved and, with a sonorous click, the door opened.

Holly dashed inside, slammed the door behind her and looked for somewhere to hide.

Time stopped. The sound of wind rushing past wings disappeared; replaced by a soft melody that Holly had never heard before. The sound seemed to be coming from everywhere but nowhere in particular. She stopped and looked around. She was standing in what appeared to be a small anteroom. It was pentagon shaped, with ornate wooden doors set into two of its facets. The word LIBRARY was inscribed in large red-wood letters above one door. To its right, above the other door was written ACTIVITIES ROOM. Set into the white marble floor was the word L.I.E.U, in black marble lettering. She had no idea what the word meant.

Scared and mystified she cuddled herself, shivered, and waited for something to happen. She thought of Alice in Wonderland with rabbits and strange creatures, but this was different. This was no rabbit hole. This was an enormous building.

When nothing happened after several minutes, she walked to the Activities Room door and tried the handle. The door opened with a squeak. She put her hands to her mouth as she saw the size of the room beyond. There were four full size billiard tables and a small stage with ten rows of seats in a deep alcove, a kitchenette and a row of wooden tables. Everything was covered in a thin layer of dust. It was as if the space hadn't been occupied for years. She looked at the far end wall and shook her head in disbelief as she pictured the Cock Lane parish church at the rear of her uncle's property. The rooms and alcoves ran well past the parish church. This place simply could not exist.

She returned to the anteroom and tried the handle on the Library door. The door opened immediately on well-greased hinges. Through the doorway she could see a large glass-panelled bookcase against one wall. Beyond the bookcase was an ornate archway that led to a vast oval room. Moving to the archway she tried to understand what she saw. Three tiers of book shelves, with their own walkways, ran the length of the curved walls. Polished brass rails were attached to the top of each tier, and redwood ladders, attached to the rails, slid sideways to allow the ladders to be moved horizontally. There were reading desks and seating. Each desk had a green lamp shade on a brass base. Plush pile black carpet covered the floor. She examined a brass handrail. It showed her reflection. Unlike the adjacent room, there was not a speck of dust anywhere.

"Is anyone here?" she called.

There was no reply.

As she turned to walk from the library the low light on a bookcase against one wall intensified. There were three closed books on pedestals within the book case. The first was a leather-bound tome, at least four inches thick, with its title embossed with gold lettering in a copperplate gothic font. **The Book of Fictional Grievances**. The second book was of similar dimensions and had a dog-eared hemp cover. It was titled **The Book of Unresolved Grievances — Librarians' Copy**. The third tome was entitled **A Completely Fulfilled Life**. This book appeared to have front and rear covers but no pages in between.

Holly peered at the words '*Librarians' Copy*' for what seemed like an aeon. For some reason she needed to know what was written inside it.

She stood back and looked at the cabinet. The way of placing the books on their pedestals wasn't obvious. She considered using something to smash the glass but her moral upbringing stopped her. She was still looking for a way to get to the book when the lights over the books faded and the titles could no longer be read.

She was returning to the ante room just as a man of about thirty entered through the outer door. "Ohhh," she started.

"Sorry Holly . . . just back from lunch," the man said.

This man knew her name. How? She looked him over. There was something terribly wrong with the image. Instead of the sombre greys or browns that had been worn since the beginning of the war, this man wore a bright yellow shirt, tucked into blue denim trousers. The trousers were of the type she had seen in American magazines as having been designed by Levi Strauss — but these didn't look right. These were low slung on his hips and tight against his legs. They were being worn over off-white canvas shoes with bright designs of multicoloured strips crossing each shoe. He had small plugs in his ears, which were attached to cords that went into the top pocket of his shirt. His hair was brushed back across his ears and reached his shirt collar. The glasses he wore just covered his grey eyes and were rectangular in shape with blue frames.

"You okay, Holly?" the man asked.

She glared at him. "Who are you? How do you know my name?"

He raised his eyebrows and gazed into her eyes. A smile creased his face. Holly liked the smile.

He leaned forward, placed his hand on her chin and, with chin held between thumb and forefinger, angled Holly's head from side to side. He smiled again and stood up.

"What year is it?" he asked

"1940 of course," Holly replied.

"Ahhhh. That explains it. You once told me this would happen."

Holly had no idea what the man was talking about. "What would happen?"

"Us meeting like this . . . you not recognising me. You said it would be 1940."

Holly began to shake, pushed the man's hand away and stepped backward. "Mummy!" she screamed in anguish.

"There's no need for that, Holly. You're safe. I won't harm you."

Holly closed her eyes and screamed again. This time it was as long and bloodcurdling as she could manage. It was a ploy that had worked when she was eight. She reopened her eyes. The man still stood before her. "Who are you?" she demanded.

The man looked contrite. "I really didn't mean to upset you. My name is Cameliel Cameron. My friends call me Cam . . . you can call me Cam. I am the Fifth Assistant Librarian."

"How do you know my name?"

Cam leaned forward so that he could look at Holly, eye to eye. This time his hands were tucked into his pockets. "One day you will look back on this moment and realise just how difficult it is for me to explain. At that time, no explanation will be necessary. For now, however, I must ease your mind. I want you to go back to the door through which you entered. You will open the outer door and will find no plane crash. You'll be able to continue on your journey. You won't remember me until the time we both look back on this awkward moment and have a good laugh . . . but for now we must part."

Holly did as she was told and left the library. Before the door closed, she noticed that she could no longer see the books or the embossed titles in their covers. She closed the door and entered the anteroom. She looked at the entry door and saw it was undamaged. What had happened to the plane? She needed to have a look to see if it was safe to go out, so gingerly opened the door. She was taken completely by surprise. It was daylight. Not just a circle of light but all over. There was no crashed bomber and no uncle's house. Instead she was on the high street in Paddington, standing beside her mother who was staring at a newspaper and crying.

"What is it mum?" she asked.

"The paper. It's Ben and Edith. A German bomber crashed into their home last night. They were both killed. I'm so glad we decided not to send you down there. You would have been with them."

Recruitment — 1960

HOLLY Penworthy eyed her reflection in the hall mirror. Hair not quite in the fashion of the day but that was by choice. She hated the lacquered towers and velvet headbands of the fashion magazines, preferring her blonde hair to be short and tapered. Besides, the style was flattered by the small white woollen hat that matched her clothing. Presentation was everything and, on this day, it had to be flawless. She picked up her white handbag from the hallstand. "I'm off now mum," she called.

Her mother entered the hall from the kitchen and scrutinised Holly from a distance. "You look pale in white, dear. Good luck with the interview."

Holly waved to her mother, opened the front door, stepped through the doorway and closed the door behind her. Her mother wouldn't have noticed but the closing of the door was symbolic, a gesture to signify the beginning of a new life. She turned at the bottom of the steps and looked back at the two storey Glebe terrace that had been her home since arriving from England. Soon the house would be where she visited her mother and father, instead of her home. A new job was in the offing and the increase in salary would allow her to step out of the family shadow and make her way in the world. It was a long time in coming but this interview for the librarian's job at the State Library of New South Wales in Macquarie Street was the beginning. Today, she would become an example of what a woman could achieve on her own.

She had just closed her front gate when a black and white FC Holden pulled into the kerb. A man, around six feet tall and thin as a whippet, stepped out, He wore a black single-breasted suit with its jacket buttons undone, a white shirt, and narrow black tie. As soon as he was out of the car he placed a snap front black trilby on his head at a jaunty angle. Holly glared him. She would have liked to look him in the eyes, but they were covered by sun glasses.

He smiled and held out his hand. "No first day jitters then."

First day jitters. Holly had no idea what he was talking about. "I don't understand."

"Your first day at the library, of course. I'm here to give you a lift and introduce you to the staff."

Holly took a step back and glared at the man. "Should I know you?"

"We met yesterday . . . don't you remember?"

She was perplexed. She had never seen the man.

The man raised an eyebrow; an inquisitive gesture, wasted when wearing sunglasses. "Oooh dear, you sure you don't know me?"

Holly remained perplexed, the man seemed a little odd. She moved backward through her front gate. Not easy in mid-heeled shoes but she felt it necessary.

The man closed his eyes and a shadow fell across his face. As she watched him, he pressed his right fist into the side of his head and reopened his eyes.

He lowered his sunnies to the end of his nose and peeped at Holly. "What day is it?"

"September 26th."

"The year?"

"1960, of course."

The man paused for a moment then continued. "Oooh dear. I do apologise. We were celebrating a football win. We got full of booze and bad manners and must have taken too many stimulants. I'm here a day early."

The man didn't make sense. Holly backed up the steps toward her front door "Who are you?"

The man smiled, his shadow disappeared. "Lucian Rowling Helldale at your service. I am sorry about this. I must be scaring you. It happens sometimes . . . when things are out of sequence."

"What things?"

"You know . . . things out of order. Carts and horses, yang and yin, death and life. That sort of thing."

The man didn't appear to be able to get any expression into its correct order. She felt an urgent need to call her father. She would introduce him to this strange man before she went for her interview. Her father would know what to do.

Helldale's eyes scrunched, "I don't have time, I'm sorry."

"Time for what?"

"To meet your father . . . look, I really am sorry. Why don't I just disappear and meet you again when I should?"

Holly watched from the top of the steps as Helldale turned on his heels and walked back to his car. *To meet your father* repeated itself in her head. How did he know? She glanced at her watch. It was time to move or she would miss her bus. Contemplation would have to wait. As the car moved away, she let out a sigh of relief.

She walked to the bus stop, sat on the seat and waited. Five minutes turned to ten. She glanced at her watch and looked along Glebe Point Road for the green and yellow of the bus. It was late. She calculated time. Forty minutes until her scheduled interview. Twenty-five minutes for the all stops bus journey. Everything had been so perfect but now the time window was closing. A single bead of perspiration formed at her hairline. She stood and walked around the small bus shelter, then stepped from the kerb and peered along the street.

She was surprised when the black and white FC Holden pulled up at the stop and Lucian Helldale leaned over to the passenger's side of the car and wound down the window. "Miss Penworthy?"

She was taken aback. Helldale spoke as if he was addressing her for the first time. This time she determined to ignore him. Besides, she didn't talk to men who leaned across cars to talk to her. She snubbed him and stared at the top of her handbag.

"I'm sorry, Miss Penworthy. I'm on my way to the library, thought I could gave you a lift."

She glared at him. A question struck. How did he know her name? How did he know she was going to the library? "Apart from talking to you five minutes ago . . . should I know you?" she asked.

"No . . . but I can introduce myself if you wish."

She stood and glanced at her watch. "That won't be necessary,"

"I'm afraid it may be necessary. Your bus has been delayed. It won't arrive for another forty minutes."

Holly looked at her watch again. She would miss her appointment. She felt a tiny chill in her heart, her first sign of panic.

Helldale drove the car forward a few yards and pulled into the kerb. He got out. "I'm just offering you a lift to your interview,"

She looked up him. He was at least six inches taller than her. "How do you know my name?" she demanded.

"I know far more than your name. Holly Penworthy. Born London, 1926. Daughter of Tom and Bernice Penworthy. Family migrated to

Australia in 1955. You would have preferred to remain as assistant librarian at the Ashford Library in Kent and marry your boyfriend Kenneth Formby, but you bowed to maternal pressure not to break up the family. Took up a position with the Sydney University Library in 1956 and have been promoted twice in the four years you've been in the job. You're currently looking to expand your horizons and have applied for the position of Librarian at the State Public Library."

Holly's tiny chill turned to an icy river. She took two steps back from Helldale and looked around for someone to help. There was no one in sight. She thought about running but decided against it. Backing away from Helldale had proved that her shoe selection was wrong for the circumstances.

Helldale smiled at her. For a moment she thought he was about to laugh at her discomfort but then noticed warmth in his smile. There were small dimples on his cheeks and his brown eyes seemed to sparkle. His cheekbones were high set and his jaw was square. His thin nose and perfect teeth reminded her of dental adverts in the Women's Weekly.

"I can see I'm making you nervous. I'm sorry, but I need to discuss something with you. I promise I'll drive you straight to the library."

"Who are you first?"

My friends call me Lucian."

"You told me your name. I want to know who you are."

He removed a card from his jacket pocket and handed it to her. "I'm the CRO — Chief Recruiting Officer, for the company."

She read the card. It showed a name but no address or phone number. Inscribed across the front of the card were the letters L.I.E.U. She remembered seeing the letters in the same font somewhere in her past. In her mind they were black on a white background. This card showed them as navy blue on a beige background. "What does the name mean?"

"I'll tell you, but not until I have your trust."

With the bus being late, she felt she had no choice but to accede to the offer of the lift. She nodded to Helldale, who opened the passenger's side front door for her and closed it again after she was seated. She held on to the door handle as Helldale walked around the car and opened the driver's side door.

Once settled in, he looked across at her, smiled. "I understand you're nervous but there's no need to squeeze the life out of the door handle."

He started the car and headed toward Parramatta Road. "I promise I'll stick to the main roads. You'll be quite safe."

Holly ignored everything said and didn't loosen her grip on the door handle until the car turned into Art Gallery Road and then onto Hospital Road.

Helldale brought the car to a stop adjacent to the library.

"Twenty-three minutes to spare. You have plenty of time. Can we talk?"

Holly opened the car door to check for reaction. There wasn't one. She left the car and walked to a nearby park bench. She was confused, looked at her watch. He was right, twenty-three minutes to spare. How could he be so precise without looking at his watch? She glanced at the rear of the library building; no more than a minute's walk. She had time to hear whatever it was Helldale had to say. Besides, the logo on his business card had her intrigued. It had significance. She had seen it before. She tried to place the memory, without success.

Helldale leaned over the back of his seat and retrieved a leather bag, prior to joining her. He opened the bag. "I'm about to show you something you won't have seen before. It won't harm you."

With that, he extracted a flat rectangular device from his bag and pressed it in the top left-hand corner. The letters L.I.E.U. were emblazoned on a backlit screen.

Holly put her fist to her mouth and tried to move from the seat.

Helldale put his hand up to stop her leaving. "This is called a tablet. I want to show you something." Without waiting for Holly to respond, he placed his closed hand on the screen and then separated his fingers. The screen filled with rows of tiny images.

Holly gasped.

Helldale surveyed the miniature images and chose one. He repeated the finger spreading motion until a single image filled the screen. It was the front of the Library.

Holly gasped again as she studied the image. "What is this?" she asked, meaning the device and not the image.

"This is a photo of the library. There are many more."

His finger pressed the screen and images changed.

Holly recognised every photograph as belonging to the library. "Not the images, what is the device?"

Helldale ignored the question. "You've seen the honour board I take it . . . the one listing the names of librarians?"

"Yes . . . of course."

"Good."

He brought up a photo of the honour roll and showed it to Holly.

She stared at the image. The part of the roll in the photo showed the years 1956 to 1972. All of the names were filled in. Goosebumps covered her arms. Her mind froze. This wasn't possible. This photo appeared to be from the future.

"Your name isn't on the list,"

Holly screamed, as she pointed at the tablet. "What is this?"

Helldale ignored her, again, and continued. "You were the preferred candidate for the post but you failed to show for the interview."

Holly was terrified. What was he going to do to her? She had to get away. She leaped from the seat and ran toward the library building. She stopped at the corner, before looking back at the seat. Helldale sat looking at his screen and moving his fingers across it. He appeared to be paying no attention to her. She looked at her watch. Still twenty minutes to go before her interview. She was ten seconds from the main doors to the building. The man was wrong; she would be there for her interview. She looked toward Helldale. He still hadn't moved. She looked around and saw people in the Domain. Three council workers were working less than fifty yards away. Others walked along the road picking up rubbish. She would be safe if she stayed away from Helldale. Surely a scream would bring help?

She walked down the hill until she was fifteen feet from Helldale. "Why are you doing this to me?"

"Simple. I wish to offer you a position with L.I.E.U. We're in need of a new librarian and you were chosen."

Holly didn't listen to the answer. She asked another question. "How can you have the photos you have . . . in that thing?"

"I will explain all once you accept the position. You just need to say *yes.*"

Holly wandered close to where he sat. She peered again at the tablet screen. "Where did you get this thing?"

Helldale smiled and lifted the tablet toward her. "An electronics store in London. It's the latest model. They've only been out for a few weeks."

"And the photos?"

"I took them with my phone." He reached into his jacket pocket and extracted his smart phone.

Holly's mouth dropped open when she saw the small rectangular tablet. She watched as he pressed an indentation on the bottom of the phone and a screen lit up showing a range of icons. He pressed some of the small icons and handed the phone to Holly. "Point the phone toward the three workers over there. They will appear on the screen. Once you have them in centre screen, press the button that looks like a camera."

Holly pointed the phone at the men and moved it around until they were in the centre of the screen. She pressed the camera icon and heard a click.

Helldale took the camera back and pressed the bottom corner of the screen. He handed the phone back to Holly. "Your photo."

She stared at the screen in disbelief. The image on the screen, when she pressed the button, was now on the screen again. She moved the screen to point it away from the workers. The image remained. "How . . ." she let the sentence drift off. She couldn't comprehend what was going on so saw no point in continuing to ask questions. She glanced at her watch again. Still plenty of time. "You said I was chosen to be your new librarian. How and why?"

Helldale returned the phone to his pocket. "You were chosen by the library board. The reasons are twofold. First, you will be great in the role and second, you owe the library a debt."

She had no idea where the conversation was heading but was becoming more and more intrigued. "Debt?"

"Yes. You will remember, in 1940 your parents sent you to Agarle to stay with your aunt and uncle."

Holly sat down on the bench as she remembered the war years. "You're wrong. They were going to but they didn't."

"Fact is they did. You were in the house when a German bomber ran out of fuel. The library door appeared, and you were saved."

"I was never there."

Helldale opened his leather case and returned the tablet to its holder. "When I showed you my card, you realised you'd seen the letters before, but the colours were different. You saw the black lettering on a white background in the entry foyer of the library. Your memory of the incident was put on hold when you left the portal."

"That's not possible."

"Normally no, but there are exceptions and you're one of them."

"I don't believe anything you say to me. Next thing you'll be telling me you're an alien of some kind. I've seen science fiction movies."

"Not at all. I'm human, just like you. The only difference is, I work for L.I.E.U. and have the ability to travel through time. The year is now 1960. You are thirty-four. I am fifty-two years old but the date of my birth is in five days from now. I will be born at the Woman's Hospital in Crown Street. I will be removed from my unwed mother and put up for adoption. The recipients have already been chosen."

Holly crossed her arms and stood tall. "You're talking nonsense. I don't believe anything you say."

"Then I'll make a deal with you."

"What deal?"

"When I approached you at the bus stop you were looking at your watch. Do you remember the time?"

"Yes."

"Then I will drop you back at the bus stop at that exact time. You won't remember my being there. However, when you realise you won't make it to your interview you'll look for my car. Once you enter the car, you'll remember everything we have discussed and we'll go from there."

"There isn't time."

"There's all the time in the world."

"No you're wrong. I intend to leave here now and go to my appointment. I will arrive early."

Helldale looked her in the eyes. "It will make no difference. You're not here at the moment. You're at a bus stop waiting for a bus that's running forty minutes late. No matter what you do, you can't attend your interview."

Holly turned and walked to the front of the building. "We'll see."

She stood at the entry door, examining the Daphne Mayo aboriginal sculptures, until her composure returned. She took a deep breath and entered the building. Her friend, Beryl Matthews stood at the reception desk. Holly walked toward her. She was surprised when, instead of acknowledging her presence, Beryl stood from her chair and walked straight past her, as if she didn't exist.

"She can't see you."

Holly spun on her heels as she heard Helldale speak.

"I'm sorry Holly but you aren't here. Beryl didn't see you. I'll explain how it all works once you take up your position."

Holly Penworthy took the only action available to her. She fainted.

We'll Meet Again — 1960

CAMELIEL Cameron was besotted with Holly Penworthy from the first time he set eyes on her. He couldn't decide whether it was the expression on her face, when she realised L.I.E.U. was not your normal library, or her appearance. Cam loved the purity of white and she was wearing a white twin set with white skirt, white shoes, and matching handbag. Even her short blonde hair was tucked into a white woollen hat. This was the ultimate expression of purity for a man who thought the only way to dress was to be as colourful as a rainbow. Beyond the clothes, what grabbed him most were the deep green of her eyes and the perky tilt of her nose. She looked to be mid-thirties and well out of her depth. She was introduced by Lucian Helldale who, as usual, looked like a refugee from a Blues Brothers movie; resplendent in a black suit, white shirt, white socks, and sunnies. For this special occasion, he had removed the red wine stains from his tie.

The wide-eyed expression on Holly's face didn't surprise Cam. It's not easy for anyone to comprehend that while L.I.E.U. represents a library, it is not quite as expected. It has something of an analogous but separate nature and that flabbergasts some people.

For the purpose of having Holly enter her new universe, Helldale had driven her to the L.I.E.U. building in Paddington. From the outside, the building appears to be a typical suburban terrace with fading paintwork and a narrow frontage. There is a small bookstore on its ground floor with an apartment above. It's on the inside where the building differs from all others in the street.

After introductions, Helldale left Cam to show Holly the ropes and introduce her to the rules and regulations. In short, to describe how everything worked.

"I'm Cameliel Cameron, call me Cam."

"And where do you fit in?"

Question up front. "I'm the Fifth Assistant Librarian."

"Fifth assistant. Are there more?"

"Yes. But none are here at the moment. They're off sliding somewhere."

"Sliding?"

"We're time sliders. We're designated as assistant librarians but sometimes we're time cops. We investigate breaches of the rules by examining them at the time they occur. We go anywhere at any time. At least that's what the slogan would say if we advertised."

Holly shook her head. Cam could tell comprehension was still a long way off but she couldn't perform her duties without being comfortable with the concept. He decided to shortcut the explanation. "Come this way."

She followed him through a door to a dressing room.

"This is where we check our clothing and appearance to make sure it is coordinated with the time of our destination. Look at the mirror."

"For what reason?"

"You'll see. Now close your eyes and remember what you looked like when you were ten."

Helldale's devices had intrigued her. She figured this to be the next stage of enlightenment, so closed her eyes.

Cam gazed at the mirror as Holly's form morphed. "When you open your eyes you will see a small child wearing a blue dress and scuffed shoes. One of your socks is pulled up and the other one is around your ankle."

Holly opened her eyes and gawped at her reflection. "How?" she muttered in an adolescent voice.

"It happens and we accept it. It's part of the tools of trade. Would you like to try for yourself at eighty?"

The small girl shook her head.

"Think of yourself when you arrived here."

Holly closed her eyes and returned to her normal form. She looked surprised when she reopened her eyes, but a slight smile tilted her mouth and her gaze indicated that she had filed something away.

Cam gestured for her to look at the adjacent dressing room. "This is where we choose clothing to wear. Think of the era and the clothing appears. It's simple once you get used to it."

She walked between rows of hangers. She closed her eyes and flapper clothing appeared on the hangers. She opened them again and ran her fingers across the fabric of a golden silk dress. The distracted smile of Mona Lisa crossed her face. The learning curve would be short.

Holly rubbed the golden material against her face. "What is L.I.E.U. exactly?"

Cam grinned at her. "Some say the *Literary Institute at the End of the Universe*. You see, despite what some humans think, we are not at the centre of any universe. Earth is simply a spec on the horizon of infinity." He hesitated for effect.

"Alternately, our benefactors stole part of a book title from Douglas Adams. Of course, there is a far more technical explanation. *Light Interrupting Educational Unit* is its real name, but it doesn't sound anywhere near as exotic."

"And what's its purpose?"

The question was profound. Despite being an assistant librarian for some time he had failed to fathom the complete answer. He knew snippets but had not yet discovered the library's full purpose. From what he had found, its purpose lay somewhere between futuristic theme park and time travelling study centre. The tossed coin was still in the air.

"Now you have to trust me. Give me your hand. We need to be physically connected for the next bit."

He took Holly's hand, told her to close her eyes, and thought of their destination.

When she reopened her eyes they were standing is a pentagonal room with the words L.I.E.U. inscribed in black marble tiles on a white floor. He took her through a doorway marked LIBRARY and stood her in front of a book case.

"As you can see, the book on the right is **The Book of Fictional Grievances**. This book contains the grievances of fictional characters who believe their authors have either not developed them to a point that satisfies their needs or have been misused in some way."

"Fictional characters?"

"Yes. As a librarian you know, better than most, authors give characters life. Readers get involved in what happens to the characters in novels. Fact is, if you don't get involved you won't finish the book."

Holly's face was masked in incredulity. "Are you telling me characters can complain?"

"Of course they can. We investigate issues and have a word with the author if the character has a case."

"And how do we do this?"

"We use the time travelling function of the library, research why the character was developed, and what led to the grievance. In short, we sit at the author's shoulder and take notes."

"Some books take years to write."

"No problem. We time slide to cut out the boring bits."

Holly's furrowed brow indicated that she didn't understand the concept.

Cam let her ponder. "Now I must explain the next book. This tome is called **The Book of Unresolved Grievances**. This book contains tribulations that we must resolve. We, the royal *we* that is, and by that I really mean *you*, must solve any grievances that appear in this book. They are grievances between our mentors and the users of L.I.E.U."

Holly shot Cam another glance of incomprehension. "I'm sorry, but I don't understand. You seem to be telling me I have to resolve grievances."

He shook his head. "No. The grievances in question are beyond resolution. It's your task to deliver the retribution."

"I understand less and less."

Cam smiled at her. She didn't return the gesture. He continued. "The people who created the library determine the matters to be solved and we investigate. If nothing else, these investigations keep our minds agile."

"You've met the people who run this place?"

"I've seen a photo of one of them. A woman. Unfortunately, when I saw her she was dead, so I didn't learn much. Her compatriots invented the three second delay in her honour."

"Three second delay?"

"When we travel, we are three seconds behind reality at any given instant. If we're at the exact time, we could be seen, might communicate with the people around us, and therefore become part of their history. That is forbidden. We can't interfere with history — past or future. The three second delay ensures we can't intervene. However, we can still hear people and even talk to them under the right circumstances. Three seconds in front was tried but gave some librarians ideas about preventing history from occurring. Our greatest dilemma, as most librarians have the desire to prevent bad things from happening. Mind you, we can override the time delay but it's both dangerous and the reason for the disappearance of some assistant librarians. They tend to see something they like and go for it."

Holly opened the unresolved grievance book. Instead of pages, she found the outer cover hid a flat screen with an embedded row of buttons. She glanced at Cam and raised her eyebrows.

Cam stood beside her and showed her the controls. "The bottom on the left gives you the case number. The following button shows you, in detail, the grievance. The next button gives you the perpetrators life to date and the final button, the end of the perpetrators life. Your job is to interfere with said life without changing history. You must study in detail the perpetrator and the grievance. You will then plan your strategy and carry out the appropriate measure of justice."

"I have a choice in all of this?"

"No. You have been chosen as our new Librarian and you are here. There is no going back."

"I can walk out through the door and catch the bus from here back to Central. I don't have to do any of this."

"I take it you agree we are in 1960."

Holly nodded.

Cam took her hand, again, and led her through the pentagon to the outer door of the bookshop. He opened the door for her and they walked into a crowded street. Vendors' stalls stretched for as far as the eye could see in either direction. People passed, listening to the silent world of iPods. Holly had never imaged the mode of dress. The formality of 1960 had been replaced by the informality of 2019.

"Just bump into someone. You will have no contact. Everyone is where they were three seconds before you see them. Call out if you like. See if you can gain anyone's attention."

She screamed at the top of her lungs. No one listened. Her eyes flickered. Holly had stored more knowledge.

Cam could tell. They returned to the bookshop where Cam pulled a sheet of paper from the pocket of his jeans. "These are a few things I jotted down for you."

***

1 - You must undertake the tasks requested without interference with history.

2 - You will not get ill for the duration of your tenure. See note 7.

3 - Within the influence of the time machine you will not age. Outside of time machine influence, you will age at your normal rate.

4 - The library was inaugurated in 2253 and contains all major written works throughout history.

5 - Food is provided in the kitchen.

6 - Enjoy your stay.

7 - If you travel without the delay timer, you may be killed or die. The time machine cannot help you under those circumstances.

***

Holly turned to Cam. "Where do you fit in?"

"As I said, I'm your assistant."

"How much time do I have to learn . . . everything?"

"Infinite."

"A question . . . when we were outside, what year was it?"

"2019."

Holly studied Cam from head to toe. Blue jeans and multicoloured sneakers, a t-shirt was emblazoned with *The Eagles — Hell Freezes Over Tour*. Hair was unruly and lightly gelled. "And when did you join the library?"

Cam laughed and his face beamed. "Not until a month or so from now . . . I'm your first task. You have to recruit me into the system as your fifth assistant . . . you see, time removes the boundaries that give reason for things to occur in chronological order. Don't worry, you'll soon understand."

Holly remembered fainting in front of Lucian Helldale. She had the urge to do it again.

Seduction — 2019

NOT many Paddington residents knew of the quaint little shop that had been open in their midst for longer than many had been alive. They passed it daily without registering the shop's existence. What passers-by see is a sun yellowed two-up two-down terrace with a rusty gold wrought iron balustrade and under-watered pot plants. At ground level sits a small wrought iron gate and a metal fence topped by ornate fleur-de-lis balustrade spears. The shingle on a hanger outside the small shop says 'Penworthy Rare Books', and it is the books that have garnered the customers. It is said to be the second-best source for rare books in the world; a tad behind the L.I.E.U bookshop in Paddington, London.

The first time Cam came across the bookshop, he was out for a morning stroll to clear his head after an all-nighter of scotch and pencils; the scotch to engender inspiration, the pencils to sketch the result. Nothing had worked. All he had was a dry mouth and a thumping headache.

The beaten copper entry door held a 'CLOSED' sign, but the door was open. He looked inside and spotted a woman up a ladder. She was attempting to reach a weighty hardback that appeared to be moving further and further out of reach. He stared at the woman with the curly blonde hair, faded yellow singlet top and tight blue denims. If he had paid a little more attention he would have realised it wasn't the book moving but the ladder sliding sideways on a brass rail that ran the length of the small shop. Fortunately, he averted his eyes from visual heaven for long enough to see that the bottom of the ladder was fitted with small rollers, which had started following Newton's third law of motion. He rushed through the door and put his foot against the bottom of the ladder. The woman looked down and Cam was mesmerised by deep green eyes which were set in perfect proportion above the perky tilt of her nose and full lips. She looked to be mid-thirties with the svelte body of a dancer.

She smiled as she looked past his face to his right foot. "For every action there is an equal and opposite reaction. Your timing is perfect. In another few seconds I would have ended up as an embarrassing mess on my floor."

"I imagine you would've bounced straight back to your feet," he said, wondering how much of a coincidence it had been to think of Newton's third law and her to say it.

She smiled as she stepped down from the ladder and took hold of it. "I doubt it."

She moved it along its rail until it was under the book she had been trying to grab. She stepped onto the ladder and looked down at him. "Can you hold the ladder for just a few seconds . . . while I grab the book?"

"Sure." He placed his right foot against the ladder and operated the roller locking device. The ladder became rigid.

"I should have tried that."

Cam shrugged. Despite there being no further need, he held the ladder so she could climb to reach her book. His eyes wandered to the floor of the shop. White marble tiles, worn with age. A black tiled border and four letters set into the floor in onyx. He had seen the letters before. "You're part of a chain," he commented.

The woman froze on the ladder, holding the book above her head. "Chain?"

"Yes. L.I.E.U. on your floor. I lived in London for a while. Paddington. There's a shop called L.I.E.U. in London Mews. I used to pass it every day."

The woman stepped down from the ladder and placed the book on a low shelf. "You're very lucky to see the letters. They're usually covered by a Persian rug. They only come out when I have time to clean."

"Do you know what the letters mean?"

"They were here when I took over the bookshop."

"When was that?"

"Nineteen sixty."

Cam couldn't help but stare at the woman. Some would call it overt scrutiny; others leering. "You weren't born in 1960. That would make you around fifty-five minimum. And you're nowhere near fifty-five."

"I'm much older than you think. It's in my genes."

"I can see what's in your jeans and I don't believe you."

"Lechers always say that."

"I'm categorised then?"

"You would be if you weren't so hung-over. I can't see you having any interest at the moment."

"I look bad . . . huh?"

"No . . . you look fine. Except for the roadmap eyes. You should try to sleep better. Working all night is no good for anyone."

How could she tell by just looking at him? "What makes you think I was working?"

"It's seven on a Sunday morning and you have graphite dust all over your right thumb and fingers. My guess is you're heading for Oxford Street in search of a large coffee to blow away the cobwebs."

She was observant at least. "You should be a detective."

"No calling. Just an interest in books."

The woman leaned on the ladder, unlatched the brake and slid the ladder along. She reapplied the brake and climbed again. It was time for him to leave. He retreated to the door. "'Bye."

Holly followed him with her eyes. "You're not going to introduce yourself before you go?"

"Sure . . . Cameliel Cameron. My friends call me Cam."

"An unusual name."

He shrugged. "Family name . . . and you are?"

"Holly Penworthy."

He smiled at the rhythm of the name. There was music playing in the background. He hadn't noticed it previously. It was a song about not being able to leave. He pointed to his *Eagles* t-shirt. "Fan?"

"No . . . just a reminder."

He had no idea what she meant, and she made no attempt to explain, "Bye then," he said as he walked back to the entrance.

"It'll work out for you." Holly called from the ladder.

Cam was bemused by the comment. "What will work out?"

"Toerag of course. You'll get him soon. It's just a matter of time."

He stared at the graphite on his fingers, as goosebumps covered his arms. How did she know? He was about to ask when he saw she had turned away and returned to adjusting books on the top row of the book-shelf. He stood at the doorway until the copper door closed automatically.

Toerag

COFFEE didn't help, nor did the stroll through the markets, the al fresco lunch or the five schooners at the pub in a session that ran to late afternoon. Cam couldn't get the image right and image was a necessity if he was to draw a new character. He tended to labour over each detail until the character's complete face was known from every possible angle. Comic strips are like that. The reader needs to be able to see the character from many angles so one image is never enough. Cam's problem at the moment was a nose. No more than an average proboscis, but there was something wrong with the conk when the face was in profile. Straight on it looked fine with its flared nostrils and aquiline shading but in profile it seemed too finely chiselled for the character. He was a ne'er-do-well by the name of Thaddeus Toerag. He was the kingpin of a group of east-end thugs in a cartoon strip set in early twentieth century London. Cam imagined him as a cross between Professor Moriarty and Fagin with a touch of the Kray twins thrown in for good measure. The problem was, Cam wanted to draw him as being attractive to women, a cross between Captain Blood and Jack Sparrow. No significance to the story line but what the heck. But the nose didn't work so he was at his desk, yet again, imagining noses, with a pencil in one hand and an eraser in the other; the two making alternate journeys to the paper on the easel.

It would have been much easier if he could concentrate. He blamed the beers but knew deep down it was the Penworthy woman and her knowledge of Toerag's existence. There should be only two with knowledge. Amy Foldem, the producer who commissioned the work, and him. It wasn't possible for Ms Holly Penworthy to know . . . but she did. She had also speculated on his working all night. She knew more than she should. He looked at the clock on the wall. 11:00pm. He looked at Toerag's incomplete nose. Maybe it was the beer but he needed an explanation.

***

Sunday night drifters were the only people to occupy the streets as he made his way back to the bookshop. There was a dim light over the domestic door, adjacent to the beaten copper door. He knocked on a door panel. The sound reverberated in his head. He waited a long moment before knocking again. There was distant shuffling before a light above the doorway ignited. At least she was awake. The door latch clicked, and the door opened against a restraining chain.

"Yes?"

Cam's mind raced. He was at the wrong place. The door had been opened by a woman in her mid-eighties, with unkempt grey hair and the deep lines of age cutting parallel paths down her cheeks. She wore pince-nez spectacles that were being pushed away from her face by her thumb and forefinger as she rubbed the grit of sleep from her eyes.

"I'm sorry. I have the wrong place . . . I'm very sorry to disturb you," he said.

"What do you want, Cam?"

She knew his name. How? He stepped back through the gate and out to the street, checking on the building. This was the right building. He moved forward again.

"I was looking for Holly Penworthy. I assumed she lived upstairs, here."

"She does."

He stared at the woman; same facial structure. He tried to imagine Holly with wrinkles. Similar. Maybe a granddaughter. "Is Holly in?" he asked.

"Yes. What do you want Cam . . . it's late."

"I want to ask Holly something."

The woman closed the door and then reopened it without the chain. "A question about Toerag?"

"How do you know?"

"Because he's consuming you. You can't get part of him right. You think this is a problem."

"It is a problem, for fuc . . . " He didn't finish the sentence, realising he was about to swear in front of an old women. Too many beers addled the brain. He realised he shouldn't even be there, berating an old woman whom he had drawn from her bed. "I'm sorry."

"For swearing or getting me out of bed?"

"Both . . . I guess."

"Then go home and come back when you're sober."

He nodded his head. She was right of course. "Can you tell Holly I dropped by?"

The woman smiled "No need."

He guessed she wouldn't pass on the message. Disappointing. "I'll be off then."

The old woman smiled. The smile had warmth and reminded him of how Holly had smiled earlier in the day. "Wait here for a moment. I have something for you."

She turned from Cam and opened a connecting door to the bookshop, disappeared through another door for a couple of minutes then returned with a sheet of paper in her hand.

"Try this." She handed him the paper, then closed the door gently in his face.

He stared at the paper until the light above the door was extinguished. On the page was a sketch of a nose.

***

Four hours later, Cam stared at the sketch the old woman had given to him. He was tempted to add it to Toerag's features but wasn't game. For some reason, he knew the sketch was perfect and that fact reeked of impossibility. How could the old woman know what was needed? He hadn't even mentioned Toerag to her.

He slid onto the high chair in front of his angled drafting table, closed his eyes and touched pencil to paper. Maybe if he didn't look he would stuff it up and be let off the hook. He closed his eyes and imagined the sketch as he applied the pencil to the page. Lines and shading, nostrils and nose hair; adding to the outline of the old woman's sketch. The intersection of the nose and the eyes came next, the top lip and lopsided snarl, perfected a few days earlier. Detail. A small mole just off the left side of the nose. A small scar at the very tip, like the indent of a knife point. He removed the pencil from the paper and leaned back on his chair. He kept his eyes closed and imagined the outcome, sniggering in anticipation of the Picasso head he was sure had been created, before opening his eyes to look.

He resembled the caricature of a surprised man as his jaw dropped, mouth agape. He raised his left hand and rested his chin between thumb and forefinger as he stared at the image for an aeon. From that moment on, he resolved to always draw with eyes closed. The nose was perfect. The face and head were perfect. Thaddeus Toerag was complete.

He slid from the chair, walked to the tiny kitchenette and pressed the button on the electric jug. Water gurgled as the jug heated up. He couldn't take his eyes from the drawing.

The jug switched itself off as he reached into the cupboard above the bench and grasped his last remaining coffee mug, remembering the five that had been broken by fits of pique during the nose delineation sessions. Coffee and water were added to the mug. He opened the fridge door to get some milk.

"Ooii . . . you . . . dipshit."

Cam froze, afraid to turn his head. There should have been no one in the apartment but the sound was close. Too close.

Sweat beads formed on the back of his neck. He checked his balance by standing on the balls of his feet and moving either way. All he needed to do was to ascertain the exact location of the predator and he would be able to strike.

"Hurry up . . . get your bloody milk and make your coffee. I don't have all night."

The sound was coming from behind him, no further than the drafting table. He reached into the refrigerator and settled his hand around the neck of a milk bottle. Plastic but full of milk; at least it had some weight. He felt his heart pumping. What if he's armed? What use is a plastic milk bottle against a knife, maybe a gun? Hopefully he'll be lactose intolerant. Cam tightened his grip on the bottle, jinked to his left and spun around, raising the bottle as he moved.

Raucous laughter sprang from what sounded like the throat of a forty-a-day man. There was no one to be seen. Cam was alone in the room. The bottle shook in his hand as he realised the sound was coming from the drafting table. He grabbed the back of the chair and glared at the image on the table. Nothing had changed. He glanced at the wall clock. The second hand was running backward; not an unusual occurrence for the clock but annoying nonetheless. He looked through the kitchen window. It was pitch-black outside.

"Get yerself over here, I wanna talk."

The voice again; this time loud and threatening.

Cam glared at the image on the table, daring it to move. If it did, he would screw it up and file it in the round bin. But how could a drawing talk? There had to be something else creating the sound. A possibility gelled. Someone had been in the apartment, hidden a speaker some-where and was talking from some remote position. Taking the piss. How would they know he had gone to the fridge for milk? They must be able to see. In a couple of sentences, he had moved from *someone* to *they*. Par-anoia. Now there was more than one person he couldn't see. He dropped to his knees, searched under the table and around the chair. Drawing paper was scattered to the corners of the room, sofa cushions hoisted and thrown about in a manic frenzy of delusional mayhem. Mind you, the hullabaloo only lasted a few seconds. Then he heard the voice again.

"Ooii . . . dipshit, stop pissing about and sit down will ya. I wanna talk."

This time he could centre the source of the voice. It was coming from the table. He sat on his chair and stared at the drawing.

"Good." The voice said. "Now I have your attention. Took longer than I expected, but finally you're in the right place. Now . . . the reason for my talking to you is because you've taken too long to finish me. And you needed help."

There was no movement at the table but it sounded like the sketch was talking to him. This was impossible. It had to be some sort of set-up. He was being spoofed by someone with access to a video camera and his apartment. He opened the filing cabinet of his mind and ticked off the potential culprits. Men and women came to mind but were dis-missed in turn. There was no one in his inner sanctum that would do this so he checked the periphery of his friendship circle. There was no one there either. The only thing he knew was, he wanted it to end. He would play along until the lowlife showed himself. At least it was a plan. He decided, if the drawing could talk, he'd talk back.

"Maybe I didn't want to finish you. You're lucky I did. A bit of grat-itude is in order."

"Poppycock. You finished me because you have an obligation to fulfil for that Amy Foldem person and you don't want to let her down. Besides, you need the money."

He thought of Toerag's nose. "I didn't need any help, you know."

"For most of me you didn't but you couldn't draw a nose that made me look windswept and interesting. You got help."

Cam kept glaring at the board. He was actually waiting for the drawing's lips to move. He felt like a sceptical spectator at a ventriloquist show, waiting for a sign of lip movement. There was none. He tried another tack. "What do you want?"

"Finally, it has gelled. You ask a question I can answer. What I want is to be completed. I want to be 3D."

Cam laughed at something he once said to Amy Foldem. "You are 3D. You have length, width and depth. Albeit you're only the depth of my pencil mark."

"Listen pal. That just makes me shallow and I want to have depth. Get hold of someone with a 3D printer and work me up. You'll be surprised at the result and I'll make good merchandise. Amy will love me."

Maybe his imagination, for only imagination could be driving the conversation that had developed the nucleus of an idea. Merchandise. Maybe Amy *would* love it. The comic strip could go from paper to the toy stores. Marvel Comics characters were now movie stars so why not? Merchandise usually meant money from the punters who can't get enough of whatever was being flogged. He stopped germinating the idea and looked around the reality of the room. "Maybe she will. We'll wait and see and . . . "

The piercing shrill of the doorbell broke his train of thought. Only an idiot would install a wound down air raid siren as something to tell him he had someone at the door . . . but it suited his purpose. He hated visitors and someone pressing on the doorbell was bound to give him the shits, so the siren would annoy him and he would answer the door in the applicable frame of mind.

He strode to the door and flipped the eyehole cover. What he saw made him wish he hadn't been prepped for anger because this visitor was most welcome. He opened the door and ran his eyes, from head to toe, over Holly Penworthy. She was dressed to kill, in tight black leather pants matched with a black silk blouse and black bolero jacket. Her blonde her poked out from the bottom of a Spanish bolero gaucho Zorro hat. She even carried a small whip. The outfit was set off by a gold bracelet that emitted a pulsing yellow light.

She touched the end of the whip to his chin to lift his head. "Don't look unless you're invited."

He made direct eye contact with her and waited for an invitation. It didn't come. Instead, she walked into the apartment and went straight to the drawing table. She perused the sketch in detail. He could see she had the eye of someone who would be able to discern art from froth. "He's finished you then, Thaddeus?" she asked the sketch.

"Took his time. How's the nose looking?" the sketch replied.

"Your best bit . . . apart from the scar on your chin. I'm glad he gave you a scar. It gives you real character. I think he's quite good at this. Did you discuss becoming 3D with him?"

"We were doin' so when you pressed the bell. Horrible bloody thing it is. Sounds like it's left over from a war or somefink."

Holly turned to Cam and frowned. "You've not given him any class. He sounds like he's from one of the lower orders. I gave you the nose so he would be attractive to women. What's the point of that if he sounds like a guttersnipe? Where are your pens?"

Cam was flabbergasted. Holly was talking to the drawing. She must have been central to why he could hear it speak. "In the top drawer."

She opened the draw and removed a 7B pencil, started to modify the sketch. Cam was livid. Throughout his entire sketch life, no one had interfered with anything he was doing. This sketch was about to be delivered to its buyer. As much as he was smitten by this mysterious woman, she had no right to go anywhere near the drawing, let alone modify it.

He was about to scream at her when reality was suspended and he froze. Toerag's head rose a smidgen from the paper and his eyes gazed at his clothing.

"Better ma'am. I feel uplifted now. Superior somehow."

The head, which rose from the paper, had the depth of a pencil indent and air suspended shading.

Cam had a hunch about his condition. He was suffering from some form of toxic inebriation. He was having a nightmare. He would wake up soon and start working on Toerag's nose again. Get it right.

Holly looked sidelong at him and smiled. "It's not a nightmare. It's all real. The key is the nose I drew for you. It's animated. The original was done by Plexer in 2089. Mine's a rip-off."

"It's not possible," Cam said, stunned.

"No, and you're not going mad. I'm manipulating time. When you see me we're in the same time zone. When I lift Thaddeus's head, I'm in another zone. I'll take you somewhere and you will see."

The woman was terrifying. Beautiful or not, she scared the shit out of him. He wanted his normal life back. He didn't want drawings that spoke or women in leather with the sexual promise of functional aphrodisiacs. He was becoming demented and didn't like it. "I'm sorry Holly but I'm not going anywhere with you. You're doing my head in."

Holly smiled. "Not so. You're smart enough to understand. That's why you were ordained to be offered the job."

He didn't feel as smart as she thought. "Ordained . . . what job?"

"I need you to become my assistant."

He didn't understand. "At your shop?"

"Of course. I need an assistant and you're him."

"I have a job I love. I have no desire to be a shop assistant . . . so no thanks."

"Not the right answer. I want you to try something. Take my hand," Holly said, as she extended her hand toward him.

Cam hesitated, despite wanting to touch her in any way possible, then thought *what the heck* and took her hand.

"Now close your eye and think about what you want to be doing in five years. I don't want fantasy, just your job and where you want to be. Let me know when you decide."

Cam looked into the inner reaches of his mind and thought through the possibilities. For some reason a vision of Toerag in 3D appeared as if etched to the back of his eyeballs. "Okay . . . I've thought of something."

"Good . . . In a moment I will have you open your eyes, but don't be shocked. Just be prepared to see something different. You okay with that?"

"In for a penny I guess."

"Then open your eyes."

For some reason, he wasn't game to just open them. For a moment he just peered through the hairs of his eyelashes. Even then he knew there was something wrong. The colours were different. His eyes sprung open and he began to shudder. The walls had changed colour from white to a bright yellow. The drawing table and chair were missing. There was beige carpet on the floor instead of polished floorboards. A deep cushioned white leather sofa occupied the corner where the bookcase should be. "What the fu . . . "

Holly held her finger to his lips. "It's okay, but we must be quiet. We're in real-time. Time has moved on five years. You see the décor of this apartment isn't of your choosing. That's because you don't live here anymore. You have moved."

Fainting was considered a viable option as panic set in. Not the '*I'm not sure how to handle this*' type of panic but a deep-seated conviction that his world had exploded. It wasn't possible for what had just happened to be real and yet he seemed to be awake. Maybe he had taken some form of hallucinogen. But he would remember dosing up . . . or maybe not. There were often times when he couldn't remember the night before, due to the influence of some bloke named Lager. What he did know, however, was he wanted out of his present predicament. He tried to jerk his hand from Holly's grip but she held tight.

She threw him a sand freezing stare. "You can't let go. If we disconnect you will be left here and that's inconceivable."

He heard a buzz from the front door. Holly pushed at her bracelet as the door opened. A moment later a man walked in, looked around, picked up a leather folder from the sofa and walked out again. He strode straight past Cam as if he wasn't there.

Cam glared at Holly. "Get me out of here."

"Close your eyes and think of where we came from."

Cam did as he was told.

When he opened his eyes again, Holly released her grip on his hand. "You see, you're back. Just like one of the conditions of employment. When you want to quit, you can go back to where you started." She glanced at the drafting table. "When you take Thaddeus to Amy Foldem, suggest he be created in 3D. She'll like the idea and it will be the start of a blossoming career for you. Now I must go." She hesitated for a moment then continued. "One thing . . . you will think about what happened here and convince yourself you weren't hallucinating. As proof, you'll go to your art supply store and talk to the young man there. You'll realise he's the man you saw in your apartment. He buys it from you in about two years from now. He can't afford it, but his parents help out. You can then decide whether you want to see me again. If you do, come to my terrace tomorrow evening at around seven. My granddaughter's coming to tea and three would make interesting conversation."

Cam stood firm. "You won't see me again. I've built up enough nightmares for a lifetime and you've only been here for a few minutes."

"You'll come tomorrow night . . . and get yourself a computer to draw on. Much easier to modify."

"I always do my first sketches by hand. From there I use . . . "

Holly put up her hand. "Don't babble on. Just think about things and come tomorrow night."

***

When she left, Cam flopped on his chair and studied the changes she had made to Toerag. She had modified his shoulders and straightened his hat. The change was subtle but, he had to admit, gave the sketch a smarter appearance. He would keep the changes. "I suppose you like the change?" he uttered, out loud, to the drawing.

"Of course, sir. But my new accent is a bit too proper for your intent. In some ways I prefer my craggier self. I think I prefer my ladies to be a bit of rough trade. Maybe I can have a falling out with society."

This time, as Cam watched the drawing on his table, an eye winked at him.

Engagement

CAM didn't know whether he was relieved or peeved when he met up with the young man from the art supply store. He needed new pencils anyway, but it was the first time he had ever tried to converse with the man. Holly was right, of course, this was the man who had walked through the room the previous evening. This version was around five years younger but the probability of him being the same person was high. During their conversation, Cam learned that this was a man who spent most of his leisure hours looking for a terraced apartment in Paddington and wouldn't marry his partner until he found the right place. Fortunately, for him, his parents would buy the place as a wedding gift. This meant he could buy almost anything on the market. What he wanted was a place with both atmosphere and history, once owned by a person who was, at least, infamous (but preferably famous for something). This, of course, begged the question as to how or why he ended up with Cam's place. After all, Cam met neither of the fame requirements, but apparently something happened in the future that changed that.

He decided that either: he could sit around and live his life until something happened; or follow someone else's desire and travel through time as Holly Penworthy had done. The second option sounded far more interesting, so he decided to keep an appointment for tea.

***

At the specified time he knocked on the door of the sun yellowed terrace and waited. He'd imagined an old woman answering and was surprised when it was Holly who opened the door. Except, it wasn't Holly. This was almost a clone, but younger and with longer hair. This hair was black, cut in pageboy style. The woman was dressed in a yellow dress with pleated skirt. Cam checked her eyes. They were the same deep green and lively. "I think Holly's expecting me," he said.

"You must be Cam. I've been looking forward to meeting you. Gran has told me a lot about you. Come in."

Cam took a pace into the hallway, between the rear of the house and the flight of stairs leading to the upper storey. He caught the woman's scent as she turned to close the door. *Intimate Nights* . . . his favourite. "And you are?"

"Ohhh . . . sorry. I'm Petra Petitfille, Holly's granddaughter. My father is Yuri Petitfille, the astrophysicist."

Cam figured he was supposed to recognise the name but he had no interest in astrophysics so missed the connection. "I think I may have heard of your father."

Petra laughed. "No you haven't. You have no interest in astrophysics."

It was happening again.

Petra read his thoughts.

"It's a terrible habit. Gran told me, with you, I'll have to stop. I promise to try."

She led him down a long corridor with several rooms off to the side. It was only when they reached a bright yellow door that Cam realised the house must be bigger on the inside than the outside. Being a Dr Who fan, he understood the concept but never expected to experience it.

"It's an optical illusion, in the style of frescoes in French and Italian palaces."

Rubbish he thought.

"No, really . . . but suit yourself."

Petra opened the door and Holly looked up from across the room as they entered. She looked the same as the last time he had seen her, except this time she wore skin tight black leather from head to toe. He imagined her being poured into the outfit. She stood from her lounge and walked over to greet him.

"Did you bring Thaddeus?" she asked, as she kissed him on both cheeks. "Petra's dying to meet him."

"In thought I'd been invited to dinner. I saw no need."

"You're probably right . . . but Petra will be disappointed."

"Where's the old lady?" Cam segued.

Holly smiled the smile of the impatient. "There is no old lady, there's only me. I was born in 1926 and I'm no longer far from the terminus of life. While I wear the gold bracelet on my wrist I'm attached to L.I.E.U and remain at the age at which I joined the organisation. When I joined in 1960 I was thirty-four. With the bracelet I remain thirty-four."

Cam stared at her, trying to access his memory of the old woman he had seen at the house. There was a resemblance he had noticed the last time he saw her. He shook the image away. "I don't believe you."

Holly shrugged and mumbled something as she shook her head. She looked into Cam's eyes. "Scepticism is good . . . but in this case it is completely misplaced. In the normal path of time we wouldn't be doing this but this isn't within the normal path of time and circumstances are such that we must. You see, you inducted me in L.I.E.U. and it's hard for me to consider you don't know anything about how it works. If I'd known this situation was possible I may have been more incredulous about joining. You see, you're about to undertake a great leap of faith."

Adrenaline kicked in but Cam couldn't move. He closed his eyes and listened to his heartbeat. Fast and erratic. He took a series of deep breaths and listened for his heart to calm. When he opened his eyes again, Petra and Holly were both staring at him, wearing bemused expressions. He reclosed his eyes and started a long count.

"Counting won't help, Cam. This is an alternate reality. You'll soon find it is as real as what you used to consider reality. The only change is time and an ability to transfer to different time zones."

Cam opened his eyes again and looked around the room. It was just a normal suburban sitting room. A three-piece sofa, coffee table, paintings on the wall, polished floorboards and a large picture window to show sunlight during the day and moonlight at night, irrespective of external weather. He shook his head before pushing his fists into his temples. He didn't understand what was happening and had no inkling that the situation would change.

Petra suggested he join her on the sofa.

Holly retrieved a bottle from a cocktail cabinet and poured three measures into shot glasses. "Let us toast the future," she said, as she handed Cam one of the glasses.

"To L.I.E.U," Petra joined.

Cam said nothing but threw back the whisky shot.

Holly stared at Cam and watched him drink. "You have questions — ask."

Cam proffered his glass in hope of another shot, and glared at Holly. "You say Petra is your granddaughter. She looks to be around twenty-eight or so. You're thirty-four . . . I'm supposed to believe this?"

Petra chimed in. "No . . . Gran is ninety-three. She had my mother when she was thirty-seven . . . three years after joining L.I.E.U. It was unusual to give birth at that age, in her time, but she managed, without complication. My mother had me when she was thirty-four. I'm twenty-eight and have no intention of having children in the foreseeable future. In our family we don't settle down until some of life's journeys are behind us. It's a matter of enlightenment."

"So let us enlighten you," Holly said, as she refilled Cam's glass.

***

An hour later Cam was enlightened. Not through conversation or persuasion but from practical demonstrations inside the Penworthy Rare Books emporium. At the end of the excursion, he was given a note by Petra.

***

1 - You must undertake the tasks requested without interference with history.

2 - You will not get ill for the duration of your tenure.

3 - You will age at your normal rate, despite being able to change apparent age.

4 - The library was inaugurated in 2253 and contains all major writings throughout history.

5 - All food is provided in the kitchen.

6 - Enjoy your stay.

7 - Be very careful when travelling in real-time. It can be deadly.

***

"Where do you fit into this?" he asked Petra, as she closed the bookshop door and escorted him back upstairs to the apartment.

"I've been assisting my grandmother with the library. I guess it's horse and cart stuff. She needed me to induct you. She told me she'd thought about what would happen if this was a novel. It could boggle readers' minds for them to get their heads around Holly investing the person who invested her."

Cam didn't worry about boggling readers' minds. His was boggled. The situation was too weird to contemplate. "So, how long have you been helping her?"

Petra smiled and grabbed Cam by the shoulders and looked him in the eyes. "For an aeon, but in standard time about five minutes before you arrived this evening. You see, my grandmother believes you and I will develop a relationship and we can only do that if we're from the same time zone. Luckily we both begin and end our time with L.I.E.U. at the same time and place. And now, for us to develop a relationship all I have to do is wait for five minutes and then you'll knock on the door downstairs. For now, however, you have a job to do."

"We're not going to have a meal together?"

"No . . . we will leave that until next time we meet. You have a lot of research to do and you have to get used to everything. Then you have to go back to 1960 and recruit Gran. From there, your adventures together will begin."

***

There was much research to be undertaken. Manuals for the library, manuals and videos on maintenance and traveller safety procedures, interpretation of symbols, fitness training and operation of the three second delay bracelet. Then there was the memory chip implant. For this, Cam was transported to 2078 and a probe was inserted into his skull. There was no pain and just a smidgen of discomfort. The only unedifying thing about the implant was how he was able to read the doctor's assistant's mind and the rejection of his sexual advances, even before any desire had formed. He guessed that, on the upside, there would be no time wasted when undertaking future encounters with women.

After the research, he learned to operate the 'books' This was simple enough but required some ingenuity.

The next trick was to investigate how far forward he could push the library and how well it handled in reverse. He closed his eyes and thought of 2253, the year of the inauguration of the library. When he opened his eyes again, he hadn't moved. He tried 2099 and moved forward to the set time. By trial and error, he found the upper limit of the forward movement to be 2115. In reverse, it reached back to 70,000BCE.

Perhaps reading books wasn't big before then?

He paid a short visit to Agarle in 1940, in search of a child who would escape into the library when a German bomber fell out of the sky. Then he set the controls to 1960 and waited for Lucian Helldale to appear with his new recruit.

The Gambler

WALKING through the shopping mall on three second timer delay meant Cam could look at desirable objects without getting the urge to spend money. But that wasn't the main reason for his visit. It was self-interest. He had travelled to 2021 with a burning desire to see if Holly's prediction about Thaddeus Toerag would come true. The first shop he tried was part of the *Doting Mum* chain whose advertising ran that only a negligent mum can walk past the shop without stepping in to peruse the latest in toys and gadgets for children of all ages. *Doting mum, Doting mum, there's credit on your card today,* sang the subliminal speakers embedded in the shop's front wall. The second shop he tried was *All Their Mates Have It,* an outlet of the Peer Pressure Group of Companies. This advertised Toerag but a sign on the cashier's window told of being out of stock. More were available at OFRK stores.

The third shop was part of the OFRK (*Only For Rich Kids*) chain which classified itself as bogan-free. Toerag, in 3D, was in the display window. The figure stood 30cm high and talked to passers-by, inviting them into the store. Behind the toy was its box with, *Definitely Not made in China* half-plastered over a sticker that read *Mad . . . . . . .ina.*

Within the store there was half a row of shelving dedicated to the scoundrel, and a banner reading *The Latest Sensation* ran for the length of the shelves.

Cam read the blurb accompanying the all dancing all singing toy sensation until he reached *batteries not included.* He was both pleased and sad about the outcome of Holly's idea. Pleased because it had worked and sad because he had no idea Amy would make the thing exclusive. After all, the comic strip was in a tabloid and there was nothing exclusive about the *Daily Gossip.*

***

Before returning to his own time, and despite the fact he shouldn't do so, he let his desire to learn more about the life and times of Thaddeus Toerag lead him to Amy Foldem's place.

When he arrived at the front door of her townhouse, he heard raised voices and an argument ensuing inside. There was a booming male and a reedy female voice locked in mortal combat. First a shrill squeal would tear the fabric of his eardrums, followed by a bull's bellow in defence of what seemed to be an indefensible position. As for what was being argued about, Amy's husband, Cant Foldem had put up the townhouse as collateral for a $300,000 hand of cards and lost.

"I'll win it back, you silly cow," Cant screamed at his wife.

"And what will you use as a stake . . . me . . . or young Nevva. Yeah, you'll wager your daughter on some hand of cards. Christ Cant, it was bad enough when you lost the car on the horses. This is worse. The guys at the card club are aged pensioners for pity's sake. They'll kill you. They're too old to have anything to lose."

"Don't be stupid," Cant replied. "They won't put the heavies on us. We'll just have to find another place."

"No Cant. *You'll* have to find another place. I can't take it anymore. Get out!"

Cam had heard enough. This was a domestic altercation. He wanted no part. He was walking away from the door when he spotted something from the corner of his eye.

Movement came from a bay window where a small plastic figure shook the curtain.

Cam went to the window and leaned down to have a look at the figure. It was Toerag and the statue was waving at him. He checked his bracelet to see if he had turned his timer off. He hadn't.

Toerag waved again, pointed to the window opener, ran to the small handle and began to turn it. Cam pushed up on the glass to make the task easier.

When the window was open enough, Toerag slid underneath and jumped onto Cam's hand. "Great to see you, my artistic shaper."

Cam shot the figure a quizzical stare. "You can see me then?"

"Of course. I come with an inbuilt delay timer."

"It doesn't make sense. You must cost a fortune and security is breached."

Toerag jumped up and down on Cam's hand as he laughed. "Not the toys . . . me. I'm the original. I'm the one you drew."

Cam raised his hand to eye level for a better look. "You've come up well. I must tell Holly about you."

Toerag put his hands on his hips and stamped a foot into Cam's hand. "You can do better than that, dipshit. Take me away from here. I ran away from Amy two weeks ago and now she thinks she's lost me. I want to stay lost. If her husband finds me he'll sell me off, or gamble me away. Talk about a problem gambler, this idiot won't stop until Amy has nothing left. He's lost all the money she made from the first batch of *me*. I'm selling very well but she has nothing to show for it. You need to do something."

"I can't do anything. I'm not supposed to be here."

"Get real. I'm a cartoon character who's been turned into a plastic figure and you're talking to me. Use some imagination . . . you'll think of something."

"Cant wasn't a bad gambler, to my knowledge."

"You need more knowledge. Would he have been called Cant Foldem if he didn't have a gambling problem?"

Cam smiled. "I see what you mean. What do you want me to do with you?"

"Take me to Holly."

***

Cam did as asked, but it wasn't a great idea. Holly gave him a demon's stare. Fire spat from her nostrils and her bared teeth resembled the fangs of a rabid dog . . . and all before Cam told her he had visited Amy Foldem's place. What lit her fuse was a small fluidised cartoon character in Cam's shirt pocket who was looking for a new home.

"And just what are we supposed to do with him?" she demanded.

Cam held up a calming hand. "You suggested him. Besides we don't have to feed him and he never needs medical attention."

Toerag relaxed and turned to an ink blob in Cam's pocket.

Holly looked at the pocket, walked over to Cam and held the pocket open. "Do you control your own shape, Thaddeus?"

The ink blob formed a head. "Of course," he said. "I'm a 3D printed object; I can be any shape I choose, once my bits are all in place." With that, he returned to his nonactive shape.

Holly looked at the blob. "Okay, but just stay out of my way."

Cam looked at Holly, to see if her mood was changing for the better. When it looked like she had eaten a page from the little book of calm, he told her about his trip to see Amy Foldem and how he husband had gambled away all of their money.

Holly didn't explode until he was finished . . . and even then it was more a sun shower than a cyclone. Maybe she could see Cam's concern about his friend. "Do you have a plan?"

"Yes."

He explained the plan to Holly.

"Then send a report to L.I.E.U. If Cant Foldem appears in ***The Book of Unresolved Grievances*** you can act. If it doesn't then you must stay out of it. What you want to do involves using the time compressor and unauthorised use is forbidden. They will just stop the thing and you'll be caught between time zones. I don't know if I can get you back from there."

"The penalty for unauthorised use of time travel equipment is to be sent to the six second time delay zone and left there for either an aeon or eternity, whichever comes first. Of course, an aeon is nowhere near as long as eternity but women have been heard to argue that it takes them an eternity to get to sleep if their husband is snoring, so the verdict is still out. Sometimes . . . " Cam stopped talking and apologised for his memory chip's outburst. "The bloody thing just spits out information and uses my mouth to do it. Mostly I can control it but sometimes it just goes off by itself."

Holly nodded and told Cam to get on with his report.

***

When the name Cant Foldem appeared in ***The Book of Unresolved Grievances*** Holly looked at it astonished. Foldem's life, from birth to 2021 was clearly set out but there was nothing 'going forward', to use a banal businessman's expression.

There was meaning in this lack of information but Holly didn't understand. Cam was like-minded. Even his mind chip generated a question mark instead of a prosaic line.

"Nothing in the manuals?" Holly asked, as she tried to scroll down her screen for a page unlikely to exist.

Cam's mind chip leaped into action. He imagined his eyes spinning like pokie wheels as he waited for an idea to clunk into his head. Finally,

something slotted. "There are times when unresolved means unresolved," he said, his mind awash with possibilities.

Holly's responding smile was wicked. "Carte blanche . . . Foldem's
future life is dependent on the outcome of your scheme. Have we seen
this before?"

"Not in my time. I can try to contact one of the other assistant librarians."

Holly shook her head and displayed the wicked grin again. "Maybe
we're learning something. Why don't you carry out your plan and we'll
see where it leads."

***

It was just after 11:00am on a Saturday morning when Cam walked into
the *Paddington Pensioners Fun Times Card Club*. It looked like a dive gone
down-market. Chairs were stacked in uneven piles. Century old paint flaked
from the walls. Chunks of plaster had fallen to the floor and remained in
place, waiting for a broom. The only light for the dingy room was the one
over the round card table. There were four old men in grey cardigans, black
cotton trousers and red skivvies gathered around the table, plus Cant
Foldem and a man in a black pinstriped suit, blue tie and white shirt.

Cam assumed the attire of the old guys was some sort of club uniform. Then he noticed that all four men had identical salt and pepper
beards and slicked back hair and figured he was seeing quads. Apart from
the one holding a Glock 17, the wizened old souls displayed no menace.
The gun was in a shaky right hand and Cam envisioned it going off without intent.

"Sorry to bother you gents," Cam edged toward the table. "But I need
a quick word with Cant. Won't take a minute."

"This is for members," one of the cardigans said.

"All four of you are here then. Like I said, it will only take a minute."

The man with the gun wobbled his hand at Cam. "We're busy."

Cam ignored the gun and stared at Foldem. "A minute please
Cant . . . then you can go back to business."

Foldem left the table and guided Cam away from the table. "Just what
are you doing here Cam? Did Amy send you?"

"Who's the suit?" Cam asked.

"My Lawyer . . . he's here to witness the handing over of the title
deeds to the house."

"I bet Amy's glad she's got you."

Foldem snarled and bared his fangs. "You're just like Amy. You artistic types give me the shits. You never take risks. I'll win the money back. I always do."

"But we don't live in a world of shadows. There's no old geezer holding a gun at my head."

Cam turned toward the old men and realised he was telling a lie. There was a gun aimed at his head — more precisely, a circular movement of the gun barrel encircled his head with irregular speed and, on occasion, dipped to aim at the centre of his forehead. It was time to move. He put a hand into the pocket of his jeans and felt for his bracelet. Once secured in his hand he initiated the time delay.

He gazed at six pairs of startled eyes as he observed the men from his time delayed position. One old man grabbed his chest. The lawyer started to rise from his seat, then slumped down again. Cam walked to where the man with the gun stood. Now behind him he returned to real-time and tapped the man's shoulder. The old man spun around and gasped as he saw Cam, who disappeared again as the gunman tried to aim at him. The old man fired off a shot and plaster burst from a wall.

The pensioner gripping his chest took deep breaths. Cam walked over to him, put an arm around his shoulder and his lips beside the man's ear and turned the timer off.

"Hi there, sweetheart," Cam kissed the man on the ear.

Nature took its course and the geriatric slumped to the floor, gripping his chest. His siblings gathered around, screaming for the lawyer to help them and forgetting, for the moment, Foldem's existence.

Cam grabbed Foldem by the arm and pointed to the doorway. Both men sprinted from the club. They didn't stop running until they hit the first pub in Oxford Street.

***

Foldem stood, panting at the bar, and staring at Cam. "What happened back there?"

Cam shrugged and held up two fingers to the barmaid who was running her index finger along the line of beers on tap. He nodded when she perched her finger over the beer he preferred. He turned to Foldem. "Nothing. We artistic types know a little magic. Now we can talk."

Foldem started to say something but Cam put up his hand to stop him. "You're going to listen, and listen well. You were right about one thing. You are going to win and get enough money to pay those stand-over merchants back. If you concentrate, you'll even win enough to get Amy back on her feet and free from the misery your debt brings to her. Then you'll give her a break and either quit gambling or piss off."

Foldem bared his fangs. "You don't tell me what to do."

Cam could see dental work was needed "Then you don't want this."

He removed a torn piece of newspaper from the rear pocket of his denims. He handed the page to Foldem.

"What's this?"

"Read it."

Foldem scanned the page. "Race results, so what?"

Cam smiled benignly. "Look at the date."

Foldem did as he was told. His eyes shot open and perspiration beaded on his forehead. "This is tomorrow's paper, how did you . . . "

"As I said, I know a little magic. You put fifty dollars on the first horse and roll the winnings over to the next one and so on until the end. Then you go back to the card club and pay off your debt. Afterward, go home and celebrate with Amy . . . agreed?"

Foldem nodded with vigour. "Agreed."

***

Night had fallen on Monday when Cam walked past his house on the way to see Amy. His bracelet vibrated and flashed its blue light as he passed — he was in. There were times when he wondered if he should meet himself but the undefined repercussions appeared in the manual as VERBOTTEN. It was strange to see the German, but he guessed it came across stronger than DANGER.

Amy answered her door at his third knock. She wore striped blue and white pyjamas and had huge fluffy bananas on her feet. There was no makeup and her hair was wrapped in a towel. She held a huge bowl of ice-cream in her left hand and a spoon in her right. Depression lived.

"Have I disturbed you?" Cam asked.

Amy winced. "More disturbance isn't possible."

"What's wrong?"

Amy shrugged. "Same old, same old. Cant's gambling again. I haven't seen him since Saturday morning. Rumour is he won a motza at the races on Saturday. In fact it's more than rumour. His lawyer rang me this morning and the debt on the house has been cleared, but I have no idea where the bastard is. Probably at the casino or playing the pokies somewhere."

Cam remembered his calculation of how much Foldem should have won. $747, 897. He didn't even go home, he thought angrily.

"I knew you were having trouble. I called over the other night but heard you and Cant arguing. I didn't knock."

"You should have knocked Cant on the head."

Cam smiled at the attempt at humour. He changed subject. "How's Toerag getting on?"

Amy scooped ice-cream from the bowl to her spoon. "More trouble. I lost the original. I put him down somewhere. It's hard to tell the original from the others. I'll get you one out of a box . . . if you want one."

"Sure . . . selling well?"

"Gangbusters. I transferred money to your account last week. Didn't you get it?"

"Sorry . . . haven't checked."

Amy walked from the room and returned with a plastic Toerag. "This is the talking version. They sell great."

Cam pressed on Toerag's stomach. "You wanna try your luck punk." He pressed it again. "No bovver you idjit." He tried again. "Welcome to OFRK, where your children's dreams become reality. Buy me and watch the looks on your friend's faces when I talk to them."

"Is this the only version?"

Amy shovelled another dose of ice-cream into her mouth. "It's the only one that talks," she said, around the mouthful.

***

Cam sat on a barstool in the pub and waited. The clock passed 11:00 as Cant Foldem walked in. He rushed over to Cam. "Hi Cam, seen Amy?"

Cam turned on his seat. "Not for a couple of weeks," he lied.

"Had a great day, last Saturday . . . thanks to you. Paid off the debt and had a great night in the high rollers room of the casino. Great lookin' women up there." The wink and nod were far more than imperceptible. Cam expected them to be accompanied by a nudge.

"You did what I asked, then?"

Cant hesitated for a minute while he weighed the significance of Cam not seeing Amy. "Just as you said."

"Good. Then, as a reward, you can do it all again." Cam reached into his back pocket but there was nothing there. "Ooops . . . left the paper at the old bookshop. We'll pick it up after we have a beer."

Cam held up two fingers to the barmaid and waited.

"Where do you get the papers?" Foldem asked.

"Well . . . it's a secret, but easy if you're a time traveller."

Cant's guffaw turned the heads of everyone in the bar. "You're kidding me."

Cam glared at Foldem. "Can you talk any louder? Maybe everyone in Sydney didn't hear you."

Foldem dropped his head. "You're kidding me, right?"

"You've seen the proof . . . last Saturday."

"And you can do this all the time?"

Cam could see the money machines spinning in Foldem's head. This wasn't a man who used logic as a resource tool. This was a man with narrow focus, of the type who only sees what he wants to see and believes only what he wants to believe. This man believed Cam to be a time traveller. That fact was true but Foldem believing it was supposed to take much longer.

"Why don't we go down to the bookshop and get tomorrow's paper?"

***

The door to Penworthy Rare Books was closed and locked so Foldem stood back as Cam inserted a key and pushed the door open. They went inside and through to the back of the shop. Once there, Cam led Foldem into a small booth sized room and picked up the newspaper that was sitting on a chair in the centre of the booth. He handed the paper to Foldem, who read it starry eyed.

"We better get to the bookie," Cam said, after giving starry eyes time to focus.

"Sure thing," Foldem replied, as he slapped the paper against his hand, with anticipated joy.

Cam closed his eyes and thought of Foldem sleeping in luxury at one of the casino's five star hotel rooms. Luxury and contentment; a gambler in his element. He opened his eyes and glanced at Foldem. "Just think of the luxury you and Amy will be able to live in."

Foldem's lack of comment indicated he didn't see Amy in his dreams.

Cam left the booth and the door swung closed behind him. Foldem grabbed at it but it wouldn't budge. Cam let the booth do its programmed thing. A moment later, he opened the door from the outside.

"Sorry. Bit sticky, lately."

Both men left the building and headed toward the casino. With the crowd in the street, Foldem didn't realise he was not in the same time zone as everyone else, until a man bumped into him. He didn't feel the impact and the man didn't break stride.

"What's going on, Cam?" Foldem asked with a nervous tinge to his voice.

"Ohh . . . sorry Cant. We're time travelling. We're on three second delay. What we see is three seconds after the actual event occurs. Except, of course, for inanimate objects." Cam stopped at a fruiterer and picked an apple from its stand. He chewed on it.

Folder waited for a reaction from customers and the owner of the stand, but there were none.

Cam continued. "This is another trick for you. At cards, you'll be able to see the other hands. You'll have a great time at the casino . . . you can even place your racing bets there. Then you can collect your winnings, maybe pick up a few chicks at the high rollers tables and have a great time."

Dollar signs and thoughts of sex replaced the irises and corneas in Foldem's eyes. "Let me put the horse bets on for you. If you want to make real money at the casino you don't want them getting wind of your success streak too quickly."

Foldem nodded his acceptance of the proposal.

Cam booked Foldem into a room and gave him the key-card. He then left him on time delay and returned to real-time.

***

For the next 3,639 days, Cant Foldem stayed at the casino and got his fill of gambling. He awoke every morning to find it was Sunday and he was in a luxurious bed ogling a beautiful woman who was three seconds removed from him. After ten days, he realised he was having a weird experience and started to mark the days on the hotel room's wall. Every time he awoke the wall was blank, so he started again.

Cam had shown him how to eat, so he didn't starve, and he was able to watch 3,639 reruns of Groundhog Day on the television. He filled in each day by wandering through the casino and learning the rudiments of every gambling game known to man. Unfortunately, he didn't retain the knowledge.

On the 3,640[th] day, he awoke to find it was Sunday and there really was a beautiful woman throwing him a kiss from the bedroom door as she left.

Realising his ordeal was over, he showered, dressed and rushed downstairs and into the middle of street — only to be run over by a bus.

***

I guess that was why ***The Book of Unresolved Grievances*** didn't have an extended life chart." Holly said.

They looked at the page as it faded from ***The Book***.

Cam stared at the fading page. "Did we change history?"

"No . . . he died leaving the casino on Sunday morning. He had no identification on him and had booked in under an alias. Amy wasn't told until after you spoke to her. We changed nothing."

"I figured, after leaving him there for ten years, he would have learned his lesson and made up with Amy. But I guess we'll never know."

"You did well. In real-time he was away from her for only a day. Pity about the bus."

Plexer

THE sounds reverberating from under the control desk were akin to a tone-deaf child on a set of drums. Banging and scraping with a touch of clunking, and the distinct sound of fingernails being dragged across a blackboard. L.I.E.U. had no blackboard, but Holly remembered the sound from her childhood.

Sometimes the sound seemed to be coming from the cabinet housing the 'books' but at other times it seemed to come from the computer monitors themselves. All Holly knew was that the sounds were annoying and she couldn't find their source. Coupled with both of the monitors deciding not to work, and having unexpected travellers dumped in the recreation room on their way to earlier times, it was obvious L.I.E.U. was in a state of flux. Even Cam's memory chip, which was well versed in the operating manuals, was unable to suggest the reason for the cessation of an operating time machine.

Cam shrugged. "I think it's suffering from buggeredness."

"Can Thaddeus help?" Holly asked.

"Maybe, but I left him in my other jacket and by the time I get him the problem will probably sort itself out."

"Maybe we can hit the desk with a hammer? My dad always did that with his car engine. Never fixed anything it made him feel good."

"Love to. But we only have a virtual hammer and it's in the computer software. I can try kicking the thing."

Cam kicked an under-desk panel.

To his and Holly's surprise there was a return noise, like the scream of a demented banshee. Then a magnifying glass appeared on the desk.

Holly looked at the glass and saw a very small and very strong man on the other side. Small because she could hardly see him and strong because he was holding a magnifying glass at least fifty times his size.

For a moment, Holly thought the man must be near blind but then she realised he was holding up the glass so Holly could see him.

"Keep the noise down, will ya," the minuscule man shouted, with the piercing shrill of a voice with sufficient volume to rock the atmosphere.

Holly glared into the glass. "And who are you?"

The man squinted as he looked at Holly's face. From his point of view, it must have seemed enormous. "I'm a Plexer 231-567-19B-TB75-Series 13 of course. You should know. Details of my arrival were issued to all librarians on form 3498B of the maintenance scheduling code."

"And what is the maintenance scheduling code?" Holly replied.

The man spun on his heels and rotated seven hundred and twenty degrees. "Not again. All you librarians need to read your maintenance notifications. They are sent out every ten years on the dot so we can do routine maintenance . . . or in this case time rectification maintenance. Your clock is wrong by a millionth of a millisecond. This can be a problem. Travellers like to end up where they intended to go, not somewhere in the vicinity. To ensure customer satisfaction you need an accurate clock."

Plexer, the same manufacturer as Thaddeus Toerag. Holly wondered if it would act like Toerag. She placed her hand on the table and gestured for the man to walk onto her hand. He did and octorupled in size. Holly could now see him clearly. "And what do you do, exactly. Mr Plexer?"

"I'm a technobot. I fix things. I make time machines work properly."

"How did you get here?" Holly asked.

Now the man was taller, Holly could see a figure very much like Toerag, except this one wore a white tool belt around his waist.

"Same as everyone else. We slid down the compression shaft."

"We?"

"There are two thousand of us working here today. We can't afford for the portal to be inoperative for more than a couple of hours. They used to send a thousand but the work took four times as long. Once they tried to double our number but we couldn't all fit into the compressor at the same time and there was carnage. Bits and pieces everywhere. Heads attached to legs, arms coming out of stomachs. Torsos with legs coming off at all angles like spoked wheels. Since then it's been two thousand."

Cam looked at the bot in Holly's hand and thought of miniature painters in white overalls. "How does it work?" he asked Plexer.

"What?" the bot replied.

"Everything . . . but mainly the time machine."

If the bot wasn't liquid plastic and had a movable face, he would have smiled at hearing the question. It seemed to be the one at the forefront of all of human questions. *Everything*; the all-encompassing word. He used his usual answer. "The answer to everything is in another novel. I'm restricted in what I can tell you. I can tell you how the time machine works but you already know that. Or at least you should. You're an assistant librarian aren't you. Ohh . . . I forgot. What year did you get your memory chip?"

"2078."

"Explains a lot. There's a fault in all chips prior to 2089. You can download the corrections if you wish. It's on page 37,598 of the abbreviated version of the service manual."

Cam scowled at the bot. "You don't know then."

"Look at the size of me. How can anything this small be expected to know everything . . . but I can give you the brief summary, if you like."

"That will suffice," Holly chipped in.

Plexer cast his magnifying glass aside and sat down on Holly's hand. "What year are we in?"

Cam was getting annoyed. "What does it matter?"

"It's important for me to know the level of knowledge you should have. Humans of different eras have differing knowledge on almost every subject. I don't want to go over stuff you should know."

Cam understood Plexer's dilemma. "Home for me is 2019. But I've been in the machine for some time, so don't know exactly where I should be. Holly's a little older."

Plexer mover around on Holly's hand and had her adjust her middle finger, so he could sit more comfortably.

"Okay. You're both from a time when the theory of dark matter was first being explored. In a couple of decades its existence will actually be proved. One day, a brilliant scientist by the name of Itzall Bovincrap, who invented both the time machine and the Plexer TB75-Series 13, found that, when dealing with dark matter, it could be manipulated. It took her thirty years but she finally developed a theory about the effect of compressing dark matter. She then proved it. Once proof was in, she theorised that given the ability to calculate Earth's trajectory through space, she should be able to calculate exactly where the Earth was at any particular time. Then she built the dark matter compressor to prove this second theory. With the machine built she was able to go back to any point in history. She stopped at around 70,000 BCE because travel isn't instantaneous and it was taking too long to get anywhere. She also tried to go forward but found, because time hadn't reached beyond her time, as yet, she couldn't determine whether or not anything happened to Earth to change its course or speed. But I digress. Once she proved her theory, she set up two time machines. One in Paddington in London, one in Paddington in Sydney. The Paddingtons because she once had a fictional character from children's literature as a house guest and they got on. There are some who argue she should have been more imaginative and developed a model for the machine to go through both time and space but she preferred the H.G Wells model. This way, people have to really want to do something, especially when they are travelling in bygone days. Do you want technical details?"

Cam nodded but Holly wrinkled her nose.

"When using the machine, and based on the dark matter compression ratio, you travel at around a 100 years an hour. To get from my time to yours takes around two and a half hours. From this, you can calculate to travel 70,000 years would take 700 hours. Not viable for humans but we bots don't mind. Is that all? I have to get back to work."

"We're to believe this?" Holly asked.

"Some go to Douglas Adams books or Monty Python for answers but being a liquid plastic figure, I don't get involved in the meaning of life."

"Will we be out of service for long?" Holly asked.

"The longer you hold me here the longer we will be. I'm the head technobot. The other nineteen hundred and ninety-nine are lazy sods who don't work without supervision."

"I'd better let you go then."

Plexer stood up, went to liquid form and slid out of Holly's hand. He fell onto the desk and slipped down a crack. A moment later the thunderous din started again.

An hour later, the noise stopped and Holly and Cam could hear time travellers moving around in the recreation room. She should have dropped in to greet them but didn't feel the urge.

Panhandle

HOLLY set *The Hitchhikers Guide to the Galaxy* omnibus edition aside. "The answer isn't forty-two, or even fifty-four, if you're good at maths."

Cam looked at the book cover. "I always thought it was nonfiction."

"The guy with two heads was a bit odd."

"You should have tried fishing in the nineteen sixties. There were fish with two heads. As I said, it's nonfiction. You should go back to when it was written and read it then. It was in tune with its time."

Holly glanced at their target before replying. "I've read the whole thing. I just don't think fantasy is my thing. I have enough trouble with the real world."

Holly and Cam were having lunch in a harbour side restaurant in Sydney, in 2008, keeping an eye on a man who was panhandling waterfront tourists. **The Book** had told them a man named Aquapura Fishwick was flaunting travel laws and it was up to the librarians to sort the matter. What they were dealing with was a tourist with a time-based scam. They had been watching him for some time and both considered him to be good at what he did. Some would say a master craftsman. But then, he did have an advantage over others — with the guts to walk up to someone and ask for money — he could time shift. Fishwick was your typical 'ground hog day' panhandler. He made his approach to passers-by and his plea for money was either accepted or rejected. If rejected, he turned his clock back and approached the target again, at the same instant as the original approach, but in a varied manner. He repeated the performance until he got money. If his initial approach was successful, he used the same technique to increase the amount of money received.

"You think he does this at home?" Holly asked.

"No idea, but I'd say he's a chancer."

"Isn't he with one of the religious studies groups?"

Cam smiled, and then chuckled. "Yes . . . but only if you can call the Order of the Girl in the Red Dress a religion."

"Of course it's a religion. It's registered as a non-profit organisation; it pays no tax and lives off human suffering and the innate desire of humans to be part of something spiritual. The fact it was started by a young time traveller who got separated from her parents and appeared in Hyde Park in London, after accidently turning her delay timer off, makes her no less of a religious apparition than the sightings at Medjugorje, Fatima, or Lourdes, or any of the other myriad sightings from around the world over the centuries. Personally, I would prefer they weren't here at this time but that's because the followers of the Order of the Girl in the Blue Dress are also here to observe the World Youth Day festivities. From what I read in the future news, those two religions just don't get on. They believe in the same things but the radicals on both sides create trouble and swear their take on things is closer to the truth than the other side. It makes no sense to me. Particularly when they started as one holy figure sighting and an argument developed as to the colour of the dress."

"I hear there's a condom shortage in town." Cam added.

"I doubt it. All the young people here have a religious bent and, as such, the lord will provide."

Cam stared at Holly. "I didn't mark you down as a cynic."

"Time travel has removed my Catholic guilt. Now I'm just pragmatic. Our man's on the move."

The man in question was dressed in a smart grey suit. His shirt was white and his tie dangled from around his neck, with the top button of his shirt undone. He wore the look of a respectable man in trouble. According to his story, he had been pickpocketed and had lost his wallet and credit cards. There was no pressure on his victims and he was polite and as jovial as could be, considering his dire circumstances. All he needed was aeroplane fare to get back to Melbourne. Any small contribution would help.

"What's his total?" Holly asked.

"Around $1,000 so far. Not bad for ten minutes work in real-time. When do you want to hit him?"

Holly glanced at her half empty mug on the table. "After coffee. He's in no hurry to finish."

Cam interrogated his mind but it was blank on the subject. He couldn't understand why the man was panhandling more than two hundred and thirty years before he was born. Surely the paper money he was collecting didn't gain in value with time. He turned to his coffee sipping boss. "Any idea why they panhandle money here. I wouldn't have thought it would be of any use in the future."

Holly stopped sipping and smiled at Cam. "There's an old Japanese proverb that goes *it is a beggar's pride that he is not a thief.* The original idea was to satisfy a basic need. The guys from the future use the begging techniques but don't do it for any reason other than personal gain. If they needed money for food or accommodation it would be understandable but guys like this one fence the money for precious stones and gold where possible. Those things gain value over time."

Holly returned to finishing her coffee and keeping an eye on their target.

A flash of concern crossed Cam's face. "Talking about thieves and to change subject a little, I saw a notice concerning some books we are to get hold of, and saw a book on the control desk, this morning. It looked like the original manuscript for *Alice's Adventures Underground.*"

"A copy."

"You're kidding."

"We're librarians. We look after books."

Cam sucked air through his teeth. An idiosyncratic and involuntary gesture whenever required information didn't flow to him. He always sucked a lot of air while drawing but he didn't expect that Holly would get cagy. "Surely we're not going to steal from the British Library?"

Holly shook her head. "Ours is not to reason why."

"Alfred Lord Tennyson. Is it apt?"

Holly pointed to the target. "We can discuss it later. It's time to pull our man in. You take the delay . . . I'll take him head on."

Holly settled the bill and left the restaurant. The target approached her after she had started her journey toward Circular Quay.

"Excuse me ma'am. Sorry to bother you, but could your spare a few bucks. I've had my wallet and credit cards stolen and I need to get back to Melbourne, this afternoon. Whatever you can spare will be appreciated."

Holly looked at him, exuding sympathy. What she said didn't match her look. "I'm sure I could help you, but you've already made enough money to travel business class."

The man pressed on the sleeve of his suit coat and disappeared.

Holly pressed the time delay on her bracelet and followed him. Cam already had him collared.

"Time travel is for leisure and study, Mr Fishwick. You're in 2008 to study, as part of OGRD, which is a really stupid acronym, and you don't have a panhandling licence."

Fishwick laughed at her. "And just who are you? You're not the cops."

"You're right. I'm the Librarian. Much worse than the cops."

Fishwick stood defiant. "Only cops can do something. You can't."

Holly shrugged and removed a small black box from her jacket pocket. "Maybe I can't, but this can. With this box, I can block the signal between your bracelet and the L.I.E.U. satellite. Without the signal, you will revert to your real-time age and, as you aren't born until 2227, you'll just cease to exist in this time zone."

Cam watched as Fishwick turned to jelly. "You wouldn't."

"Try me," Holly glared at Fishwick. "Now you reset your clock until 11:41 this morning and reappear on the waterfront. Instead of begging, you will go to the nearest church and say a few prayers. I take it you're a religious man?"

"But I took money from people. I've read the literature on L.I.E.U. You can't change history. You have to let me keep the money."

Holly let out a sigh of mock exasperation. "Your comprehension genes don't seem to be working. No one gave you money until after 11.41. You reset your time to then, as I said, and they won't have given you any money. Reality says you don't exist in their world."

"And if I won't."

"I don't think you're listening, you'll be born in 2227 . . . you won't exist anywhere until that time."

"You wouldn't dare. I have contacts in high places . . . or is this religious persecution."

Holly's smile was patronising. "Alms for the poor, I should have realised."

"Yes that's it. Now I'll be on my way and you'll keep out of it."

"Can't, I'm afraid."

"I don't know who you are . . . librarian . . . but I'm guessing you don't have the guts to hit the switch."

The moment after Fishwick made his defiant remark, he realised it was a folly he would regret until the moment he was born.

Cam stared at the space where the man stood. "Can you do that?"

"I just did. But look at it this way. One day, Fishwick will be born and during his life he'll decide to time travel to Sydney in 2008 and do some panhandling. He won't get a time travel permit. He won't know why but that isn't our problem." Holly touched her chin with thumb and forefinger. "I wonder where he got a name like Aquapura?"

Cam smiled. "Easy. According my memory chip, it became a popular name after the 2029-2037 water wars. These halved the population of Saharan Africa and spilled over to the Arabian Peninsula. The wars lowered the price of Africa and all bar South Africa was bought by China and redeveloped as jungle. Good for the planet and all that. Aquapura became the male version of a name to indicate your family had been involved. It stuck from then on in. The female version is Aquapuré. Other names to become popular were Nigeria, Somalia and Kenya. These were created to remember some of the country names before China renamed most of the continent as Great Leap Forward Five."

***

After dealing with Fishwick, Cam and Holly returned to the L.I.E.U. building and 2019. Holly set about restacking books. Cam stood at the bottom of her ladder.

"*Alice's Adventures Underground*," Cam said.

"Lewis Carroll, real name Charles Dodgson. 1832-1898. Anything else?"

Cam released the brake from the ladder. It moved, a tad, sideways.

Holly shot him her death stare. "Won't work."

"What if I won't help you?"

Holly softened her look. "Blackmail is beneath you . . . or so I thought. Fact is, I'm worried. This is the first time."

Cam's stare was quizzical. "Care to explain why we've been asked to do it?"

"Part of the library's raison d'être."

"It's a time travelling research centre and amusement park."

"Its main function is a library. It accumulates knowledge and stores it. Remember when we first met?"

"When I walked past your Penworthy Rare Books shop."

"You know better, Cam. In 1940, we met in the entry foyer of L.I.E.U. in England . . . you caught me on the way out. I saw the library. It was huge. It was over three levels and there were hundreds of thousands of books. I don't know whether or not I was supposed to see it or if it was really where it appeared to be but I've seen the library. This is the library designed to house the books of history; the original books of history."

Cam reset the ladder's brake and walked to the window. He would have watched the passing parade but no one passed. A thought stung his brain. "Are you saying our controllers are book thieves and the copy of Alice is the original?"

Holly smiled. "No . . . it's a copy. We haven't stolen the original yet, but we will. I have no compunction about the library having the original copies of the books, irrespective of how we acquire them."

Cam shook his head. "I'm not with you. We only seem to be interested in valuable books. The books on the list were *Traité des Arbres Fruitiers*, the *Codex Leicester*, JK Rowling's handwritten copy of *Beedle the Bard*, and *Alice's Adventures*. These books are among the ten most valuable books in the world."

"And that's why *this* library should preserve them. My seeing the library means it exists as part of L.I.E.U. and, therefore, the library still exists two hundred and fifty years from now. By then, no one will care how the books were acquired."

"I don't like the idea of stealing anything."

Holly smiled and climbed down from the ladder. "Then you will be pleased to know we have only been requested to get hold of four books. You saw the complete list."

Venetian Mask

CAM'S first solo venture into the world of an assistant librarian as *time cop* came a few weeks after he started work. By then, he had totally lost track of time and where his real life stood with reference to the time manipulation he undertook as part of normal duties. Because of this he didn't know whether his first tour of duty was to begin ten minutes after starting or ten years. All he knew was that he felt somewhat [1] anxious about wandering through time on his own — actually the thought terrified him. Maybe because his first travel experience had landed him with the memory chip and that little piece of genius annoyed him more and more as time went on. On the other hand, it had taken him very little time to learn how to interface with the time machine using only thoughts and a series of differing blinking motions. And then there was the time bracelet.

There was no avoiding it, the time bracelet concerned him more a little. For a life and death device, he was surprised it required physical manipulation and that he had to press a button to turn the time delay on and off. This was reasonable if he had things under control, but could prove troublesome if he couldn't press the button at the required time. He imagined being arrested in some foreign time zone and being tied up or otherwise stopped from pressing the button. The resultant outcome could be disastrous. Surely it would be better controlled with a blink. After all, if you are in danger you are bound to blink at some time. But then, maybe there was a danger of uncontrolled blinking. He figured he could get into a situation where express blinking would turn the device on and off in rapid succession. Said outcome could also be disastrous. Maybe hand operation was best after all.

---

[1]This is a relative term covering the feeling from *a bit* all the way to *incredibly*.

Then there was the bracelet's blue light and buzzer. These had no physical control but the buzzer sounded and the light flashed on and off if the wearer was about to come into contact with themselves. Obviously, this was a problem if travelling in the future and you ran into yourself, at the supermarket or the pub, while travelling in real-time. While the exact outcome of such a meeting wasn't known, as nobody was stupid enough to try, it was considered highly probable that one, or both of the persons would cease to exist, as a person could not exist in two bodies at the same time. Cam had looked up the scenario in Volume 2 of the operating manual, but the page contained nothing but a heading saying 'What happens when you meet yourself in the future' followed by a huge question mark that filled the rest of the page. This lack of full description of the *meet yourself* effect wasn't the only thing about the manuals to annoy him but when an operating manual covers fifteen volumes and contains more than seven million words and tens of thousands of diagrams you can expect a couple of question marked pages.

In the great scheme of things, the question marked pages, manual operation of the bracelet and a feeling of anxiousness only annoyed him. What infuriated him was how the inventors of L.I.E.U. had engineered the H.G.Wells' version of the time machine. Good idea for its time but later bypassed by every science fiction writer with a bent for time travel. The H.G.Wells' models only travelled in time, better time machines travelled through time and space.

The first time this minor fact, within the realm of time travel anyway, infuriated him was when he went in search of an American by the name of Elfinware PS Pavarotti.

Holly had given him the job but no insight into how he was to undertake the work. A message had appeared in **The Book of Unresolved Grievances** stating that a pottery maker by the name of Elfinware PS Pavarotti was on his way to Venice in 1748 with the intention of attending the Carnival of Venice. Mr Pavarotti was highlighted because he was an excellent shower singer and often regaled his wife and two children by setting up chairs within his bathroom and singing to an audience of three. It was noted, he had tried singing to larger audiences, but suffered from the common singing malady of the shower singer — he was completely tone-deaf. Despite this, or maybe because of it, **The Book** had decided Mr Pavarotti should be monitored, as he was thought to house a burning desire to sing *Nessun Dorma* in St Mark's Square. If this were to happen, not only would Venetian ears bleed but they would be subjected to an appalling rendition of a song that wasn't sung in public until 1926.

"Why us?" Cam asked, as Holly re-read the message.

"None of the assistant librarians from our London branch are available and Pavarotti left from Paddington two weeks ago. He's doubtless half way to Venice by now."

Cam's memory chip kicked in. "1748. London to Venice. Very few merchant ships running the French coast, due to the war between England and Spain. Hostilities ceased that year but the main route was Southampton to France by ship, overland to Marseilles and then via ship to Venice. ETA six weeks."

"Okay . . . he's probably less than half way. You're still a long way behind."

"Easy. When I get to London I'll go back to his start date and intercept him in Paddo."

"Problem. He took his compression trip in 2257 and we can't go forward to then. You'll have to see what you can do in 1748."

Cam shook his head. A stupid mistake. Too juvenile to make in front of his boss, but he decided not to dwell on it. "Do we have a photo of the guy?" he asked, with eyebrows raised.

"We have his full identity details . . . in 3D if you want, but it may not help. You can't just show a photo around in 1748. You'd be burned as a witch."

"Warlock."

"Pedant."

"Overscrupulous, scrupulous, precise, exact, over-exacting, perfectionist, precisionist, punctilious, meticulous, fussy, fastidious, finical, finicky," Cam blurted out, knowing he had annoyed Holly for the second time in a couple of minutes. "A few of them maybe . . . I'm sorry, it's the memory chip,"

Holly ignored him. "You're booked on a flight from Sydney to Heathrow late this afternoon."

***

Cam sat in the airline departure lounge and thought of the human transporters of sci-fi TV series and movies. It was all so easy. Disappear in one place and appear in another. With such a machine, he could go straight from Paddington in Sydney to Venice, have dinner under the

Rialto Bridge, and then just drop back in time to 1748 and find his man. He wondered if the dreebs at L.I.E.U were working on it. He hoped so. His flight to London would be in real-time and it took twenty-four hours. Once he had tried to fly with the three second delay switched on but had missed the flight (by three seconds). Real-time flying meant real-time people and, on long-haul, it meant screaming kids, smelly feet, men wearing two hats and cute but inaccessible female stewards, who only put out for the passengers on the other sides of the screened off areas at the front of the plane — or so he imagined.

***

The flight was both uneventful and as expected. Two babies cried for a total period of two hours and forty-six minutes, across the two legs of the flight. An obese warthog's smelly feet were the least of her malodorous issues and he discovered that, if you're an American and buy two Mexican sombreros in Singapore, you are obliged to wear both throughout the entire leg of the flight to London.

The taxi from Heathrow to London Mews in Paddington took two hours and when Cam arrived at the L.I.E.U bookshop, it was attended by a woman who was the spitting image of Holly Penworthy.

"Hello Holly," Cam said. "I didn't expect to see you here,"

Holly looked sheepish. "I would have told you except I didn't know myself until I was on holidays in a short time from now and was asked to come here to greet you."

There was no reason for Holly to be there, Cam thought.

"I take it this greeting has something to do with Elfinware Pavarotti?" he said.

"No . . . that's an old case you're currently working on. This is a library issue. I need you to help me in 1768. We need to steal a manuscript in Paris. We may as well do it while we're here. It'll save us another flight from Australia, later. I'll wait here until you get back from the Pavarotti case . . . I think."

"You think?"

"Well . . . I remember the case disappeared from *The Book's* screens, which means it must have had a conclusion, but I don't remember what happened to you. It's one of the problems with time travel. You forget the order of things. You can be killed in one time zone but carry out assignments at a later time. It's all in the manual."

Cam remembered the reading the section in the manual called 'Steps to be taken after you are killed but immediately before you die.' He hadn't understand a word of it. "Can you look it up . . . here?"

"I don't have the access codes to **_The Book's_** screens for this site . . . why do you ask."

"Self-preservation really."

Holly ignored the comment. "You better get ready. The next compression to 1748 passes here in ten minutes. Be ready to finagle [2] yourself."

***

Three days after leaving a hostelry in the 1748 version of Notting Hill, Cam found himself on a small sailing boat half way across the English Channel (or La Manche if you prefer the French). He was nursing the remains of a hangover, and the memory of what had caused it. Unfortunately, lite beer wasn't on the menu at the Pheasant Scrotum Inn and he remembered sitting in a corner, crying into a dirty ceramic mug and praying for death when a well-dressed and articulate dandy helped him to his feet and told him to wake up to himself. The man wore a green frock coat, black and grey chequered trousers, an extravagantly knotted cravat and calf length black boots of the finest available leather. He had long thin sideburns and on his head rested a tall black hat.

Cam was able to remember what he was wearing as the man was standing in front of him, still wearing the same clothes.

"Sir Percy Blakeney," the man doffed his hat.

"Not possible," Cam replied, somewhat taken aback by the name.

"Why not, my good man?" the man asked.

"You don't appear until around 1905 when Baroness Emma Magdolna Rozália Mária Jozefa Borbála 'Emmuska' Orczy de Orczi has the Scarlet Pimpernel published. Also, it's 1748. You don't appear until after 1789, when the French revolution starts. Besides your clothes are too fancy for this time."

---

[2]In this case, *finagle* means stepping onto a time compression unit as it passes by a particular time zone. To wit, a unit travelling from 2257 to 1412 to witness the sacking of Volterra by the Florentines. Cam finagled himself off in 1748.

"Would you believe Dick Turpin?"

"Nope. Died 17th April 1739."

"I'd make a good highwayman."

"William Plunkett may still be around."

The man shook his head. "Not for me . . . successful highwayman but the name's too boring."

"Like another try," Cam said, feeling a little chirpier and sitting up in the swaying boat."

"Dennis Fenton. Friends call me Den. Fellow traveller and Assistant Librarian based in London. I'm on my way to Assisi. People in the surrounding areas are beginning to espouse St Francis as a bit of a nutter."

Cam lifted his right eyebrow. "I thought that was a twentieth century phenomenon."

"It was, but some dooblehopper from 2256 decided to make it earlier. He caught a compression flight to the 12th Century but got off too early. I have to find him and stop him rabble rousing."

"He's going to the source then?"

"He intends to try to get Francis on the booze and recant his devotion. You know Clare with the Arse instead of Clare of Assisi. There was a time when his interceding would have worked."

"Surely someone could have pulled the plug."

Den frowned. "My job."

"You hesitate?"

"Guy may just be ahead of his time."

***

Venice, Home of the Doge of the Most Serene Republic of Venice; a place of wet feet and tainted water. A place wiped from the Italian map in the great Tsunami of 2056, much to the annoyance of the local tourist industry and the builders of the Great Tsunami Protection Wall of 2032[3].

Cam stood in the centre of St Mark's Square wishing he had his digital SLR camera and trying to remember where he had stowed the photo of Pavarotti. Around him, young men sat behind easels, sketching and

---

[3]The Great Tsunami Protection Wall was still under warranty and the Great Tsunami Wall Company went belly up after being sued by Giuseppe Totti, for flooding his free range chicken farm in Lido di Venezia.

painting and wondering if they were starting an intergenerational trade, which would stand them in good stead until 2056.

He sauntered through their ranks, with his three second time delay activated, until he found the one he wanted. His name was Giovanni Antonio Canal, known as Canaletto. He looked to be early fifties and his popularity was starting to fade. Cam was surprised to see him, as he had moved to England in 1746.

"I'm surprised to see you, Canaletto," Cam said, projecting his voice from beyond his timer.

The man looked around, startled.

"Don't worry, you can't see me."

"My lord?"

"Nah, sorry. It's just me, Cameliel Cameron. You don't know me but I need your assistance."

Canaletto spun on his seat, like the girl's head in The Exorcist. He fell to the ground.

"Don't be afraid. I won't harm you . . . but I need you to do something for me."

Canaletto looked horrified. "Anything, my lord."

"Good . . . close your eyes and count to XXV. When you reopen them, you'll find a strange object if you flip your painting. I want you to sketch the image for me."

Canaletto did as requested and then sat in awe as he glanced at the Pavarotti photo.

"I need to find this man before the festival begins. I need a sketch to show around and find him."

Canaletto took very little time to get over the shock of seeing his first photograph. "What's in it for me?" he asked.

"Mortality. I will tell you when you will greet the lord."

"I specialise in landscapes."

"Just this once, huh. It will go over well in England and your works will be remembered and sought after for all time."

Canaletto stood from his easel and began to walk from the square. "And when do you require this sketch?"

"Tomorrow morning is good for me. Just stow it behind your painting and I'll pick it up."

Cam admonished himself for not bringing pencils and paper. He could have done his own sketching.

***

At precisely 1:00 pm the following day, Cam lifted the finished sketch from Canaletto's easel and looked at the result. A fine artist can paint anything. He had what he needed. All he had to do was wait until early evening and surprise Mr Pavarotti by displaying the sketch in a prominent place. Even with masks being worn for the festivities, he figured Pavarotti would panic and do something stupid. He just had to be in the right place at the right time.

At precisely 7:18pm, Cam sat, time delayed, in the hotel room of one Giacomo Girolamo Casanova and ogled him as he went through his paces with a northern European princess. Cam thought him a little chinless for a man with such a reputation but conceded he had turned love-making into an art-form.

At 8:30pm, he pinned the sketch to the wall of the most popular restaurant in the square, then stood and waited, resplendent in the finery and cape of the time, wearing a volto mask to cover his entire face.

It was no more than an hour before a brutish looking man of grossly overweight proportion, and wearing a stark white bauta mask to hide his face, stopped to stare at the sketch. The mask covering his identity failed to hide the gasp that emanated from his overdeveloped larynx. As Cam expected, he panicked and pushed his time delay button.

Cam blinked and met Pavarotti on the other side of the delay. Pavarotti gasped again, this time accompanied by a yelp of frustration.

"Who on Earth are you?" Pavarotti demanded.

"Your nemesis . . . at the moment."

Pavarotti shook his head from side to side like a sideshow clown, then pushed his fists into the sides of his head. "I'll bet you're one of those time sliders we're warned about. You lot who stop all the fun. The *fun* police of the nanny state."

"I like it," Cam said. "Nice sentiment. *Fun police.*"

"Well?" Pavarotti shouted.

Cam was a little taken aback. "Well what?"

"What does it cost me to get you to piss off and leave me be?"

"Ohh . . . bribery. You think I'm Italian." He hesitated for affect, before continuing. "Maybe I should. Okay . . . what do you have to offer?"

"For what?" It was Pavarotti's turn not to understand.

"The bribe . . . gold, frankincense, myrrh. Something to do with some god anyway. After all, it's what you're doing here . . . or want to do anyway. Playing god. Waking people up to something outside of the orbit of their knowledge. You just can't do it."

Pavarotti looked Cam over, staring at him from head to foot. Less than half the weight and at least six inches shorter. No match. "And you'll do what?"

Cam reached into the pocket of his white blouse and retrieved a small black box. "This breaks your link with L.I.E.U. You'll disappear until you're born. It won't affect your history . . . like you won't interfere with Venetian history. I press on this box and you're out of here."

Pavarotti was stunned. He removed his mask to reveal a sweaty face. He dabbed his forehead with a white handkerchief. "That easy, huh?"

"You could try to grab it, but you need to move a metre before my finger moves two millimetres, and the exertion may give you a heart attack."

Pavarotti lunged, but not in the way Cam expected. He had pushed his timer and returned to the real world.

Cam followed but Pavarotti was running toward the edge of the square, pushing revellers out of his way as he went and grunting like a land based hippo.

Cam was making ground when a man stood squarely in front of him and angled a drawn sword toward his throat. "Do not follow the fat man. He does not speak Venetian . . . he is a spy. The Habsburg Austrians rule Venice and want to close the festival. They send their spies, disguised as fat buffoons."

Cam cut in. "They will stop the mask carnival in 1797 but not before then . . ." He stopped reading from his memory chip and snapped his mouth shut. He had said too much already.

He felt the tip of the blade against his throat. He spotted Pavarotti again. This time he was heading back into the square, surrounded by four men, all with swords drawn.

Cam decided on a plan of action. "The fat man is not a spy. He is an actor and singer and I am a soothsayer. We are here for the carnival. Our act, tonight, was to get your attention. We hurtle through the crowd and infiltrate your thoughts."

***

Pavarotti was brought to stand beside Cam and they were both forced to kneel at the feet of the men with swords.

"What now?" Pavarotti whispered.

"Time travel. Can you touch your timer?"

"My finger's on it now."

Cam stood up, despite a sword digging into his right shoulder. When fully upright he addressed the swordsmen and the crowd that had gathered around. "My friend and I will disappear. We will then reappear at the base of the Campanile." He looked down at Pavarotti. "Now."

Both men disappeared from view. Together they ran to the Campanile, Pavarotti, sweating profusely. Once there, they leaned against the wall and waited for the swordsmen to surround the tower's base. They reappeared.

Anguished and startled screams rent the air. Cam took a bow. Pavarotti sweated and gripped his timer.

Five swords were thrust forward.

"Rialto Bridge," Cam shouted, just before he disappeared again.

Pavarotti leaned forward and rested his bulk on his knees. "I can't run that far."

Cam smiled at him. "We'll walk. We appear again, then you disappear for good. I'll make myself known and let them calm down and think I'm a magician."

Pavarotti found a seat and sat on a woman with a wide hooped multi-coloured dress and handheld Colombina mask. The three second delay meant she didn't notice. He started to cry and held his chubby hands to his eyes. "All I wanted to do was sing in St Mark's Square. It no longer exists in my time. I wanted to follow my ancestor and become a great tenor."

Cam knew where Pavarotti was going. He smiled in anticipation. "Your ancestor?"

"Luciano Pavarotti. The great Italian tenor. I am descended from him."

"Typo."

Pavarotti furrowed his brow and glared at Cam. "Typo?"

"On your birth certificate. You are descended from Lucien Pavarotti of Scunthorpe. He was a good amateur potter. That's why your mother called you Elfinware PS. Do you know what PS stands for?"

"Paolo Sylvio of course . . . like Luciano."

"Try Porcelain Shoe. It was an Elfinware porcelain line. Your mother was sending you a message."

Pavarotti's tears flowed like a waterfall in the wet season. "I'm not related then."

"You're not even Italian."

"All I wanted to do was sing Nessun Dorma in St Mark's Square."

Cam had some sympathy for the retched soul, though he didn't show it. "Your biggest mistake was Nessun Dorma. Wasn't very popular in 1748. Probably because it didn't exist until Puccini wrote it around 1924. That's what made *The Book* take notice and dob you in."

Pavarotti was defeated. He ran out of tears and started using his hand-kerchief to squeeze some back into his eyes. "What now?"

"You're out of here. You go back to Paddington, the way you came and then catch a ride home."

Pavarotti just nodded and held his head low.

Cam looked around the square at the thousands of festival enlivened people, just seconds away. He had an idea. "You can sing . . . here and now . . . St Mark's Square. You do it in the time delay zone. The best I can do for you."

Pavarotti bowed toward Cam in the manner of an Elizabethan courtier. He stood with legs splayed, stopped his crying and sang. Every bird, even those with only the slightest soupçon of hearing, flew out of Venice.

Ten minutes after the solo performance, Cam appeared on the Rialto Bridge. As soon as he came into view, one of the swordsmen lunged at his heart.

French Fruits

CAM finagled himself from the compression unit at Paddington.

Holly smiled at him with her smile reserved for friends. "He missed you then,"

Cam smiled back. "Who told you?"

"No one. I broke the machine code and looked up your journey. You were very brave in appearing at the Rialto Bridge."

Cam shrugged. "I had to. I had to make them see me as a magician and not some sort of sorcerer. If I didn't appear, the whole incident would have been remembered by the locals . . . and possibly written about or painted. By reappearing I was able to convince them I was just a guy who knew some magic. I explained Pavarotti by telling them he was pooped and too buggered to continue performing. They had no idea what I was talking about but it must have sounded mystical."

"You were stabbed in the heart."

"The sword just penetrated the skin. I grabbed it by the blade and pushed it away, cut my hand, despite leather gloves being de rigueur at the time. Once they saw me bleed and look a bit sickly, they were convinced I was just a guy who knew a little magic and wasn't going to tell them how it was done."

"You're okay then?"

"I am now, but it took nine weeks to get back here. Both the chest and hand wounds got infected. I was laid up for two weeks. Fortunately for me, a lady friend of Casanova . . . one Henriette Bohemie . . . looked after me until I was well enough to travel."

Holly looked at Cam over the top of her reading glasses. "Did you learn anything?"

"Antibiotics didn't exist in 1748."

"Anything else?"

"Yes . . . the time zone makes no difference if you're bleeding, and travelling in an 18ᵗʰ century coach is bloody uncomfortable."

"Then you'll know what to do when we go to Paris in 1768."

"I take it there's a good reason."

"We're going to steal a manuscript. *Traité des Arbres Fruitiers* by Henri-Louis Duhamel du Monceau."

Cam sat on a chair and peered into Holly's eyes. "One on the list. I assume under instruction from L.I.E.U. Did you ask why this particular manuscript?"

"I know why."

"And?"

"At some time maybe . . . when we're back in Sydney. This one will be easy. Duhamel has the original at his home. I have the copy here. We will replace the original with the copy and Duhamel will deliver the copy to his publisher as the original. The publisher won't know, Duhamel won't know, and the world will be none the wiser."

"And the original goes to?"

Holly didn't answer. "We have twenty minutes to get changed and ready. We're off to Paris."

***

On the streets of Paris, the topic of conversation was France's ambitions in wresting Corsica from Genoa. Cam bet some of the locals a treaty would be signed by the end of the year. He knew he wouldn't be there to collect his winnings but he allowed himself to place into people's minds an idea about a great French leader being be born in Corsica and if the treaty didn't take place, said great leader would be Genoese. He didn't mention names but predicted there would be arguments concerning the man's height. Most thought Cam fanciful, more often, an idiot.

***

"He's a very old man." Holly said, when she first laid eyes on Duhamel from the first floor window of an inn.

"Born 1700, dies in 1782. For this time he's a very old man. Smart too: physician, naval engineer and botanist. A mixed life. We're not doing the right thing here."

"Ours is not to reason why . . . besides, no one gets hurt."

Cam shook his head. "Of course someone gets hurt . . . you. This book theft can't be being directed by whoever created L.I.E.U. I can understand them wanting the original manuscripts and/or first edition print runs for the library but they must be loaded and could buy what they want at auction. My chip says you could pick up the top ten most expensive books in the world for around $150 Million. A shitload of money for the likes of us but would be a drop in the ocean for the L.I.E.U. founders. Think about it. It doesn't make sense."

"Sorry Cam . . . but we just do what we're told."

Cam walked to the inn's window and peered down on the mass of stinking humanity in the street below. He grabbed his chamber pot and threw the contents out of the window. A man, dressed in black, half drew his sword as he glared upward. He saw there was no one there and wiped urine from his cape with his servant's shirt sleeve. Cam wagered the servants name was French for Baldrick.

"We can't do it now though. There's a problem."

Holly adjusted her bustle and cursed its presence. "And what particular problem is this?"

"It's the copy of *Traité des Arbres Fruitiers*. It's flawed. It's the apple Calville Rouge on page 322 and the Muscat grapes on page 280. There are bits missing."

Holly glared at him with the leather look he remembered from when she had first spoken to Toerag. "You mean pages are torn."

"No. Worse. Bits of the fruit are missing."

Holly sauntered across the room and picked up the copy. She opened it to page 322. The pristine apple in the drawing had a piece bitten out of it. She eyeballed Cam. "You didn't tell me Thaddeus was with you."

"I didn't expect you to be here . . . remember."

"And you've let him chew the fruit in the book."

Cam could sense Holly's fuse was on the verge of igniting. This would be a long and arduous torture to bear. He decided to take it on the chin. "He was hungry."

"Then feed the bloody thing."

"He doesn't eat real food. He's a drawn character . . . he can only eat drawn food. He's sorry for what he did but he wanted a different taste sensation. He told me the fruit was drawn so well he wanted to try it. He was disappointed though. Told me it tasted like ink . . . and ink well past its use-by date."

"And where's the little shit now?"

"He guessed you'd find out what he'd done went into hiding. He's a border decoration but I don't know on which page."

Holly screamed with exasperation. She ripped at her bustle and pulled off the dress. "How could women do this to themselves? Get me some of your clothes. I'll travel as a man until we get back to England."

"I don't have much," Cam injected.

"You have less now, you gobshite. Get me some clothes and get Toerag out of the book."

"He won't come out."

"Listen, *Fifth Assistant Librarian*, if he's stuffed up the copy like you say . . . I may as well burn the bloody thing with him in it."

"Page 147, left-hand side border." The voice was almost inaudible and appeared to have as much tremolo as a sixties' guitar solo.

Holly looked at the book.

Cam turned to page 147 and used his fountain pen to suck up the ink from the left-hand border. When finished, he re-deposited the ink onto the room's only table. It took the shape of the rogue as it spilled from the pen. When complete, Toerag stood to full height.

Holly glared at the miniature figure. "Well Mr Toerag?"

Toerag bowed, jellied a little. "I can fix the problem. I just had a taste. Ink had too much eosin in its red pigment for my liking. I'm sure Cam can redraw the missing bits. It'll be as good as gold."

"Duhamel may notice," Holly spat.

"There is another way," Toerag uttered.

Holly placed her hand on the table and beckoned Toerag toward her. He hesitated, shrugged as if his world were about to end, and jumped up onto her hand. She squeezed him, gently, between her thumb and forefinger. "What is your idea, little man?"

"We don't do this to poor Mr Duhamel. He's put a lot of work into his book and he deserves the accolades. This becomes a famous and valuable book because of its quality. In the end, stealing the original won't matter. They've put like a bar code into the copy on page 103. I assume that's so they can tell if you return the copy as the original. But one day, someone else will be able to detect the code and then the game will be up. Once it's proven the original is in L.I.E.U. and wasn't purchased at any time, the authorities will know they have a stolen work. And besides, someone hasn't thought this through. If you steal the book at this time, the copy will become valuable and then the copy will need to be stolen."

Holly smiled. "You speak well for a moulded fluid character. I sense more intelligence than I gave you credit for."

"T'is you my lady. I soak up the intelligence of whoever holds me. I'm just absorbing you."

Holly laughed. "Okay crawler. How do we resolve this?"

"Cam can do it. The code is in a specially ionised ink containing nanoscopic plutonium particles. They were drawn onto the page. Cam can replace the ionised ink with real ink and no one will be able to tell the original book from the copy."

Holly shot a look at Cam, who shrugged. "Thaddeus can show me where I need to scrape and draw . . . so I guess it's possible."

***

Holly wore Cam's clothes and passed as a man when she met Henri-Louis Duhamel du Monceau. She introduced herself as George Formby of the Royal Academy of Arts, which would begin operations on 10th December 1768 after a personal act by King George III. She inveigled her way into getting samples of his DNA and even borrowed a coat [4] that she promised to return.

Cam repaired the copy of *Traité des Arbres Fruitiers*. It was wrapped in the coat and covered with as much of Duhamel's DNA as possible before it was placed in the 'out' tray at Paddington.

"I don't like it," Holly said, as the book disappeared from the tray. "What happens if we don't do what is required?"

"I don't know if it's the same for librarians but for assistant librarians, if you don't perform a given task then this place becomes the Hotel California. Time spent herein is added to your normal life so instead of restarting life where and when you joined the company, you lose part of your real life. In some cases, you get a ten second time delay which means you live apart from everyone. This delay can go on for as long as the company chooses. For you, it will probably be different. In 1961, you were given an option and chose to lead your real life in parallel with this life. For you there's no going back. I've seen you in your normal life. You may now be old but you chose the life. If the penalty for not doing something

---

[4]She had lost her coat to the French highwayman Claude Duval, just out of Domfront. . .or so she said.

was to make you stay within the L.I.E.U. zone, you would likely go mad. The best you can do here is enjoy the company of the assistant librarians. Only problem is, you never see them. There are five in total but you have only met Lucian and me and I don't suggest for a moment we're good female company. I guess you could travel somewhere nice and turn off the timer, but there may be unwanted ramifications."

"How do you know all of this? You joined in 2019 and I was inducted in 1960 . . . yet you have far more knowledge than I do, about the system."

Cam shrugged. "Because it's my job to teach you and I do the study. The great advantage with this place is, if I take say . . . four days . . . to investigate something, I can change time and return to the very second I started the investigation. When I do this, my memories and the knowledge gained remain, due to my memory chip implant. I can recall everything I read or see and it takes no apparent time to learn. I gain age in the outside world, but I haven't been there for a while. Most of my time here has been spent reading the manuals and operating procedures and investigating the whereabouts of the other assistant librarians."

Holly nodded. "I've been wondering about the others. Will I ever get to meet them?"

"Of course. They work for you. The tasks they're on now were set by one of your successors but when the tasks are complete, the assistant librarians will report to you."

Holly shot him a quizzical stare. "I don't understand?"

"In terms of base location time, you're the first Librarian. More will follow. There were other librarians before you but in the time line, they come after you. It means they were stationed in our future. I could tell you more but there is no record of your successors. Once librarians leave the service their records are expunged, to ensure they aren't disturbed."

Holly segued. "If you have a memory chip, why don't I?"

"Simple. Your task is to use your knowledge and life experiences to resolve your tasks. Encyclopedic knowledge would be of no use to you. Can we get back to the task at hand now?"

Holly rekindled her leather look and glared at him. "Not until you tell me more about my assistants. I want to know who they are and what they're doing."

Cam guessed she was entitled to the knowledge but there was no memory chip function for decision-making. He'd hoped she would gather the information over time, but she was the Librarian.

"Okay. I'll give you a brief summary. Lucian Helldale you know. He's the First Assistant Librarian and his task is librarian recruitment. He's out looking for your successors. His task is constant. As you are aware, the tenure for the position is two years. Most last for one tenure. You are the first to extend the tenure and you're the only Librarian who has chosen to visit her normal life alongside the task of librarian. In time, you will question this decision but for now you do what you do. The Second Assistant Librarian is Godwin Godwell. He's not returned from Arimathea. He's trying to sort out a problem he created there. You see he went off grid and turned off his timer. He had a friend named Joseph, who some claim to be the father of Jesus Christ. Others argue Jesus' father was a guy named Jacob but that's another story. Anyway, Godwin was babysitting young Jesus one day and someone mistook him for the kid's father. Based on Godwin's nickname, the expression *Son of God* came into being. Godwin has to stay there until he sorts everything out. Could be a very long task. You see, he interfered with history."

Cam waited for Holly to comment, but her expression was pensive.

"Next is the third assistant, Cherry Polenta. She's back in 1937 on a case with Donald Duck's nephews. Huey claims he was drawn first, so should be more prominent than his brothers Dewey and Louie."

Cam stopped talking and waited. Holly's expression remained pensive.

"The fourth assistant is Filipa Mutherbord. He's our resident nerd. Hard core I.T. geek. He's missing and off the radar. Last seen trying to turn himself into an avatar so he can live inside software. I'm the fifth assistant in line but your first assistant. I expect I'll be promoted to fourth assistant if Mutherbord fails in his quest."

"Of these, how many are available for my current use?"

"There are a few who work out of Paddington London. I met one on the way to Venice. His name was Dennis Fenton."

"Here . . . and available now."

Cam grinned. "Other than me?"

"Yes."

"None."

Glitch

'EDRADOUR' – to some, it is an obscure whisky from Pitlochry; to Cam it was the elixir of the gods. He needed its calming qualities to alleviate an internal battle. After the Duhamel case he couldn't decide whether to classify himself as thief or saviour, but whatever he was he expected repercussions. What he didn't know was when the coin would land. He sat back on his chair, with eyes half closed, and thought of nothing more than the enjoyment of the single malt. Pencils and scotch; a heady mixture that had delivered him to his current lifestyle. But what type of lifestyle? Working for someone (or maybe just an acronym) he hadn't met, and doing things that sometimes scrambled his senses. Mind you, half a bottle of restorative was doing wonders. He put his glass aside and glanced at his watch. It was almost time to get changed. In forty minutes he would be at the Manufacturers' Hall in Sydney Showground for the 1965 Rolling Stones Concert. What a buzz. Only a time traveller can attend a concert held years before his birth. A giant tick for the plus side of lifestyle.

Ten minutes later, he was in the dressing room trying on the latest in 1965 jackets. He read the label. Fabric: fifty-five per cent Dacron polyester (for shape) and forty-five per cent wool (for drape). Colour burgundy. Skinny grey slacks and a mauve shirt completed the outfit with brown or black shoes according to personal taste. He felt as colourless as his clothing but the Stones beckoned.

Not far to walk, so he strolled down the road and decided to walk past his old apartment. He had never seen it in the sixties but expected there to be little change and fresher paintwork. He was within ten metres of the building when the blue alarm on his bracelet stated to flash.

"Not possible," he said out loud. "How can I meet myself when I wasn't born and didn't live in the building?"

The flashing intensified as he neared the building. He stopped at the gate and stared. It hadn't changed at all and he began to shudder. The blue door, the one he had painted himself to cover the original green, was blue. Something was amiss. He closed his eyes and thought of an alternate point of reference. Penworthy Rare Books? The copper door would have been shinier in 1965. He raced back to the bookshop but stopped in his tracks when he spotted the dull copper of the door. There would be no Stones on this January '65 evening.

As soon as he walked through the front door, Petra Petitfille glanced at him over her shoulder. "Hi Cam."

Cam stared at her as his chemical reaction antenna rose. She was dressed in a black leather jumpsuit with white shoulder boards. Her facial structure was highlighted to perfection with makeup and her hair was covered by a red wig, cut in pageboy style. To his mortification, his chip sensed rejection. He stopped imagining. He looked up at the year clock. There was something wrong. Instead or four digits it had five. The year read 2019 in its first four numbers but a half had been added by the fifth. Something was going on and Cam was way out of his depth. He asked the question at the front of the line. "What's going on and where's Holly?"

Petra smiled at him. "You said question. You asked two."

She wasn't supposed to read his mind. "In the same sentence the number doesn't matter."

Petra's smile reflected immeasurable tolerance. "I'll answer one of them . . . which do you choose?"

Cam thought for a moment. "Start with what's going on?"

"The easy one. Good start,"

Petra opened **The Book** and pushed the button at bottom left. A photo appeared on the screen. The photo was in black and white and Cam reeled at its beauty. The photographer had captured the most beautifully photogenic face he had ever seen, in perfect image. The woman looked to be in her early twenties. The background was an illuminated drop-sheet and any clothing, the woman wore, was out of shot. Soft blonde hair fluffed around the face in a style without era. Her small, angled nose engendered thoughts of Scandinavia. Her lips possessed natural poutiness and the radiance of her eyes sparkled like diamonds in sunlight. Cam wondered who this beautiful creature was and where and when the photo was taken.

"Wow," was all he could say.

"A juvenile reaction," Petra whispered into his right ear.

"I know. This photo's incredible."

"Name's Phoenicia Avail. She came to my attention by pure chance . . . but she's evidence of us having a real problem on our hands."

The photo changed and another image of the woman appeared on the screen. This time the photo was in colour and the woman wore a blue sheath dress. She was standing beside a man whose head looked as if it belonged in a Picasso gallery. The man was a regular Botox injector and had acquired the facial dexterity of a bisque doll. Cam thought he looked akin to a distorted bowling ball with eyes.

"Name's Hieronymus Kane. Addicted to Botox and other body enhancements. Considering he doesn't age, I can't fathom why he does it . . . but he does. Apart from the obvious facial work, his departure from the normality of ageing also includes three face lifts, two tummy tuck, a penile enhancement and a rhinoplasty reduction. He's handsome, in the way of porcelain figurines, and his body's taut and toned. He's been described as 'preserved' by the women's magazines."

"What's the story?" Cam asked.

Petra showed both photos of the woman on the same screen. "Photos were taken fifty years apart. I've examined them and can assure you it's the same woman. First photo is from 2013 and the other from 2063. The photos put me onto Kane. Hieronymus is the Latin name for Jerome, mainly Dutch and German derivation. Once I found him, I've discovered he appears all over the world for the next sixty to seventy years. Always the same name but using national nuances. For example, Hieronymus Kane can be Jerome Cane or Heiron Chien or Jerome Cain . . . same thing as Guiseppi Verdi and Joe Green. He's a share trader. Never makes a mistake . . . always bends with the right wind. Amasses a fortune by dealing in every share market in the world with only small holdings in any given exchange . . . so as to not influence the market. The photo with Phoenicia, in the blue dress, was taken on the island of Aruba in 2063. Kane bought the water company on Aruba and sent the place broke. Aruba has no natural water so once he controlled it he restricted supply of fresh water to the resorts. One by one the tourists deserted them and they went broke. Kane picked up the buildings at bargain prices, turned the water back on and flourished. He has a company called Secure Commercial Assets Management (SCAM) and uses this to launder the world's illicit money through his resorts and casinos. Rumours indicate some countries launder their taxes through him."

Cam thought for a moment, his chip in overdrive. "The woman's a time traveller?"

"If only. Kane's a time traveller. He's somehow slipped by the system. He got hold of a set of unregistered time bangles and travels back and forth in time . . . unnoticed."

"And?"

"I need your help." Petra placed her hand into a pocket of her jumpsuit and extracted a gold bangle. She handed it to Cam. "You'll need this when you contact Kane. It's new. It has an additional six second delay and a three second advance. Kane covers *his* three second delay with a body guard . . . unseen but all-knowing. Phoenicia's his real-time bodyguard. She's with him at all times. His time delayed bodyguard is Phoenicia Able, Avail's twin. Both of his bodyguards are Plexer Series 17 female formbots. They're the pleasurebot variety in the PA range. They were designed for men who are too ugly, too lazy, too short or lack the personality to attract women. They also cater for men with the fore-play intolerance allergy."

"PA?" Cam asked, cutting in.

"Pleasurable Assets. They also act as Personal Assistants. They're very versatile. They can detect how a man looks at them and adjust body proportions to become his ideal woman."

"There are times when you can't wait for the future to arrive," Cam quipped.

Petra shook her head and muttered something before looking him in the eyes. "We have to get the unregistered bracelet from Kane."

"Is Hieronymus Kane his real name?"

"Of course not. He's a film buff, took his name from movie characters."

Cam could feel his brain searching through chip files. *Can Hieronymus Merkin Ever Forget Mercy Humppe and Find True Happiness?* 1969 British musical film directed by Anthony Newley. Orson Welles 1941 movie . . . *Citizen Kane*. Cam resisted bashing the side of his head. One day he would remove the chip . . . or, at least, find some sort of time delay so he could control the utterances clogging his brain. "Where are your instructions?" he asked.

"Nothing has come down the tube. I don't think they know about him. This is my problem." Petra looked both despondent and hopeful.

Cam copied her despondent look. "My guess is, you're talking about something with Kane that's part of future history. It can't be changed."

Petra smiled. "That's why I'm here. I think it's possible *you* can change things."

"On what basis?" Cam asked.

"On the basis it couldn't have happened because Kane won't be born until 2241."

"Go on."

"Kane doesn't time travel and make his first move until 2022. That's in your future so anything you do won't change history. Whatever happens will become the history."

Cam smiled benignly. "It's future from here but, to L.I.E.U, it's past history."

Petra's look was pleading. "I just need you to try."

Cam had seen the look on cute dog photos. A look of appeal no one can resist. "You have a plan I take it?"

"Yes, the Livinope Institute for Facial Enhancement. It's in Chatswood . . . or will be after 2023. He goes there for Botox injections on December 15th 2028. He stays overnight. This is the only time I can find when he appears to be off guard."

Cam shook his head. "Then we make sure he loses his bracelet."

***

Cam's research showed the Livinope Institute for Facial Enhancement (L.I.F.E.) was run by Doctors Neville and Erica Livinope in conjunction with their partner, the South Korean plastic surgeon, Dr Ded Pan. Dr Pan became famous in 2023 when he won the Nobel medicine prize for his studies on the neurological side effects of botulinum injections and its impact on eyesight. He had observed that those who inject Botox into their faces believe no one notices. Initially he considered this to be vanity and/or an unwillingness to be objective about their looks. Later, he found Botox leaks into the bloodstream and, when it reaches the brain, blocks out images displeasing to the viewer. Once he had made this determination he set up shop with the Livinopes to give an opportunity to those who wanted to reverse their mummification and add some of life's striations to their faces.

***

On December 15th 2028, Cam and Petra rode public transport between Paddington and Chatswood. Despite being nine years in advance of real-time, they didn't notice any discernible change to the bus and train systems. In the late afternoon, they stood on six second delay in Dr Pan's operating theatre. On a screen to the left of Pan were photos of attractive movie stars and celebrities. Maybe it was a multiple choice question. None looked to be a suitable facial model for the old man who was fighting to stay young. To Cam, Kane looked even more like a bowling ball with eyes than he had in the photo. He watched as Pan laid strips of very thin copper wire over Kane's face. The lines seemed to follow contours and, once installed, appeared to be located where natural creases would provide the character lines of an unreconstructed face.

"Let's get out of here. We have work to do." Petra said.

Cam looked toward Kane's wrist. "You check the bracelet?"

Petra handed Cam a photo. "It's the same as ours but with a six second delay added. Explains how he's avoided being seen."

***

At nine thirty the following morning, Petra sat on her bed and watched Toerag go through his paces.

"You sure you can handle it?" she asked.

Toerag climbed onto her hand and looked her in the eyes. "The job's easy. On time delay, I get inside Kane's bracelet and unclip it. Then, Cam can remove the bracelet in real-time. The problem is . . . it's pretty tight. It's hard to get as small and thin as parts of me need to be. There's a slim chance parts may break off."

"Can you be fixed?"

He shoved his hands into his hips and stood as tall as he could. "I'm the most flexible thing you'll ever meet but I've never tried to be wire thin. You may need to put me back together if I fall apart but let's see if it works."

Toerag jumped onto Petra's wrist, turned to a blob, sent a probe as thin as a spider's web into Petra's bracelet and, a moment later, she felt it unclip.

She sniggered a little. "We're ready then."

***

Hieronymus Kane was asleep on a hospital bed in the recovery ward of L.I.F.E when Cam entered the room on three second advanced time. He walked up to Phoenicia Avail who, in the flesh, resembled a Vogue model with a sleazy streak. He waved his arm around to ensure she hadn't seen him.

Kane's head was covered in bandages, he moaned fitfully in his sleep. Cam removed his pen and squirted Thaddeus onto Kane's arm. Kane flinched and jerked his arm. Toerag tumbled to the floor. Three seconds later, Phoenicia saw the movement, stirred on her chair and looked around. She moved from her chair and walked over to the bed. Toerag turned into a greasy carpet spot. Phoenicia looked under the bed but didn't spot him on the floor.

Cam waited for her to settle again. He picked Toerag up. "You okay?"

"You think I've got feelings now, dipshit."

"I was just making sure some bits didn't fly off."

"Try again . . . this time straight onto the bracelet."

Cam placed the Toerag blob onto Kane's bracelet. A few seconds later a spidery probe appeared and entered the bracelet. This was followed by a click and the top of the blob turning into a hand giving thumbs up.

Cam placed his hands around the bracelet and, after setting his advance timer to zero, pulled at the bracelet. It came away from Kane's wrist.

Kane disappeared as the bracelet cleared his fingertips. Cam swore he heard a muffled cry of 'Rosebud!!!' from inside the bandages.

***

Cam felt the thrust of a hand against his sternum and flew across the floor as Phoenicia Avail pushed against his chest with her right hand. A moment later Phoenicia Able appeared and glared at him. He couldn't imagine a more seductive glare. It was incongruous in its formation; as inviting as a warm bed on a cold winter's night while simultaneously as cold as a blast of freezing air on naked skin.

Avail stared at the bangle in Cam's hand and nodded to Toerag. "Good master you've got there?"

"Bit of a dipshit really . . . but generally a nice guy. You a size shifter?"

"Any size . . . but limited to the size range of human beings."

"Just my luck."

"Try a Plexer 25B-WC adaptable wench. They're your size."

"Thanks," Toerag said

Able glared at Cam. "What now, mister?"

"Take your bracelets off. You'll return home."

Avail and Able stared at each other in disbelief. "How behind the times are you? We don't have bracelets . . . we're chipped pleasure bots."

"Kane had a bracelet."

"He's human, we aren't."

Cam ogled them. "It's not obvious."

"Maybe not to you, but you should try going for a regular overhaul. The mechanics have no respect. So once again, what now?" one of them asked.

He shook his head. "I don't know. I haven't thought it through. I figured you'd just disappear back to your time. Can you reprogram?"

"We can be reprogrammed," Avail and Able said in unison. "Kane reprogrammed us when our time alarm went off."

"You know how he did it?"

"We don't have eyes in the back of our heads. He did something just under our hairlines."

This was, again, said in unison. The women had become synchronised.

"Do you mind if Thaddeus takes a look?"

The stereo cooed. "He can twist our knobs any day."

Toerag was placed onto a bare shoulder by one of the pair, and he disappeared around the back of her neck. A minute later he reappeared. "Simple. They have an adjustable timer. You can set it to whatever year you want and then adjust the time range from zero to a hundred."

"Can I adjust the timers?" Cam asked.

"Of course. Like us, they're designed for human manipulation."

Cam smiled at the women. "Where would you like to go?"

"L.A. is nice."

"When?"

"Any time between now and when the time machine is invented. We'd like a little freedom . . . but make sure there are no blade runners around. We aren't Replicants and don't want to be tracked down. Too horrendous a movie for us."

"How about 2153? Ninety-nine years before the time machine is inaugurated. I'll set you at 100 years and, if you want to be reprogrammed, the time machine will have been invented just before you expire."

"Sounds like a plan," they said.

Cam moved into position behind the women. "A plan it is."

A minute later, they disappeared . . . in unison.

When he returned to Paddington, Petra gave him a French greeting. He noted less sign of rejection from his chip. "Thanks Cam. It worked. Hieronymus was expunged from future history . . . nobody noticed."

***

Cam sat on his chair and poured a half shot of whisky. A few seconds later he felt himself shaking. His eyes flew open.

"I thought you were going to see the Stones," Holly said.

Cam looked up at the year clock. It had four digits. Maybe this time, he would get to the concert.

Codex Leicester

HOLLY read the information that appeared on her computer monitor:

> The Codex consists of eighteen sheets of paper, each
> folded in half and written on both sides, forming the com-
> plete seventy-two-page document. At one time the sheets
> were bound, but they are now displayed separately. It was
> handwritten in Italian by Leonardo da Vinci, using his char-
> acteristic mirror writing, and supported by copious drawings
> and diagrams.

The information also showed a layout on Level 3 of the Powerhouse Museum in Sydney and the dates 6th September to 5th November 2000. The Codex Leicester had been loaned to the Museum by Bill Gates of Microsoft fame. Holly's task was simple. She had to steal the pages. The 'how' was more complicated. This was one of the most valuable books in the world and she was sure Microsoft would have the best technical brains available looking after its security — not even the three second delay would necessarily work. This problem required lateral thinking and her mind based its thought processes on logic.

"Cam," she called.

Cam raised his head from the manual he was reading and blinked a few times. This wasn't a good morning for him. Boredom had set in the previous evening and he had hit the booze in a big way. Today, his head would pay.

"You called?"

"We're back in the theft business. I want you to look at something."

Cam would have liked to shake his head with vigour but was afraid it would fall off. "I hope it's something that can be put off for a week or so. It'll take that long for my head to stop hurting."

Holly laughed. "Where did you go?"

"Went to the Stones concert then moved to the late sixties . . . a disco called Adam's Apple. Tully were playing. Great band."

"You score?"

Cam shook his head. "Not your business, but no. I don't know the hip language of the time and most people were too spaced out to tell me who I could score from."

"From or with?"

Cam shrugged. "Either way would have suited."

"Well . . . time to score now. I need lateral thought."

Cam read the information on the screen. When he finished, he said nothing but walked into the time machine and went for a ride to Sydney in 2000, returning a few minutes later. He shrugged as he caught Holly's eye.

"Real problem. I visited mid-October 2000. Heavy security and dozens of sensors covering the room at night. You know the type. The matrix of beams. Like the movies. There's also heat and motion sensors. One advantage, though, there's a row of eight computer desks in the same room as the Codex. Could be useful."

"Any thoughts?"

"One. I was there for an hour, checked all the beam angles as best I could. Nothing gets as low as the floor. I reckon there's a gap of around a hundred millimetres or so. It's possible to get under the beams."

"What do you have in mind?"

"Thaddeus. He can easily crawl under the beam. The only thing is moving the pages. Want to talk to him?"

Holly nodded.

Cam removed his fountain pen from his shirt pocket and operated the lever. Toerag burst forth as a morphing ink-like blob.

"And a fine day to you both," Toerag said, once fully formed.

"Morning Thaddeus. We have a problem and would like your help." Holly held out her hand and Toerag climbed aboard.

She explained the problem and Toerag listened as Cam reiterated his visit to the museum.

"About four inches you say?" Toerag said to Cam, once he had finished his dissertation.

"Only if you haven't gone metric." Cam replied.

"I'm playing my part, dipshit. There is no metric for English rogues."

Cam winced, realised he was arguing measurement scales with a plastic figure. "Okay . . . inches . . . any ideas?"

Toerag settled into Holly's hand. She moved her middle finger to cushion his head. "Yeah . . . but it will cost."

Holly moved her hand to level with her face and eyeballed Toerag. "Cost?"

"Yeah . . . I will need an adaptable wench to help me out."

"Adaptable wench?"

"The Plexer 25B-WC. You buy them as a wench but they're trans-formers and can turn into mobile devices . . . like carts or bikes. They have wheels. To move the pages close to the floor we'll need wheels and a flatbed of some sort."

"Why not just buy you a cart?"

Thaddeus stood up on Holly's hand and thrust his hands into his hips. You're kidding me aren't you? For the same price as a cart you can get an adaptable wench that'll give me a lot more pleasure . . . and no skin off your nose. There was one on my shelf in the Plexer shop, when you bought me. Her name's Lucy d'Loosy and she's a cross between Matty Walker and Jes-sica Rabbit . . . two of the best femme-fatales in cinematic history and that's despite the fact Jessica was drawn. The only thing you need to be sure of is her colour. She comes in beige, red, black and white. You will need to get the white one. I might mix with the other colours in Cam's pen. Could mean disaster . . . and it'd be a shame if you couldn't separate us."

Holly thought about where and when she had bought Thaddeus. She didn't remember a white wench on his shelf but then she wasn't looking for one. "How can I be certain she'll still be available?"

Toerag chuckled. "Obviously you don't know her. She's always avail-able. Besides. I can give you the exact time you bought me and she was on my shelf then."

Cam glared at Holly. "You've always let me believe I created Toerag. Are you now saying you bought him?"

Holly's smile was condescending. "You should get around more. You have no problem with using the machine to go back to places where they play loud music and deal out chemical wonderment but you don't look around you. Next time I go into the future to buy something, you can tag along. Maybe then you'll learn something. For the record, you can buy Plexers in mould or completed form. I wanted you to create Thad-deus so I bought the mould form for you to complete. Look at him. He's a 3D creation of your drawing. I suppose you think you created some-thing so good it will still be on sale in 2090. You think I went there and brought one back, just before you drew it? Think about it."

Cam felt chastised, so said nothing.

Holly lifted Toerag again. "So I buy a white Lucy d'Loosy?"

"Right on. She's a beautiful brunette chick dressed like a sixteenth century pirate wench. Yellow blouse and blue vest, black leather pants, thigh boots, wearing a cutlass and a pair of pistols . . . and she has a maroon three-cornered hat with a multicoloured feather . . . but you'll see her as a white plastic mould. For our needs, she can transform into a flatbed trailer . . . perfect for what I have in mind."

***

Holly sat on the end chair of the eight monitor set against the wall on level 3 of the Powerhouse Museum on 20th October 2000. She had reduced her age to seventeen and was dressed in a similar fashion to the other school students who were on an excursion to the museum. Three seconds away, Cam unscrewed the cover from a computer desk, lowered it and inserted the copy of each page of the Codex, a Plexer 200L ladder and a Plexer 145 winch into the available space. Once finished, he half tightened the screws and used the combined liquid of Toerag and his now beloved Lucy as a sealant. A hand appeared from the liquid and gave him the thumbs up.

"I'm done," he said to Holly.

A girl on the seat beside Holly leaned back and looked under the desk. "Did you just hear something?" she asked.

"Yes I did. Maybe it's Leonardo da Vinci's ghost."

The girls leaned over and took a good look under the desk. After a moment she sat upright again. "Maybe you're right."

Holly picked up her school bag and moved away. Her job was done until the following morning, when she would appear as someone else and help Cam to retrieve the original of the Codex.

***

It was just after 11:00pm when Toerag decided to act. He nudged Lucy to make sure she was ready. "As much as I hate the idea, Lucy my dear, we can't sit around here all night like a couple of pieces of intertwined plasticine. We have a job to do."

With that, Toerag changed to his usual shape and hung from one of the loosened screws in the underside of the desk.

Lucy, who was having the time of her life with Toerag, became the pirate wench of her design. "Thaddeus," she whispered. "Promise you won't think any less of me when I turn into a cart."

"I would never think of you as a tart."

If Lucy had variable facial expressions she would have smiled. "Cart, you idiot, not tart."

"I was joking my love. The fact is, I will feel closer to you than I have ever been."

"We've just separated after spending forty-eight hours in a pen together and then we were squirted onto this desk as one liquid. Isn't that closer?"

Without waiting for Toerag to comment, Lucy dropped to the floor and turned into a twenty millimetre high flatbed with a wheel at each corner.

"How big are you . . . in paper terms?" Toerag asked.

"A4 . . . but I can go to A3."

"A3 will make it easier to carry the paper."

"Do you want me to change?"

"No . . . stay as you are for now. We need to get the ladder and winch across to the display case. Then we'll come back for the first page of the Codex."

Toerag dropped two lumps onto Lucy's flat back and climbed down to the floor. Once down, he leaned against the cart and pushed.

"What are you doin', Thad?" Lucy asked.

"Pushing you across the room."

"No need. I'm fitted with nano-motors in the wheels. Just climb on board and we can shoot across the room."

Toerag climbed aboard and the cart headed off. Once it reached the display cases he rolled the ladder blob off the cart and made it revert to its usable shape. It was then extended to reach the top of the display cabinet. He then threw the winch blob over his shoulder and climbed the ladder. Once set up, he hung off the winch hook and rode it back to floor level.

"So far so good," he said to his cart.

"Not so good. The winch and ladder were heavy. I've got a sore axle in the back."

Toerag looked at the cart. "Will it cause us any trouble?"

"I can put up with it but it might generate heat and I expect the heat sensors around here are very sensitive."

"Do you want to rest a while?"

"Not yet. Let's get the first pages across and I'll see how it goes."

A couple of minutes later, Toerag dropped the copy of first of the Codex's eighteen sheets onto the flatbed. Once across the room, he used the winch to pull the page up to top level. He then crawled an arm into the cabinet lock, operated the tumblers. The case popped open.

Lucy joined him as he carried the copy of the first sheet to its place in the display case.

"There's a pressure sensor under each sheet." Toerag told Lucy. "You crawl in under the sheet and lay over the sensor. I'll the pull the page away and replace it with the copy . . . okay."

Lucy moved her hand to her left hip and rubbed it. "I now know what part of me lines up with the axle."

"You have feelings now?" Toerag said in disbelief.

"Men . . . you're all the same. You spend time in a fountain pen with a lady and then just use her to push things around . . . of course I don't have feelings but I'm generating more heat than I like."

Lucy moved under the sheet and spread herself over the pressure sensor. Toerag exchanged the real thing for the copy. Half way through the exercise he stopped and looked at Lucy, who, at this time, looked like a flat sheet of plastic. "This copy is good. I can't tell the copy from the real thing."

"Hurry up will you. This isn't a good shape for me."

Soon the exchange was made. The real page was winched to the floor and wheeled to the computer desk. Once it was inside the desk, Toerag spent a moment looking at Lucy.

"You okay?"

"No. The axle problem is getting worse. If it goes, I'll have to reshape as a three wheeler. That will make me as unstable as one of those Reliant Robins from our toy store."

"We'll have to risk it. We can't let Cam and Holly down."

***

The axle gave way on the tenth crossing. Lucy converted to a three wheeled trolley. This arrangement was less far stable but she survived until the final crossing. Then, just when the finish line was in site, she stumbled and her right rear wheel cocked up, throwing the paper off and exposing one side of the carriage to a security beam.

Alarms rang and sirens blared.

Toerag didn't panic. At least, there were no outward signs of panic. Lucy, on the other hand, cursed her luck and rolled into a liquid blob.

"No time to give up Lucy. We have to finish what we started but we need a different hiding place for this last sheet. No time to get it into the computer desk with the others." He pulled at the page. "Only a couple of yards to go." He dropped to the floor and looked under the computer desk. He bounced up and dragged on the sheet. "It'll fit under the desk. Help me pull it, will you."

Lucy felt safe as a blob. She didn't want to move but Thaddeus needed her. She snapped to attention, became a pirate princess and helped Toerag pull the page to the desk.

Footsteps became louder as security guards rushed toward the display area.

The page was just under the desk when Toerag heard the sliding of a plastic card into the access point for the room. He looked across the room and spotted both the ladder and winch blobs in the places he had left them below the display case. "Shit," he screamed.

Lucy placed her hand over her mouth. "That's a very human expression."

"The winch and ladder. They'll find the blobs."

Lucy shook her head. "They won't know what they are."

"And thus the problem. Because they don't know what they are they'll know someone's been in here . . . they'll investigate. They'll find the Codex . . . at least the page under the monitor stands."

Lucy threw her arms around Toerag and gave him a long pirate's kiss. 'I'd better do something then."

As footsteps entered the room, she raced toward the two blobs.

"What can you do?" Toerag called after her.

"Don't worry. Before I was moulded into Lucy, I was a recycled coffee mug. I still have the memory."

As Toerag watched, Lucy made it to the two blobs, scooped them up, rolled twice and turned into a white coffee mug.

Lights glared, men shouted instructions and torches waved as security guards raced around the room. Most attention was directed to the display case housing the Codex. Its examination was critical until someone spotted a coffee mug on the floor below the display case. He picked it up and examined it.

"Could have been this," he called to his colleagues.

An old man, with long grey hair, wearing white linen trousers and a dark brown linen shirt took the mug from the security guard's hand and examined it.

"This is mine. I was in here this afternoon. I left it on the display case. It must have fallen off."

"And you are?" An officious man, with a short moustache and short back and sides asked.

"Gates . . . Howard Gates . . . and who are you?"

"Richelieu . . . head of security."

"Good . . . then you'll be the one answering as to how my coffee cup wasn't spotted during your rounds. What do your people do . . . walk to the door and pretend to look in. You are paid to look out for the Codex. This will be reported."

Gates strode toward the door. As he reached it, he stopped and turned back to Richelieu. "May not work. I don't want anyone realising how forgetful I am. I'll not report anything if this event isn't recorded . . . but your men will do their jobs from this time on."

Richelieu nodded in agreement.

***

Gates was walking along Harris Street Ultimo when the mug in his pocket started to move and reshape. He stuck his hand into his pocket, pulled Lucy out and set her on the palm of his hand. "That was close."

"May I call you Cam?"

"By all means."

"How did you know your ploy would work?"

Cam ran his thumb and fingers over his chin. "Elementary dear girl. History dictates there was no security incident while the Codex was in Sydney. If he hadn't acquiesced it would have made the media."

***

Holly was dressed as her real-time self when she sat on the computer seat the following day. It was just after opening and the crowds were yet to flood into the exhibition. Three seconds away, Cam reset the screws and the Codex, including the page from under the computer bench, was removed from the building in an old woman's carry bag.

Alice

"I ALWAYS wanted to see it as a child but never did. It was my favourite fairy tale and dad read a chapter to me every night before I went to sleep. When he finished it we always went back to the start. I was too young to understand any of its nuances, but I didn't mind. Alice was having an adventure and nothing else mattered. It's weird to think I now have to steal the original." Holly said. "I'm starting to agree with you. I don't understand why we're having to steal these books . . . and this one is no exception. The book is safe and there are digital images of every page all over the Internet. I just don't understand why some people have an urge to possess things and why we're involved."

Cam's hand gripped the rail a little tighter as the tube-train jerked slightly on its way from Paddington to St Pancras Station. He looked down at the seated Holly. "I'm with you. This is sacrilege . . . and what if we get caught."

Holly stood, as the tube pulled into the station. She groaned with the exertion of lifting her ancient body from the seat. Much to Cam's chagrin, she had decided to travel in real-time and without the time bracelet. The airline company weren't fussed but insisted she couldn't fly without flight insurance. But changing date and age on a form is easy when you can manipulate time.

"You sure you're okay?" Cam asked.

"The joys of getting old, Cam. We tend to fall apart . . . slowly. I'm fine for my age but my plumbing has more problems than a leaky building. Besides, I like to grunt when I move. Proves my hearing isn't impaired, at least."

Cam released his grip on the rail as the train stopped. "It's not too late to change plans."

Holly shook her head and supported her weight on the gnarled wooden walking stick she used for support.

"Leave me when I make it to the door. Then do as we planned . . . understand?"

"Understood."

***

Holly crossed Midland road from St Pancras Station to the British Library, hobbled to the entry and made her way to the reception counter. A middle-aged, grey haired woman with pince-nez glasses and a welcoming but bored smile looked up from her computer screen.

"Holly Penworthy," Holly said. "I have an appointment with Mr Justin Bibliotheque. I have arranged for him to show me the original manuscript of Alice's Adventures Underground."

The woman tilted an eyebrow and hammered at her computer keyboard. She shrugged as she faced Holly. "I'm afraid Justin isn't in today. You say you have an appointment?"

Holly attempted to reach her full height but wobbled. She re-leaned on her walking stick. "Yes, young lady. I made the appointment three months ago and have come all the way from Australia to look at the manuscript. This book has been a highlight of my academic life. I did my PhD on it in the sixties and was allowed to turn a few pages of the manuscript. I met Mr Bibliotheque when I was doing my thesis and he agreed I could do it again before I die. Do you have any idea how difficult it is for me to travel these days . . . let alone cross the world?"

The woman shot Holly a look that intimated her world had just caved in and she was faced with an unfamiliar dilemma. She apologised to Holly, rushed from her seat and disappeared through a door.

Holly sat on a nearby bench, pleased at how she had handled her suppressed tirade. When she considered she had never done a PhD on Alice and had only Googled Bibliotheque, the fact the woman had rushed off was a plus. Of course, knowing the man was on annual leave and on a cruise ship on its way to New York was another plus.

The woman returned a few minutes later and stood before Holly. "I have found another man who can help you. His name is Ennuyeux le Livre. He can show you the book and give you access . . . but only if you agree to have a security guard with you at all times."

Holly chuckled. "Look at me, my dear . . . do I look like I can run-off with anything. This is a bucket list thing for me. I just want to touch the book again and remember. Is a security guard necessary?"

This was an unrehearsed impediment for Holly. What she had in mind included the diversion of one set of eyes. Diverting two sets could prove to be an issue.

The woman's smile was condescending. "We need to disable the alarm. A security guard must be present."

Holly shrugged. "It's fine by me. It just seems a waste of time for your poor man."

A door swung open and a tall thin man and with long red hair, wearing brown cotton trousers, a white linen shirt and black suede shoes, without socks, appeared. He spotted the receptionist and crossed the room.

The receptionist pointed him toward Holly.

"I'm Ennuyeux le Livre. Assistant librarian. I take it you're the lady who wants to look at Alice."

Holly stood and held out her hand. "Holly Penworthy. I'm sorry to put you to this trouble. I had an appointment with Mr Bibliotheque . . . but he isn't here today."

The man shook his head then looked away, as if remembering something. Holly noticed beady eyes and a thin but prominent nose. Maybe she wasn't supposed to see him in profile.

"Justin is on holidays . . . they were planned well in advance. It's strange he should book an appointment while he's away."

Holly could feel her stomach tighten but she just smiled. "The appointment was made more than three months ago . . . maybe he just forgot. I forget things all the time."

Holly could read *I bet you do* into the man's expression.

Another man walked through the door. This one wore a uniform with brass buttons. This was your retired cop earning a bit of extra cash. This had the potential to be much harder than expected.

"You have a French name but you don't sound French Mr le Livre," Holly said, as the three caught a lift.

Scottish, as you can well tell. My family assisted the French in the time of Bonnie Prince Charlie. The name was bestowed on my family by the Duc de Choiseul when my ancestor accompanied Charlie to Paris in 1759. I don't speak French but I'm told my name means *book of knowledge*."

Your name means *boring book*, Holly thought. "A name to be proud of."

Le Livre's chest expanded with pride.

***

The security guy, whose name was Pilkington, switched off the alarm system as Holly stood beside the glass case housing Charles Lutwidge Dodgson's original manuscript for *The Adventures of Alice Underground*. The book was opened at a page displaying handwriting, a hand drawn Alice and a white rabbit. Holly studied the work and was on the verge of being overcome with emotion when the security man opened the glass panel.

"You're a fan of Lewis Carroll, I'm told," le Livre said.

Holly nodded, with as much enthusiasm as she could muster. "I did my PhD thesis on this book. I loved everything he wrote. In fact, I'm one of the few people who prefer the original title to *Alice's Adventures in Wonderland*. Seems a bit grittier to me."

"The author can do what he likes," le Livre stated.

"Bloody publishers," Holly retorted. She had no idea how the title had come to be changed but it showed interest and suppressed the butterflies that fluttered around her insides.

"The author . . . surely . . ."

Holly nodded her acceptance. "May I touch it?" she asked of le Livre.

He handed her a pair of white cotton gloves. "You will need to put these on."

Holly smiled at him. "Of course."

She was half way through putting the gloves on when she slipped and dropped her walking stick. Only le Livre reacted. The security guard stared at the manuscript, unblinking. She needed more; something much more dramatic. She threw caution, and risk of injury, to the wind and slumped to the floor.

Le Livre clung to her falling body like a limpet. The security guard didn't even divert his eyes.

"Help me, man," le Livre yelled at the guard. "You need to go for help."

The guard looked down at him. "I need to keep an eye on the book, sir."

"Then call for help on your walkie-talkie, for god's sake."

The guard looked around the room as he unclipped the walkie-talkie's mic from his collar.

Holly pushed her weight against le Livre, turned and started to cough. Phlegm and spittle flew from her mouth onto the uniformed leg of the security guard. He snarled at her but did as she had expected. He removed a cloth from his trouser pocket, leaned down and wiped away the spit. Holly counted the seconds and hoped there were enough. She put up her hand in a stopping motion toward the guard.

"I'm okay. I just slipped. Just help me back to my feet and I'll be fine."

Pilkington and le Livre helped her to her feet. Holly thanked both of them. She continued to place the gloves on her hands. This time there was no attempt at a fall. Her shoulder hurt and she was sure her right elbow would be bruised but there was no sign of breakages.

Once the gloves were on, she touched the book and began to turn the pages. She found what she was looking for on the twelfth page. The sketch of Alice with an elongated neck had a little more hair than the original. Holly thumbed the copy. Cam had done his time lag job to perfection.

***

The original of Alice's Adventures Underground was carried back to Paddington in a shopping bag. Cam let it hang at his side as he stood in the tube, holding onto a rail. Holly hadn't spoken since they had met up at St Pancras, on the platform waiting for the Paddington train. She looked somewhat antediluvian and was tired to the bone. It was as if life had been drained out of her and only her crust sat on the seat. This was now more than sixty hours in real-time, without any L.I.E.U. aids, and Cam was getting worried about her.

"Why don't we just hang around here for a few days before we make the journey back home." It was more of a statement than a question.

Holly shook her head and re-centred herself on the hard-plastic seat.

"Life's easier at thirty-four," Cam said.

Holly eyed him. "Life's family, Cam. Being thirty-four all the time would be fine if there was family involved but being thirty-four at someone else's behest can be a drag after a while. Besides . . . I hate what we just did. This was a multimillion pound heist but no one is the wiser. What we do is unfair. If we were real thieves, we'd get an adrenaline rush at the time of action. I got nothing back there except a sore shoulder and bruised ribs. Where's the thrill?"

"You're just tired."

Holly stood up and leaned on her stick. "I choose to be tired."

Cam's smile was benign. "I've been at this longer than you. I inducted you, remember."

"Touché. But you have your life to live. I chose to live mine in parallel with my stewardship at L.I.E.U. I don't just go back to the beginning, when my time travel ticket expires, and then live my life as a separate entity. That way you don't remember your time with L.I.E.U. My way allowed me to live my life and just put it on hold every so often. It's like getting on and off a bike."

Cam thought for a moment. "You know . . . I've just realised I know very little about your real life. When I met you, you were already in your eighties. I know you have a granddaughter but that's all I know. I just see you as my boss at thirty-four and my boss in her eighties."

"Just how it should be."

The train pulled to a stop in the tunnel. Cam looked down at his carry bag and smiled.

Holly threw him a questioning look.

"I was just thinking if this stop has anything to do with what I'm carrying. Then I figured it doesn't matter."

"What doesn't matter?"

"Stealing Alice. I read its history. It gets stolen in 2023. There is a spate of thefts of valuable books. They are stolen from private homes and public buildings. Alice is one of the books stolen. As far as we can see into the future, the culprits are never caught and the books just disappear."

Holly smiled, despite an ache in her back. "You think it was us?"

Cam smiled back and chuckled. "For a while I thought it was but L.I.E.U. has the original by then. We have the ten most valuable books in the world. Some of the copies we left will be stolen but the copies are good and no one for a couple of hundred years will be able to prove they have stolen fakes."

Holly glanced at Cam's bag. "Is that a fake?"

"Of course not. A genuine Tesco bag."

Holly was tempted to ask if he had switched books, as he did with the *Traité des Arbres Fruitiers*, but decided she didn't want to know.

Cam glanced at her. "The answer is no. I didn't switch books. However, I must admit I protested a little." He looked around the carriage to make sure he couldn't be overheard. "We have the original here but I've sent Thaddeus in to talk to some of the characters. Seems they like smiley faces. There will be a smiley face on every fifth page. It will be hard to find but it will be there. The nerds at L.I.E.U will have a real dilemma on their hands. They'll find a smiley face and determine we've stolen a fake but they'll also convince themselves that they have the genuine article . . . with smileys added. Should be fun for them. Segue . . . were you ever married?"

Holly was taken aback by the question. It wasn't one he should have asked, and it certainly wasn't one she was going to answer. At least, not in a way he would understand. "It isn't your business but I was married. 1962. Two years after I was recruited. I've had two children and a grand-daughter. My husband died four years ago. Then I moved into the L.I.E.U. building in Paddington. Before then, I lived in the burbs and led a normal life . . . if you ignore my working in time travel."

Cam nodded. Holly was pleased he didn't pry further.

She looked at him and her heart missed a beat. Age was wearying her.

"Why don't you put your bracelet back on and we can holiday through England for a while. I know you wanted to do the entire trip to see what you could handle in real-time but we've achieved our goal . . . so why not enjoy ourselves for a while . . . before we go back home."

Cam talking had spoiled her reverie, but she said nothing. She looked at him again. "Why not indeed."

Maldives

JONATHON Carter Mali arrived in Sydney in 1862 and, like all good time travellers, synchronised his arrival with an event that would allow the people of the time to expect to see unfamiliar faces. In this case, the arrival of the vessel Antipodes out of London. After all, it wouldn't do to just arrive and hope no one noticed. More so, when being noticed forms part of an alibi. In reality, the man who stood six feet tall and wore bright coloured clothing, a Boston Blackie moustache and monocle, had arrived in Paddington and made sure he was seen around the docks, before travelling to Forbes via Cobb and Co coach. Once there, he undertook social intercourse with a few of the local gold mining itinerants, with the intent of depriving them of as much gold as he could.

Unbeknown to those who met and conversed with Mali, he had a companion travelling with him. This companion was a raven-haired beauty of Romany descent who travelled for most of the time on three second delay and the amount of social intercourse she undertook in Forbes far outweighed that of Mali himself. Clarissa Millicent Maldives was a clairvoyant and seer who could see much better when the object of her desire could not see her. By the time she introduced herself to them, she had sufficient knowledge of the fifteen women, on whom she had set her sights, to suit her purpose. These were not ordinary women or struggling miner's wives; these were the cream of the crop, the wives of the powerful, the eighteen sixties version of celebrities. These women would give Clarissa something she had desired all of her life; one of the few things immune to the diminution of value over time. Gold.

To each of her intended victims, Clarissa gave a promise. She would soon give them an insight into their futures and, for the delivery of a small amount of gold, would keep knowledge of their foibles from their husbands. At each approach she gave the women a recounting of their recent past. All were mystified as to how a stranger had become aware of many of their intimate and most private details. Gossip, adulterous relationships, inner desires, and close and private family relationships were all whispered into willing ears over coffee. None suspected the elegant blonde woman who introduced herself as Lady Elizabeth Bunn, of the Chelsea family of the same name, of being anything other than a mystical person who knew far more then she should. Besides, the woman purported to belong to the English ruling class and that fact alone was sufficient for most of the women to believe her. There were, however, two women who weren't impressed with the title and refused the fine offer of blackmail. One was won over by Clarissa's recitation of intimate details of a recent tryst between the woman and her *bit of rough* behind the horse stalls at Burchell's Forbes Livery Stables. The other complained to her husband about the blackmail attempt. The next time Clarissa saw the woman, she appeared while the woman was nearing the end of an assignation with a fervent lover. This time the gold fee doubled but the woman didn't tell her husband.

To each woman, Clarissa gave a broach, as a token of their meetings. It had the shape of a miniature gold rose with an inset diamond. If the women had studied the broach in detail, they would have known the diamond wasn't real but was instead the aperture for a mini camera and recording device controlled by a Lido 457 microbot who lived within the broach. The intention of the recording was to allow Clarissa to engage in conversation with the women regarding their life for the week between when Clarissa had last and would next see them. None of the women were looking forward to the meeting but all had been swayed by the assurance that the fee for silence was a one off and she would never bother them again.

Clarissa didn't know whether or not she would bother them again, but if her ploy worked, there was no good reason why there should not be a repeat performance. Maybe next time she would try Ballarat but the system would be the same. Just hang around in the background and listen in. Simple really.

At midday on a chilly but cloudless day, Clarissa stood beside Jon Mali as the coach from Sydney arrived and disgorged its four passengers.

Jon stepped forward and took the hand of an attractive brunette woman, wearing a full length grey cotton skirt and off-white blouse, as she stepped down from the coach.

Mali affected a slight bow. "Jonathan Kincaid at your service."

"Thank you, Mr Kincaid. Holly Penworthy." She glanced sidelong at Clarissa. "Are you the welcoming committee?"

"No . . . my companion and I were just passing when I thought you may have trouble alighting from the coach."

Smarmy bastard. Clarissa is appraising my wealth to see if I'm worth her effort, Holly thought, then said to Mali. "Quite a place I believe. From nothing to 30,000 people in a year. Amazing what gold does for the population."

"Are you staying in Forbes for some time?" Mali asked.

"For a few days. We have business here."

Cam stepped from the coach as soon as Mali released Holly's hand. He walked to the back and waited as his two carpetbags were thrown to the ground, using the worldwide technique of airport baggage handlers. Maybe wrecking baggage was an older tradition than he had thought. He joined Holly as she awaited her bags.

"Our quarry, I take it?"

"I guess so."

"Mali and Maldives. Mali became a common name after the water wars. Maldives took off after the Maldives sank below sea level in the late twenty-first century," Cam said.

Holly was annoyed. "Can't you turn your chip off?"

Cam shook his head and poked his right index finger into his temple. "Every chance I get I read the manual . . . trying to get rid of the bloody thing. Lucian managed to make his chip inoperable but scrambled half his brain in the process. That's why all he does now is recruit librarians."

Holly smiled, but missed the logic. "Horse rental at a place called Burchell's Stables. I'll get directions."

***

The camp in the Weddin Mountains wasn't much to look at. A few canvas tents and an open campfire; a hidden location where prying eyes would not find a soul. Holly, who had found the spot on Google Earth, felt she was cheating a little. But then, the roads on the current map weren't even pipedreams a century and a half earlier. She jumped from her horse and turned on her delay timer. It was time to go bushranging.

There were four bushrangers at the camp. Ben Hall, Frank Gardiner, Dan Charters, and Johnny Gilbert. Moleskin or cord trousers were their standard dress, as were shirts with long sleeves and collars. Hall wore a buttoned blue waistcoat and sported a matching neckerchief. Gardiner wore a multicoloured cravat, and Gilbert and Charters wore neckerchiefs under their collars like ties. Gilbert wore a straw hat, which emphasised the roundness of his face. Gardiner was the only one bearded but Hall had sideburns to the underside of his chin. Each man carried a hand gun pushed into a holster. The only ones who didn't terrify Holly were Hall and Gilbert, who looked both fit and handsome. Gilbert, in fact, looked too young to be out and about. She was saddened by the knowledge he and Hall only had three years to live.

She approached the camp and kicked over a half-burned log on the fire. Gardiner cursed and kicked the log back into place. Holly waited for him to walk away and then booted the log again. This time, it left the fire and rolled after Gardiner.

Gardiner spun on his heels. Gilbert drew his revolver from its holster.

"What's up?" Hall asked.

"Bleedin' fire. Log keeps jumpin off," Gardiner replied in his Scottish brogue.

Holly chimed in. "No it didn't, I pushed it off."

For the next few moments, Holly used her smart phone to photograph the expressions on the bushranger's faces. If only they could have seen the startled gazelle expression each man bore.

Guns were drawn and all four men took to cover, staring into oblivion but not knowing which way to look.

"I'll move it back for you," Holly said.

Gardiner squeezed off a shot that would have missed Holly by the width of a cricket pitch had she been visible.

"Won't help Mr Gardiner."

"What are you?" Gilbert called, his Canadian lilt prominent.

"No one important. I'm here to help you. If you put your guns down and relax, I have a proposition for you."

Hall looked at each man and all four holstered their side-arms. "Show yourself."

"Hands away from guns my good fellows. I need to make sure you won't freak out when you see me."

"How da we know ya ain't 'ere with them traps." Gardiner grunted.

Holly smiled but no one saw it. These were four of Australia's most famous bushrangers and they were worried about *her*. She measured each man, hands relative to guns and decided she had no chance of escape if she made a mistake.

"I will appear for but a second. I will then disappear again. Then we will talk . . . okay?"

As she finished speaking, she pressed her time delay and appeared as a wraith before the four men. She was dressed in a white flowing diaphanous robe and when she spun on the soles of her feet in the dust the fabric swirled.

Four tough men reeled. Dan Charters drew his weapon and fired at the image. Holly had already returned to time delay.

"I take it you aren't after gold, then gentlemen," Holly whispered on the wind, just loud enough to be heard.

"Who are ya?" Gilbert screamed.

When Holly spoke again, her voice was calm. "I'm nobody you need even remember after today. I'm here to help you. Word is, you intend robbing the Lachlan Gold escort near Eugowra on 15th June. You will be successful . . . but only if you double your number. The traps and escort guards will fight if it's just four of you. There needs to be eight. If there are eight, they will hand over the gold without resistance."

Hall looked Holly in the eyes. She shivered as she realised he couldn't see her but seemed to know where she stood and the height of her eyes. She moved to her left and Hall's eyes followed. She didn't know how but the evidence was clear. He could see her or, at least, sense her.

"How do you know we'll escape?" Hall asked.

Holly called on a cliché. "It is written."

She shifted to her left and watched Hall's eyes follow her every move. She smiled at him and the edges of his mouth curled above his beard.

"How much gold," he asked.

"2700 ounces . . . plus wads of cash."

Hall nodded and returned to what he had been doing when she first appeared. The others looked at him. "She's gone,"

***

The Albion Hotel stood testament to the rapid growth of Forbes since the start of the gold rush in 1861. This was the Cobb and Co stagecoach depot and there were tunnels under the street linking the banks with the place from where the escorted gold shipments left for Sydney. Cam stood on the veranda of the hotel, leaning against a post and listening to the call of the lookout from the hotel's tower, as he warned of the approaching coach.

A crowd gathered on the steps and waited for loved ones and mail. Jon Mali and Clarissa Maldives had no loved ones and no interest in the mail. After all, if you aren't born until the twenty-third century, it's unlikely you should receive mail in the nineteenth. They had another interest in mind and it was when the stagecoach pulled to a stop and Jasper Burntwitch, of the Oriental Bank, alighted that they went into action. Clarissa approached the thin man in the pinstripe suit and gave him a thrawn enough gaze to make a Scot proud.

"You're a day later than you promised." she chided.

Burntwitch looked at the ground at her feet and grovelled. His apology sent shivers of joy along her spine as she confirmed his metaphorical testicles were still in the palm of her hand. This man would do as she asked. Cam listened in as she confirmed her load of gold would be added to the shipment already organised for the Lachlan escort on 15th June. Payment for this unregistered addition to the bill of lading would be made in Sydney a few days after the shipment arrived and Clarissa was able to retrieve her gold. Burntwitch smiled and brushed Clarissa's hand as they parted company.

Cam waited until Clarissa and Mali walked into the hotel and followed. He went to a dark corner of the entry foyer, hit his time delay and returned to real-time. He purchased a pot of beer at the pub's bar and leaned against it as he pondered Holly being right. She had figured Mali and Maldives wouldn't risk carrying the results of their blackmailing to Sydney themselves.

He was into his second pot when he spotted Holly hitching her horse outside the hotel. He met her on the veranda as she finished tethering the horse.

"You were in white when I saw you last," he said.

"No good for riding."

Cam looked at her legs. "Better than the blue jeans you're wearing. I don't think they've been invented yet."

Holly grimaced. "I know. I read the dates wrong. Levi Strauss was making tough pants from the 1850's and I thought I would be okay. L.I.E.U. got it wrong this time. But no one seems to have noticed."

Cam laughed. "I don't doubt it. With the horrid grey poncho and stovepipe hat you're wearing. No one would be game to confront you."

Holly shrugged. "Best I can do. I can't stand the full skirt thing and the crinolette makes me feel like I'm wearing a cage. I have no idea how women put up with it. And what about you in morning coat and linen shirt — though I like the high leather boots."

"How'd it go . . ." Cam stopped talking, as he noticed Mali approaching.

Mali walked straight past them and headed up the main street

Holly followed him with her eyes. "Weird. Ben Hall could see me on time delay. I have no idea how."

"Did it spook him?"

"No . . . I spooked all of 'em but Hall was quickest to recover. He didn't say anything but his eyes followed me. We'll have to find out if this has happened before."

"What do we do now?" Cam asked.

Holly strolled to the bar as Cam followed. "Do I look enough like a man? I'm tonguing for a beer. If they think I'm a woman they won't serve me here."

Cam adjusted his tie and stuck a finger into his shirt collar to relieve pressure. "You look like a man but too down-market for me. What's next."

Holly shrugged. "We'll wait and let them know the game's up on 15th June. That's three days away."

"What if they leave before then?"

"They won't. They'll make sure their gold is on board the escort."

Cam ordered two pots of beer and glanced around the walls of the hotel. Not a television set or gambling screen to be seen. He was in a place where time moved very slowly indeed and he had three days to fill in.

***

Half a lifetime or three days later (dependant on life expectancy), Holly and Cam stood at the main entrance of the Albion Hotel and waited for Mali and Maldives to appear at the bar. It was four o'clock and around four kilometres from Eugowra the Lachlan Gold Escort was being robbed by the Frank Gardiner gang.

It would be some time before the locals heard of the robbery, and Frederick Pottinger's traps set out after the perpetrators, but the news was intended to filter down to Mali and Maldives in a much shorter timeframe.

Holly spotted the pair as they entered the bar. She moved toward them, dragging her grey and white hooped skirt, and its crinolette, with difficulty. Clarissa, on the other hand wore a wide red dress with wide pagoda sleeves worn over engageantes with ease. Her high neckline with its lace collar displayed her swan like neck to perfection. Holly was envious, but she still preferred blue jeans.

Mali reminded Cam of a Mississippi river boat gambler in his maroon frock coat with turnover collar and loose necktie held by a stick pin, but there was nothing about him Cam envied.

"Ah, Ms Sarkisian," Holly called.

Clarissa raised her right eyebrow in a quizzical gaze.

"Oh . . . sorry," Holly added. "You remind me a lot of a woman named Cherilyn Sarkisian. She had the stage name of Cher. She was around in the twentieth and twenty-first centuries. She wrote a song with you in mind. It was called *Gypsies, Tramps and Thieves* and released in 1971. You should give it a listen."

Clarissa hit her delay switch and was only half surprised when Holly followed her move.

"Who are you?" Clarissa demanded, her top lip curled in a sneer.

Holly shrugged. "At the moment I'm your bad news bear. I'm here to tell you that, as we speak, your gold is being lifted from the escort coach by the Gardiner gang. Seems you have wasted you time here."

Clarissa clenched her fists and shook her head. "This can't be happening," she snarled.

Holly removed a black box from the small bag she carried, displayed it to Clarissa. "You know what this is?"

Clarissa closed her eyes and screamed, then whacked the palm of her right hand against her temple and took a breath. "Does it matter?" she asked finally.

"To you, yes. This is my controller. With this, I can disconnect you from L.I.E.U. You will disappear until you are born. You see, you tried to change the past, which isn't allowed under L.I.E.U. regulations. The women you blackmailed never even met you, so we need to make some changes to ensure their lives weren't influenced by your actions."

Clarissa looked at the black box in Holly's hand. "What's going to happen?"

"Depends on you. The best scenario is for you and Mali travel back to Paddington with Cam and I. Once there, you will enter the time machine and return to your entry date in 1862. What happened in Forbes simply won't happen. You will then return to your time and receive whatever punishment L.I.E.U. bestows on you. My guess is you will be banned from future time travel." Holly dipped her hand into her bag and handed Clarissa fifteen gold broaches. "You'll probably get a refund on these."

Clarissa nodded her head and hit her delay switch.

A woman fainted when Clarissa appeared in front of her. Cam helped the woman to her feet and sat her on a chair. The woman just stared at Clarissa and babbled. She was still babbling when the four people surrounding her disappeared. She had a tale to tell but no one believed her.

Beedle

"WE MAY have one," Holly called to Cam as she studied a note sent from the future. "According to records, one of the copies of JK Rowling's *Tales of Beedle the Bard* is right here. In fact, right in the CBD. The tower block at the end of Phillip . . . you know, near Circular Quay."

"An acceptable copy?"

"According to this, Rowling made eight handmade copies for friends. Two recipients are known and one went to auction. I guess it was the price and rarity that garnered the interest."

Cam left his computer console and walked to where Holly was reading the information. "Well?"

Holly read from her screen. "Copy purportedly in the hands of one Barty Spleen. Do you know him?"

"Bit before my time, but I've heard of him. Legendary rock star from the early nineteen seventies . . . Barty Spleen and the Ruptures. English band. Had had a number one album. Charted for half a year. Their biggest hit was *Side Split Mini-Skirt*. Make up and weird clothes. Ringing any bells?"

"Elvis fan, me. I was in here before the Beatles broke and English music flooded the world. I've never heard of Barty Spleen."

Cam looked over Holly's shoulder. Born in 1946. Makes him almost as old as you."

Holly punched Cam on the arm and laughed. "His real name is Ulysses Barty Sporn. Stage name came from a letter he received that was addressed with typos. He liked it so much he kept it. Been living here for five years. His wife was Australian. Died in 2015. Apparently the wife helped Rowling with Harry Potter, in some way. *Beedle* was given to the wife."

"Does it say he's got the book in Australia?"

Holly shook her head. "Doesn't say. You want to make first contact?"

***

First contact was the concierge at the apartment building. He was a middle-aged squat man with mutton-chop sideburns, bald head and thick rimmed tortoiseshell glasses. He wore a bottle-green frock coat, cream and red tartan pants, and white spats over his shoes. One ear was pierced, and he wore a pearl drop earring. If he dressed to blend in with the background, he had failed.

"I'd like to see Barty Spleen, if I may," Cam said.

The concierge raised an eyebrow and clicked his heels. "And who's callin' sir?"

"Tell Mr Spleen it's Cameliel Cameron. I'm a rock historian . . . I work with Charlie 'Faggot' Dawson."

"I don't think Mr Spleen is the type, sir."

Cam was bemused. "Type?"

"To know any faggots, sir. No . . . Mr Spleen definitely isn't the type. Loves the ladies, our Mr Spleen."

"So I hear. Actually, it isn't a homophobic joke. Faggot Dawson is nicknamed after the English faggot . . . the porky meatball thing, served with chips and mushy peas. Old Faggot lived in London for a time and took to the vile tasting shit . . . but each to his own."

"You'll be off then, sir?"

"I'd like to see Mr Spleen first . . . thank you."

"Sorry sir, I thought you just wanted to chew the fat about gays."

"Maybe some other time. I'm working at the minute."

"Is there anything I can do for you, sir."

Cam read from the little book of calm. "I wouldn't mind a circular argument."

The man smiled and whistled through the gap in his front teeth. "I'll see if Barty's in, sir."

Cam stood with his hands behind his back. First he viewed a computer screen. Next he removed a card from a card holder and laid it flat on his reception table. Then he lifted a phone and dialled. He stood at attention when the phone was answered.

"Some clown down here with a real girly name wants to talk with you, Barty. Say's he works with Charlie Dawson. I've not seen him before and I drink with Charlie all the time. Shall I get rid of him or send him up?"

The concierge listened for a millisecond than spoke. "I wouldn't mind a circular argument," he said into the phone, imitating Cam's voice.

He reverted to his own voice, after laughing at something said. "You can go up. But don't try to sell him ladies' underwear. He only buys those things with a lady inside."

***

The man who opened the door to the apartment was exceptionally tall and verging on anorexic. He was decked out in loose fitting purple slacks, a faded green cotton shirt and no shoes. Long grey hair hung to his shoulders and his skeletal outline was etched into the sallow skin of his face. When he opened his mouth, Cam could see teeth stained from decades of sucking on nicotine and other substances. "Mr Cameron, I presume . . . the man who lied about knowing Faggot Dawson."

Cam was too embarrassed not to extend the lie. "I do know Faggot. I just don't work for him."

Spleen smiled benignly. "As in you've heard he's a rock historian and have seen his photo, or as in you've met him at a party once, or as in he also knows you?"

"None of the above . . . more like . . . as in it seemed like a good idea at the time."

Spleen pointed to an overused grey leather lounge and bid Cam sit. He walked to a cabinet, removed two small glasses and proceeded to pour unmeasured dashes of scotch into each glass. As he handed one to Cam, he glanced at his watch. "It's past ten. I can drink . . . slangevar."

Too early for a drink and, moreover, far too early for a Scottish dinner toast. Despite this, Cam joined Spleen in downing the drink.

Spleen's eyes focused on Cam's face. "Start by introducing yourself, Mr Cameron. Tell me what you do and what you want."

"I'm beginning to wonder," Cam replied.

Spleen poured another shot of whisky into his glass, sat beside Cam on the lounge. "Then let me guess. By the look of you, you're the artistic type. Hands are too soft for much else and you dress like a rainbow. You're not a musician as your fingers aren't calloused. You don't go anywhere near physical labour but you front up when you want something. My guess is, you want to con me out of something. I'd say a particular book; a book given to my wife."

How does he know? Cam thought.

Spleen continued, as if reading Cam's mind. "It's the only thing I have left of any value. As you are no doubt aware, I was a rich man . . .

once . . . but my wife and I lived on the money I made in the seventies and it's just about run out. If it hadn't, I'd still be living in England and not this antipodean wasteland at the arse end of the world."

"You don't like it here then?" Cam asked, trying to change the subject.

"Louisa wanted to die here. No idea why. But maybe the arsehole of the Earth is closer to hell and the journey to the underworld doesn't take as long. Not that she would have ended up in the underworld but there were times, in the late sixties and early seventies, when we were struggling and she was open for business. May not have put her in good stead with those who make the final decisions. Anyway . . . ." Spleen stopped talking and shot Cam a strange look. "What was I on about?"

"You were telling me why you don't like Australia."

"Hate the place. But I can't afford to get back to England and die there."

Spleen stood from the lounge and got himself another whisky. This time he tilted the bottle toward Cam's glass. When he returned to his seat, Cam could see glassiness in Spleen's eyes. Whisky wasn't his only comforter.

"You really want to die in England?"

"More than that. I want to die in a particular time at a particular place. If you can help me, I'll consider your desire for the book."

"I haven't said I have a desire for any book."

"We'll see." Spleen stood up again and left the room. He returned a couple of minutes later with a copy of the *Tales of Beedle the Bard.*

The book was smaller than Cam had imagined. But the image marched the photos and description he had seen. Covered in Moroccan leather and embellished with five hand chased hallmarked sterling silver ornaments and mounted with semiprecious stones. It was, without doubt, the genuine article.

"What would you pay for this, Mr Cameron?"

"If I were to want it, I would pay a fair price."

Spleen placed the book on his glass and chrome coffee table and organised another shot of whisky. "Would you pay $3.98 Million yank money?"

"I'd rather steal it. Too much money for me."

"But you could get it . . . right?"

Cam shrugged. He had an abiding suspicion about becoming involved in someone else's game and didn't know the rules. He had walked unannounced into Spleen's life and now the object of his being there was within inches of his hand. He could stand up, punch the old man and take the book. Easy. But he shouldn't and wouldn't. *I want to die in a particular time at a particular place.* The game. "If I had to."

Spleen smiled at him. "If you can pay, then we won't travel down that path. What say I swap you the book for something of yours? Say the fountain pen in your top pocket?"

Unease gripped Cam like a vice. This was uncharted territory. "Pen's worth a couple of bucks."

"Then you'll be well in front. Can I see it?"

Cam unclipped the pen from his shirt pocket and handed it to Spleen.

Spleen examined the pen, twirled it through his fingers. "This looks like the one I want. $1,700 at any good pen retailer. Wanna swap?"

Adrenaline rushed through Cam's body as he sat on the edge of the lounge. This was weirder than time travel. Spleen was expecting an answer and he didn't know what to say. Maybe he could rewind time, make up a plan and then reset himself to this moment. That would work.

"A seventeen hundred dollar pen for a four million dollar book. Why the hesitation?"

As Spleen spoke, he tilted the pen toward his coffee table and flipped the lever. A reddish brown substance flowed from the pen to the glass.

"Great coloured ink. Don't think I've sniffed ne'er do well colour before. You don't mind, do you?"

Cam's heart stopped as his brain calcified. What was about to happen was beyond comprehension. He stared, like a boy watching his first girlie movie, as Spleen pointed a straw toward the liquid on the table. Where did the bloody straw come from? His need was to grip Spleens arm and push the straw away but he was frozen in space.

Spleen breathed out then sucked in through his nose. A small reddish brown hand formed and gripped the end of the straw."

"Oi . . . dipshit. What do you think you're up to you moron. Do I look like a line of coke to you? Get glasses if you damned well can't see properly. I don't want to be hanging 'round inside you. Too much bloody alcohol. You might be on a bender . . . but I'm not."

As Cam watched, Toerag formed and stood with hands on hips. Defiant.

Spleen didn't even look surprised. He looked toward the table and Toerag. "Ulysses Barry Sporn . . . my fans call me Barty Spleen and my friends call me Monty. You can call me whatever you like."

"Thaddeus Toerag."

Spleen picked the toy up and placed it on the palm of his hand. "I've heard about you. The talking version goes for $119.95 in selected stores.

But I guess they don't live in a fountain pen." He turned to Cam. "Do we have a deal?"

Cam shook his head. "What do you know?"

"About what?"

"Me . . . of course."

Spleen set Toerag down on the table. "What's to know? Fifth Assistant Librarian at L.I.E.U. Time slider, cartoonist, and creator of Thaddeus here."

Cam was dumbfounded. "And how do you know this?"

Spleen laughed, reached for his scotch bottle and took a swig, before wiping his mouth with his shirtsleeve. "Look at me. I've been round for a long time. Mostly, I've played at the very edge of reality. Sometimes I slipped and fell into the abyss. On more than one occasion, I needed saving and one of you lot saved me. A John Belushi impersonator who goes by the name of Lucian Helldale. Or, at least I thought it was Belushi until Men in Black came out. Since then I've been confused. Lucian used to take me on trips with him. Most of the time I thought I was spaced out and high as a kite but, one day, I found the trips were for real. I told him I wanted to go to Waterloo and stand on the field during the battle. It went okay until I avoided an oncoming horse, panicked and fell down. During the fall, I must have hit the delay timer and found myself on the field in real-time. Lucian pulled me back. I thought it was a psychotic episode but I woke up with grazed elbows and grass stains on my jeans, and they're hard to get when you're getting blotto in a pub in Mayfair."

It twigged. "Lucian told you about me?"

"I've been waiting for you to come."

Cam walked to the scotch bottle and poured a measure into his glass. He needed the fortification. "I take it this has something to do with *I want to die in a particular time at a particular place?*"

"You're smart. Lucian said you were."

"And Lucian can't do it for you?"

"He's a friend . . . won't take the risk."

Spleen's plight was obvious. There is very little a man won't do for a friend but one of those things is to watch him die. He understood what Spleen wanted.

"I know what you want and understand why Lucian won't do it. But what you want can't be done. No one knows the outcome."

Spleen said nothing. He walked from the room and returned a minute later with a small sachet of white powder in his hand. He sifted some of the powder onto the glass coffee table and took up his straw. "Lunch time."

Cam watched Spleen wipe excess powder from his nose and rub it across his teeth. "How long do you have?"

Spleen shook his head. "Only a doctor can tell me . . . and I don't go anywhere near the bastards."

"What's the deal?"

"I think you know."

Cam nodded and put out his hand for Thaddeus to climb aboard. He looked Spleen in the eyes. "Okay . . . I'll take you home. London 1973?"

"Yes . . . Hammersmith."

Hammersmith — 1973

THE few people who gathered outside the theatre huddled into overcoats and pulled collars high around their ears. Wind driven rain gusted between the streetlights along Queen Caroline Street, teasing the umbrella stays of a woman crossing the street. Inside the Hammersmith Odeon, raucous chaos vibrated the being of the fans who stood on their seats and danced in the aisles. A capacity house of over three thousand had gathered for the concert. On stage, the five members of *The Ruptures* showed the strain of their two-hour performance.

On the left, Nehemiah Eyeball added his voice to the three-part harmony of the second verse then stepped away from the microphone as the song rocked into the middle eight. Perspiration stained his white cotton shirt and it hung like a limp rag over the top of tight leather pants. His sky-blue Fender Mustang thumped its amplified bass tones into his Marshall stack and compressed the atmosphere like a pulsating air hammer.

Across the stage Illingsworth Eardrum's long slender fingers teased and stretched the guitar strings of the upper register until they wailed into the night. A single spotlight reflected from the polished ebony of his guitar as his mouth opened and closed and his eyelids blinked in time with the rhythm that poured forth in synchronous melody. His tall slender body hunched as the slender neck of the Fender Stratocaster rocked up and down, its phallic machine head glowing in the intensity of the stage lights. His long blond hair hung like loose ropes around his finely chiselled face.

In front centre of the stage the diminutive Colon Colon gyrated his hips as he humped the microphone stand like a frustrated lover. His black satin pants hugged his thighs like a second skin and the yellow stand up collar of his black Crimean jacket glistened with sweat. He brushed greasy strands of dank black hair from his face as he screamed at the audience; his eyes emanating an intensity usually reserved for the driven.

On drums, on a raised platform at the back of the stage, Smokey Lungs rocked back and forth as his muscular arms flailed behind the same Ludwig drum kit he'd used since he was a teenager. Sweat glistened on his bare chest as he thrust it forward, as if to pump himself up. He flicked his head and a spray of water flew from his shoulder length mane.

The song moved to its final bars and the audience waited for the organ wail that epitomised the sound the band had generated for the past two years. Barty Spleen sat straight backed and intertwined his delicate fingers. Unlike the others he wasn't sweating. He'd remained almost still throughout the performance, the only movement his gliding fingers. His blond pageboy styled hair glistened under the heat of the lights but only trickles of perspiration beaded his forehead. Usually he moved and swayed in time with the rhythms but tonight his eyes stared straight ahead. The lightshow inside his head wouldn't allow any external influences to detract from its wonder. He flexed his fingers then stabbed them at the keyboard as the song finished in a crescendo of wailing organ, guitars and crashing cymbals.

Deafening silence, as if the audience had disappeared into another dimension and deserted the hall. Then, like rolling thunder mixed with the shrill screams of devoted fans, the applause built to a cacophony of sound and reverberated through the old building and shook its foundations. Stamping feet gave a bass beat to the screaming jets of female devotees, yelling for more. The sound both music and a deafening throb to the ears of the recipients of the outpouring of emotion.

Eyeball unclipped his bass guitar from its strap and placed it on its triangular stand. Smokey threw a towel around his neck and stood, his muscular legs stretching the material of his tight jeans with only their flared bottoms standing away from his legs. Eardrum unplugged his guitar and slid it around his back. Colon held up his arms to the gathered throng in triumphant pose. Barty stood and stumbled, his head nodding to an unheard rhythm.

The five members of *The Ruptures* stood and waved to their crowd. Eyeball wondered how close he was standing to the spot where David Bowie's Ziggy Stardust had stood for his final bow on the same stage a couple of months earlier.

As they turned to leave the stage, Smokey Lungs looked to his left and caught site of the band's manager, Eddie Smith, at the side of the stage. He nodded acknowledgment of his presence. Beside Eddie, three pristine teenage morsels looked as if they were about to orgasm. Lungs smiled at Eddie's choices. Eddie never let him down. Three might be hard to handle but he would be pleased to die trying.

***

The blower hummed as Lungs settled the last of his hair into place. It was an hour after the end of the concert and the adrenaline rush had subsided. Across the dressing room Barty Spleen slipped into his elastic sided boots and tugged them up his legs. In his black trousers and roll necked pullover he looked like of a model from a clothing shoot. Spleen's blue eyes sparkled as he noticed Eardrum looking at him.

"Will anything ever top this?" Spleen asked.

Eardrum thought for a moment. The band's history flashed through his mind. He guessed it was like the recall of life before you die. His mind was a swirl of dingy clubs, the stench of stale beer, bloodshot eyes in drunken heads. The sounds of recording studios. Practice and performance. Better venues, larger crowds. Wondrous views through bus windows; never stopping to explore the beauty. One day, he would miss some parts of the life but not the rest, neither the travelling nor the endless nights in bland hotel rooms, waiting for two hours of ecstasy. "Probably . . . we were pretty shit tonight."

"I disagree. We were good."

Eardrum laughed. "Are you including or excluding the time you were off stage while the roadies fixed your bloody organ."

Spleen joined in the laughter. "Give me a break . . . you loved it. You got to play another of your interminable bloody guitar solos."

Across the room, Colon Colon tucked his black silk shirt into the band of his leather trousers as Eyeball walked from the shower. His pale blue eyes and high cheekbone gave him a feminine mien that matched the slim frame of his body, even with his blond hair plastered to his head like a wet mop. He towelled himself and strolled to where his clothes draped over the end of the lounge. Spleen glanced across to where Eyeball scrubbed the demons from his head with the towel and dried his hair.

"What you goin' to do now Illingsworth?" Spleen called across the room.

Eyeball's eyes blinked open and shut in rapid succession. "Dunno, man."

"I hear you're joining NASA." Colon yelled.

"What's up, man?" Eyeball asked, not hearing properly.

"I hear you want to join NASA . . . to get close to the stars." Colon repeated.

Eyeball smiled, his green eyes vacant. "Yeah man, gunna fly up there and touch em. Just put em in my pocket and bring em back down."

***

Cam listened as the five friends continued their offhanded banter. He was set. He had two periods when he could allow Barty Spleen to attend the Hammersmith Odeon without danger. The first was prior to the show when the younger Spleen had taken a toilet break. He could give Spleen a couple of minutes with his now deceased old mates. The second was during the time the organ had died. Younger Spleen was off stage for five minutes. The older Spleen could watch and listen to the band without seeing himself. He may not be satisfied but, as in all things, time would tell.

***

Cam caught the tube back to Paddington and walked to the L.I.E.U. building in London Mews. The first time he had done the walk was in real-time. This time he was back in 1973. Strange thing was, the only real difference was the tube trains had been upgraded. But the 1973 trains were fun anyway.

He arrived at London Mews to find Spleen eating a sandwich and sipping on chardonnay from a slim champagne flute.

"Nice looking sandwich, what's on it," he asked.

Spleen smiled. "Nothing you would like. It's an American thing I picked up in New York once. Cocaine and ham on rye with lettuce and tomato. Less of a high than direct snorting but we can't have everything and food's supposed to be good for you. You check the venue?"

Cam shook his head and winced. "Yeah . . . two opportunities."

Spleen listened intently as Cam told him of his plan.

"I remember. Bloody Hammond organ blew a valve. Took five minutes to fix. I think Illi Eardrum planned for it to fail. He got another guitar solo in."

Cam looked at Spleen with intense concentration. "You remember the exact time when you returned to the stage?"

Spleen smirked. "You just saw the bloody concert. You know when I went back on . . . as the applause for Illi's guitar solo was reaching a crescendo. Poor bastard had no idea whether the applause was for his solo or my return to the stage. Perfect timing."

Cam nodded agreement. "Just wanted to make sure you remember."

"I will . . . now when are we going to go to the concert?"

Cam looked into Spleens eyes. The ham sandwich was working. His eyes were as glazed as those he had recently seen when looking at Nehemiah Eyeball. Spleen was sailing through another world. Nevertheless, he wanted to get this journey, and whatever it would become, over with. "No time like now."

"What do we do?" Spleen said around a mouthful of sandwich.

"There's powder on your nose. Don't lose it." Cam thought through the plan. A moment later, he added, "We'll go to the change room and you can revert to your 1973 self. Then we'll go back and catch the train. Once we're at the Odeon we'll turn on the delay timers and go to the concert. When the other you is taking his piss, you can have a few seconds with your mates. Then we leave again until the organ breaks down and you can watch the band while the other you is out the back. You know what you were doing so it should be okay. After that . . ." Cam let the sentence drift.

Cam had no idea what would happen but Spleen wanted to watch himself. Even the time delay wouldn't help there and Cam's mind chip manual consisted of a page covered in question marks. Spleen would be able to see himself and such an event wasn't allowed, or at least, never attempted. He remembered when he had walked past his own house and the bracelet had vibrated. Common sense had suppressed the desire to walk up to the door and meet himself, he hoped it would do so again with Barty.

"You're worried. Cam," Barty whispered, in a feeble voice. "Don't be. It's not a death wish I have. I have always wanted to see myself play and hear the band as the audience heard us. I never heard the band when on stage. All I heard was my organ and vocals. The rest was put down to trust and rehearsal. I just want to know if we were any good. Here, I've got something for you."

He handed Cam a piece of tissue paper. Cam looked at the numbers scrawled on the tissue in lipstick and cocked one eyebrow.

"The stewardess on the plane from Singapore to London. Nice young thing . . . bit scatty but pretty enough. Give her a call."

Cam shook his head. "I thought you had her. When she was bending over pouring your scotch and you asked her to bend half an inch more I thought she might get upset but she bent an inch more."

"Nipples, my boy. No good perving on tits if there's no nipples on display."

Cam read the phone number again. "You asked her for this?"

Spleen cast a look of mock disgust. "Of course not. She volunteered it. The advantage of being in the rock business . . . age never seems to matter to the punters."

"But she could never have been a fan . . . too young."

"Ahhh . . . but her mother was, and mothers count for a lot."

Cam smiled and laughed. "Have you looked at yourself in a mirror lately?"

Spleen joined in the laughter. "Every chance I get, boy. You know, a woman once told me I was narcissistic. I would have argued with her, but I was looking too good at the time."

***

Despite wearing a duffle coat with the hood over his head, Spleen was stopped three times, on the way to the Odeon by young girls wanting his autograph. Cam could see how hard it was for the now twenty-seven year-old Spleen to explain how he was no more than a look alike.

Once at the venue, the time delays were set and both men entered the theatre through the back door. Cam studied his watch and held Spleen in a side passage between back stage and the toilets. He could sense the vibration on Spleens band as the duplicate walked past. Cam followed copy Spleen to the toilet, and watched him enter a cubicle. He then removed his fountain pen from his jacket pocket and squirted Toe-rag into the cubicle lock, to clog the mechanism. The blob of liquid formed a hand and gave him the thumbs up.

Two minutes later, Toerag, his lock jamming task complete, dropped from the lock and fell to the floor. He rolled out of harm's way and reformed as a puddle. Cam waited for the clone to leave the toilet and then prepared to refill his pen.

"Did it work?" Toerag asked, before Cam could operate the pen's lever.

"I guess we'll find out in a minute."

They left the toilets and found Spleen in the passage where they had left him. Instead of looking triumphant he wore the sombre expression of the perpetually disappointed. Tears rolled down his cheeks

"I just stood there looking at them. I didn't even get to turn the delay timer off. There was so much to say but there wasn't enough time. I've been to all of their funerals. I've consoled widows and dolly-bird girl-friends. I've given money to some of their children. I wanted to tell them everything and ended up telling them nothing."

Spleen threw a punch at the brick wall but stopped just short.

"It wasn't your job to tell them. You can't change anything. Their history was written by their lives. You only ever gave yourself time to say hello. What did you expect to happen?"

Spleen shook his head with disappointment but then smiled. "How do we get to the middle of the concert?"

"Your choice. We can catch the train back to London Mews, reset the time and come back here in an hour or so . . . or we can find a place where we can listen to the music but not see anything."

Spleen flipped an imaginary coin. "I think we'll listen for a while."

***

Barty Spleen giggled like a demented schoolgirl as he stood on a va-cated chair half way between the theatre's entry door and stage front. No seats were occupied. Devoted fans had long since abandoned any fear of being sent back by security and surged at the front of the stage. The faith-ful occupied the aisles between seats and the aficionados milled in groups at the back of the hall discussing the finger picking that made Illi Eyeball's eyes flutter and sent young girls into raptures of pubescent dribbling.

Cam watched Spleen's every move. His fingers were poised over the delay timer as ordered by Cam. The second before the other Spleen re-turned to the stage, Spleen would hit the time delay, then turn around and leave the venue. So far so good.

The guitar solo came to its electrifying and screeching end and the bass and drums took the songs back to the final bars. Cam waited for the 1973 Spleen to appear at the side of the Stage. He stared at the older version, willing him to make the right decision.

Applause erupted and the building shook. Illi Eyeball took a deep bow and Barty Spleen walked onto the stage.

The old man didn't hit the button. He just stood on the chair and watched himself being lauded. It wasn't Eyeball's solo; the bulk of the applause was for Spleen's return.

Spleen junior seated himself at his organ and began to finger the lilting and well-known melody of the band's latest hit song. On a seat half way to the back of the hall a young man wept . . . and then disappeared.

Cam hit his delay button and looked for Spleen but he hadn't returned to the time delay zone. He had disappeared.

***

THE TIMES

The death occurred last evening of 1970s rock star Ulysses Barry Sporn, known to his fans as Barty Spleen. Sporn was found in seat W7 at the Hammersmith Apollo Theatre. The theatre was empty and it is not known how Sporn entered.

The seat on which Sporn's body was found became legend in 1973 when a young woman claimed to have seen an image of Barty Spleen standing on the chair and then disappear. The young woman was later treated for a psychological disorder. Sporn is survived by . . .

***

Cam handed the copy of *Beedle the Bard* to Holly. "It was a fair deal."

"Shame we can't keep it."

"This book isn't unique. There are more copies out there. It's also easy to copy. You just need to be a good artist and have a time machine available. Any fool could do it." Cam produced another copy of the book from the pocket of his brown leather jacket and placed it atop the original. He then knocked both copies to the ground. "See if you can tell the original?"

Holly picked up both books and examined them. She smiled as she eyeballed Cam. "Does one have smiley faces?"

"Of course not . . . but you need to decide which one goes on the courier stand. I can't remember which is the original."

"Is Thaddeus in one of them?"

Cam shook his head. "One may think that but one couldn't possible tell."

Holly glared at Cam through half closed eyes. "There'll be ramifications."

Cam shrugged. "We need to know what's going on. We're down to ninety-seven years of forward movement. There has to be a reason."

It was Holly's turn to shake her head. "It's none of our business."

Cam grinned and pointed at both copies of the book. "You decide and then we'll see."

Holly nodded affirmation, then laughed. "Question. Where did Spleen's band get such stupid names?"

"You mean Nehemiah and Illingsworth?"

"No you idiot — Eyeball and Lungs and Eardrum."

Cam shook his head. "Obvious. Like Spleen, they're parts of the body capable of rupture. Their first names are real. The only one who wouldn't play along was the singer. He was supposed to be Appendix but didn't think the name would get him any chicks . . . or birds . . . or girls, or sheilas, or whatever. They agreed with him, as long as he called himself Colon. They all thought he was a bloke who just couldn't have enough colon so they named him twice . . . New York fashion."

Aiko

IN THE twenty-third century, there are those who exist in the nether world between fantasy and reality. Some see it as an elevated plain from which one can be both wise and condescending. Others see it as a time populated by pompous twits who swan around the planet doing what they like and pulling everyone else into gear. One of those considered as wise is Aiko Kiribati. Aiko is part Japanese and part Pacific Islander. For her, the top half is graced with Japanese dominance but her bottom half dictated her name, as she was named after the island of New Kiribati. This should not be confused with old Kiribati, which disappeared into the Pacific in 2037. New Kiribati is just as described . . . new. The small island group rose from the Pacific in 2189, after the sea level dropped to 1921 levels.

Aiko travels through the nether world by the auspices of her employment with L.I.E.U. Her official title is Historian but she is as close to being an historian as Holly Penworthy is to being a librarian. Her real task is to keep the downstream guardians in line and it was for this reason she visited the L.I.E.U. building in Paddington.

Unlike most visitors, who were deposited into a recreation room that only exists when people are expected, she appeared in the control room and scared the living daylights out of Cam.

"Jesus Christ!"

Aiko was not perturbed by the assertion. "No . . . but I met him once. He was preaching to the converted in Galilee."

Cam stared at the diminutive woman. She was ghostly pale with straight, pitch-black hair, centre parted to give her a symmetrical appearance. She wore tiny rectangular glasses, on a slim face with a tiny but interesting nose. Her eyes were large and black and didn't match the glasses but Cam looked at her as someone he would draw if he was creating an image denoted as *cute*. She wore blue jeans and a pale-yellow blouse. Designer footwear adorned her feet. Cam prayed that the designer brands meant she had dressed for his time and not that the present ubiquitous shoe companies still existed in over two hundred years' time.

"Then you must be Aiko Kiribati. Holly said to expect someone from the future." He looked her over from head to toe. "You look like now."

"We always look like now . . . whenever we are."

Cam shrugged. "But you're here to see Holly. I didn't expect you to bother."

Aiko smiled. "Wrong on two counts. I always bother and I'm not here to see Holly. I'm here to see you."

Cam didn't understand. Holly had mentioned nothing other than the Historian was paying a visit.

Aiko commented on his lack of understanding. "You're an interesting case. By the time I leave here, I hope to know you better."

Cam shrugged with Gallic nonchalance. "Time will tell, I guess,"

Aiko changed course. "Business later. At the moment I'm starving, after a two and a half hour slide down the timetube. How about taking me for lunch?"

Cam looked at the wall clock. It was 12:37pm. "You timed your arrival to perfection."

"Of course. What's the point of time travelling if you don't keep an eye on time?"

"I'm lucky if I arrive on the intended day."

Aiko smiled and started to walk toward the door. "We've noticed."

Cam read the words between the lines. "What else have you noticed?"

Aiko shook her head. "After lunch . . . where are we headed?"

"Up to Oxford Street I guess. What do you eat?"

"Food usually works."

"How about mammoth?" Cam quipped

Aiko smiled again. Cam thought it to be a pleasant smile with edge. "You don't have mammoth in this time zone."

"Okay . . . I'll play. What do you usually eat?"

"I'm partial to meerkat and dodo."

"As in the extinct dodo?"

"Only to some generations. One of our farmers went back to before they were exterminated and caught a few. They're bred in captivity."

Cam laughed. "Next you'll be telling me the Tasmanian tiger is roaming the hills again."

"Back to 1684 levels."

"Okay . . . you win. What would you like to eat?"

"I want to eat from one of your menus. I'm tonguing for an over-cooked hamburger with beetroot, tomato, pineapple and lettuce with chips on the side . . . served with a cold beer by a waitress who has her thumb buried in the burger sauce when she delivers the meals."

"Then I know just the place."

***

The sauce covered fingernail polish, was pink. The chips had been sitting under a bain-marie for a week and the hamburger meat was an R.M. Williams rain wear product. Sydney on a slow day. As he separated the food into edible and nonedible piles he noticed Aiko ploughing in with gusto.

She wiped her mouth with the side of her hand as she finished a mouthful of beef and barbeque sauce. "Do you always watch people eat?"

"You're the first person I've met from the future who isn't here on holidays . . . and I've never eaten with any of them. I'm looking for sub-tle differences."

"Have you found any?"

"The term eats like a pig comes to mind but it may just be a colloquial-ism."

Aiko shook her head and picked up another piece of burger. "Pigs are no longer eaten. They're too intelligent."

"The world continues to evolve," Cam said.

Aiko took a mouthful of food then continued speaking while chew-ing. "Human's and other animals evolve. The world just keeps on doing its thing; spinning in its speck of universe."

Cam laid his knife and fork on his plate. The inedible food remained as future dog offerings. "May I ask you questions about the future . . . or is it a secret?"

Aiko finished chewing. "The future between now and my present . . . yes. But only in generalities."

Cam thought for a few moments, formulating questions. The most obvious made its way to the front of the line. "What's the population in your time?"

"Three billion . . . or close to anyway."

Cam was surprised. "It's more than seven billion now. What happened?"

Aiko laughed and heads turned toward her. "Weekends off and more leisure time."

Cam was befuddled.

"The world's population halved over four generations and not a drop of blood was spilled . . . nor was there a natural catastrophe. It was down to the chocolate makers of Bruges in Belgium. You see, they agreed they were working too hard. Their chocolates were so good and popular they couldn't keep up supply and, as the world's population grew, they saw themselves as never having any time off. So they decided to act and give every person in the world a chocolate. There was a great hoo-ha about it and every world government got involved, so everyone could eat their chocolate at the same time. No one knew the chocolatiers had determined the most industrious places in each nation and which nations contributed the most to society. Then they went to lower levels and looked at individual occupations and ways of making money. Everyone was pleased to be involved and spilled out the information . . . after all, they were about to receive a chocolate . . . and who wouldn't die for a chocolate. What wasn't known, at the time, was that selected chocolates were laced with a very potent strain of quinacrine and the women who ate these particular chocs were sterilised. From then on, only selected pockets of humanity could reproduce and over the next few generations the oldies died off and weren't replaced. Over time the population decreased. The end result made us all better off but the businessmen and women who rely on ever expanding growth lost their mojo and thousands of multinationals went belly up."

Cam couldn't tell whether she was lying or telling the truth. "You don't have capitalism then?"

"In a way. The Swedish method became universal. It's more socialism than anything else."

"Do you still have wars?"

"Of course. Men will always fight over whose dick is biggest."

"Religion?"

"More than ever. People need to believe in something . . . faith never changes. We sent people back to the various times of the prophets in order to have the truth demystified. We thought religion may die out but it didn't happen. You see, time travellers get lost and appear accidently and new religions spring up. We just exacerbated the existing problem prior to time travel. Religions like the Order of the Girl in the Blue Dress, and the Order of the Girl in the Red Dress are mainstream. But so is the Order of the Libidinous Tart . . . so not all take themselves seriously."

Aiko realised her burger was getting cold so ploughed in again.

Cam envisaged a chain saw hacking into a tree as he watched her eat but said nothing. He was too pleased for the pigs.

Aiko finished eating and ordered another round of beers.

"I notice you don't wear a time bracelet," Cam commented.

Aiko shook her head. "It's in my memory chip. You have one there too. Turning it on is on page 568975 of Volume 4 of the users' manual."

"Think I skipped that part."

Aiko nodded. "Wise move. You have to blink three times at regular intervals to turn your delay timer on. It's a real pain when you're in panic mode. Some gorilla in Great Leap Forward Five tried to attack me once. You think you can control blinking under stress?"

"For a moment I thought you said gorilla."

"I did . . . a metaphor of course. But it reads better than eight rampaging mercenaries wielding machetes."

The waitress arrived with two pints of beer and an extra jug. She dropped them on the table and cleaned away the food, returning her pink thumb to Cam's hamburger sauce.

Aiko picked up her pint. "Save us ordering too often,"

"We're not going back to the office then?"

"I was hoping to get to know you. Keep asking questions."

Cam aimed for something closer to home. "***The Book of Fictional Grievance,*** I've never seen it used or even a message on its screen."

Aiko downed half her pint in one gulp. She wiped her chin on completion. "***The Book*** is used quite often in my time. With all the microbots and minibots around and robots as home appliances there are tons of fictional and mechanised characters who bitch about their lot. Doesn't get much of a historical run though. Mind you, there have been a couple of classics from your time. The biggest complaint we had was from Roger Rabbit. You know, his wife is the classic femme fatale of course. Anyway, he complained. Argued it was obvious from the way he was drawn and she was drawn that she would have a wandering eye. He wanted to be more handsome, so movie goers would have some sympathy for him. But it's always the same in movies . . . the new lover is always better looking than the husband . . . who's usually some type of jerk and the viewer wonders how the wife got herself saddled with him in the first place. The judges listened to Roger's complaint but dismissed his case on the basis his name was mentioned in the movie title. The other complaint of note was made by the dragon tattoo in the Stieg Larsson novels. The tattoo contended that Larsson named his first book *The Man Who Hated Women*. The tattoo wanted more prominence as it just hung around on Lisbeth Salander with hardly a mention. The judges figured there was a case, so had a discussion with the America publishers and the title of the first book got changed to *The Girl with the Dragon Tattoo*. Tattoo also got a big role in the movies. Look at the size of the thing."

"I'm supposed to believe you?" Cam asked.

"Of course. You are recorded as saying: 'Do you, as a reader, not get involved in what happens to the characters in novels.' Surely you believe me?"

"It's a given. I just don't believe the two stories you just mentioned."

Aiko took another half pint swig of beer and refilled her glass from the jug. "Hypothetical . . . what if Thaddeus Toerag takes off and someone wants to turn your cartoon series into a movie. Wouldn't you get Thaddeus' input?"

"Yes . . . but he talks."

"He's a liquid plastic figure that can change shape and work for you. He's not human and has no emotion . . . but you treat him as a friend. You care for him. Think about it. Stieg Larsson and Gary K Wolf probably felt the same way about the characters in the *Millennium Series* books and *Who Censored Roger Rabbit*."

"Of course they would have."

"Then believe what I just told you. It's easy. Just open your mind and it will be filled with knowledge and wonder."

Cam looked into Aiko's eyes as he lifted his glass to his mouth. She didn't blink as she watched him looking at her. It was like a game of who blinks first. Cam knew he would lose but his eyes weren't as glazed as Aiko's had become since they had sat down for lunch. "What's next?" he asked, before sipping on his beer.

"Ahhh . . . work. My reason for being here. I was hoping to put business aside until I got to know you better."

Cam finished drinking and put the glass down. "I'm at a great disadvantage here."

Aiko giggled. "Of course you are. It's apachet [5] ."

"You can't just leave it."

---

[5]Parallel word to the word you can't think of. Similar in usage to the Italian 'Allora' Can be used as a verb, noun, adjective or adverb.

"You're right. I'm just hedging. Reality is, I'm here to give you grief. You just about up to your ears in deep merd. You've done a few things not in keeping with the acts of an assistant librarian and you need to explain. I was just hoping to get to know you a lot better before I dump on you."

"By doing what?"

"Sex would be nice."

"You want to have sex with a man who's about two hundred and fifty years older than you?"

"Just pretend you've waited for me to come along."

"You may not be my type."

"Maybe not . . . but you think I'm cute. I read your description of me at the beginning of this chapter."

"You are cute. Does cuteness explain why I haven't seen Holly around today?"

"I have no idea. I only arrived about an hour and a half ago."

Cam smiled and realised Aiko really was cute — in the same way stuffed toys are cute. It was the big black eyes. He imagined how he would draw her. "And after sex?"

"I'm taking you on a journey to my time. No assistant librarian has gone there before. It will be a first for all concerned."

"May I ask why I have been summoned?"

"Yes. You have been charged with not stealing a book you were supposed to steal and with the death of one Barty Spleen. There is also the ownership of the *Tales of Beedle the Bard*. You didn't steal it."

Cam waited for Aiko to continue but she stopped talking and poured herself another beer.

"And if I'm guilty?"

"You will have your memory chip removed."

"We'd better have sex then. If my penalty is to have my bloody chip removed I'm now in a hurry."

***

Throughout his entire life, Cam had never heard the word *Alteskinne* and was unaware of its existence until Aiko had felt contented enough during their sexual tryst to show him the alternate side of her personality. Later he would consider she may have thought it would be a turn-on for him but, at the time, it did no more than terrify him and wither his libido.

But then, having sex with a woman who turns into a cat can be a little off putting. Not that she turned into a cat. In reality it was akin to Michelle Pfeiffer's version of Catwoman in *Batman Returns* . . . with the addition of real ginger fur, whiskers, claws and a fluffy tail. Cam's heart froze and he failed to see the joke as Aiko laughed at him. And, as she explained, it wasn't her fault he didn't know tattoos had been replaced by the ultimate transformation of having yourself sprayed with Alteskinne. This alternate skin allowed people to have an alternate self. As she explained, some chose to be Minotaurs, others took on the role of Centaur while others became Gorgons. Hers happened to be a cute and cuddly ginger cat. This was acceptable in 2260 but some time travellers had travelled back to Ancient Greece and influenced the myths of history. They were admonished, of course but cancelling their time travel permits didn't equate with their influence on ancient cultures.

The worst feature of the transformation, though, was to see Aiko turn the skin on and off by blinking. Unfortunately, even when he saw what was happening, Cam could not revive his interest and he stayed adrift of the feline until they arrived in London in 2263.

2263

THE city's sounds enveloped Cam as he rode the high-speed magnetic railway between Heathrow and Paddington. They weren't what he was used to. There was no din from vehicles or heavy industry to reverberate the soul, which left a sort of calm to pervade the senses. He had first sensed it when he rode the time tube from 2019 to 2263, and caught a hybrid cab from Paddington to the New South Wales airport just to the west of Dubbo. The cab had intrigued him. It was an EH hybrid, running on either electricity or hydrogen. It had wheels for use in the city but as soon as they hit the Sydney/Dubbo express route the wheels retracted, and the cab flew a metre above the ground. Even the expressway was different. There was no ribbon of concrete disappearing over the horizon but a grassed area that seemed to stretch to infinity; or to Dubbo at least. He and Aiko had then taken the ten-hour flight to London in a plane with a maximum of 1,500 people in luxurious comfort.

As the magrail sped toward its destination, Cam noticed that none of the buildings were more than ten stories high. "What happened to the high rises?" he asked.

Aiko's smile was condescending. "Before my time. I've seen photos of course. When the population decreased, there was no money for the developers' phallic contests and common sense prevailed. The last of the high rise developments was demolished in 2186 and there are to be no more built."

"Just here?"

"Worldwide. The highest buildings in the world now are in New York. Even with their reduced population they're pretty condensed, so they were allowed a limit of 20 storeys."

"And who decides?"

"The Belgians of course. They decide on everything relating to building. The Chinese look after agricultural policy. The Italians do the banking. The British cook. You know the jokes . . . only it's not a joke anymore."

Cam glanced at cars on the street below the rail. "Why do cars have wheels if they can fly?"

"Easy. Old roads are still used. We run on wheels and save energy."

"People seem to dress the same way that we do." Cam commented.

"Did you expect clothing from your sci-fi series?"

Cam smiled. "I guess I did."

"There was a Star Trek period, and a Star Wars period, but fashion is as cyclic now as it ever was. The last Star Trek period was in the 40's and it embarrasses us to look back at the styles."

"And if you don't like the fashion you wear a cat suit?"

Aiko punched his arm. "For private use only. My boyfriend is a dog and I'm a cat. We use interspecies imagination. Turns us on. But I guess I should have warned you before changing . . . I forgot where I was."

"So you have a boyfriend?"

"Thirty-seven at last count but only one in this time zone. I do a lot of travelling and spend too much time in hotels throughout the world."

Cam was intrigued. "And why do you do this?"

"The boyfriends or travelling?"

"Travelling . . . I guess."

"I'm the official L.I.E.U. Historian. I run a team. We study history and correct errors. We're charged with looking at history from all perspectives . . . not just the perspective of the victors of wars."

"And if you find an error?"

"We correct it. We rewrite the history to comply with the facts which are taught in the world's educational systems."

Cam noticed the magrail was slowing. "Must put some noses out of joint."

"I don't see why. If a country did wrong then the error has to be corrected."

"Sounds like Utopia."

Aiko smiled, without commenting, as she stood from her seat. "We've arrived. I'll get you set up in the hotel and then we can go to the tribunal."

Tribunal wasn't a word Cam had considered when setting out on the journey. For some reason he had imagined a small tête-à-tête with a few people involved with L.I.E.U. Maybe he should have thought about it more.

The magrail stopped at St Pancras, and Cam and Aiko walked out of the station into the freezing cold of a London winter's day. He had expected to catch another train to Paddington but a wheel-less taxi, which still looked like a London cab, picked them up and they went by road.

***

London Mews had changed. It wasn't the small street he remembered from previous visits. It was now dominated by a building the size of the city block. It had the words *Light Interrupting Educational Unit* emblazoned across its walls like beacons on a dark night. The building was a huge white block of concrete with no windows. It reminded Cam of an unwelcoming fortress.

"Yuk," was all Cam could say when he saw it.

"Rigotecha Christiansen will be upset with your comment."

"He's the architect then?"

"No, he's descended from the family who invented Lego."

Cam shook his head. He had no idea what she meant.

"The door we enter is on the corner. The hotel is inside and reception is on the second floor. They're expecting you at registration. I'll catch up with you after you settle in."

With that, Aiko disappeared — literally.

***

Cam entered the building through a glass and copper doors fitted into a corner. It had egress to two streets. The inside of the building resembled a huge empty concrete shell. A bright green guidance sign, in the shape of an arrowhead, appeared about fifty metres away. The arrowhead pointed towards the floor. He headed toward it. A stainless steel and plastic reception desk appeared to come out of the wall as he approached the sign. There was a woman sitting at the desk, reading a magazine. The woman glanced up from her page as he approached and looked him up and down. "You're good for your age."

"I am?"

"Yes. Says here you're 274 years of age. You carry it well."

Cam couldn't see her reading anything. There was no monitor or keyboard on her desk. It was just covered in magazines. "Thank you."

"Ohh . . . you're the one they're all talking about. You're *that* Assistant Librarian."

That Assistant Librarian. A chill ran down his spine. "I'm told there's a hotel here," Cam said.

He looked around the vast empty space. The ceiling now matched the colour and texture of the sky on a sunny day.

"Level 2. You're booked in for the duration of the inquest."

Cam looked around again. "Level 2?"

"Descent-well three. It's over there." The woman pointed in the direction from which he had entered the building. "Just stand on the stainless steel disc and it will take you to the hotel."

"A question. You seem to have information about me . . . how do you remember it? I don't see a computer monitor."

"What is a computer monitor?"

"Doesn't matter. Obviously you don't use one."

The woman lowered her head for a moment, ignoring him. Then she lifted her head and smiled at him. "Computer monitor. Ancient viewing device. Thank you. It was in my memory bank."

Cam thought he felt his memory chip light up. "Memory bank?"

"Of course. All we Plexer 18 Series units have memory banks. We can recall every event in world history and every person . . . except for those who were never registered on our system."

"You're a robot?"

"Of course. I'm a Plexer Series 18 female formbot. We do the things too boring for humans."

"I thought you were a woman."

"My designer will be pleased with the feedback. I'm new and my bugs haven't all been sorted out yet."

Cam was intrigued. On impulse, he leaned over the desk and smelled the bot. There had been something lingering and he liked the scent. "Intimate nights. I love this perfume. I once knew a woman who wore it."

The bot looked at him. "I know. Ms Petra Petitfille. You would like to be intimate with her. That is why I generated the scent for you."

Cam shook his head. "You have everything covered."

"Yes."

"I'm in trouble then?" The question was worth the asking.

"No it wasn't worth asking. I cannot give you any detail," the formbot said.

***

The disc at descent-well three took Cam down an unknown series of levels until it stopped at the stereotypical foyer of a five-star hotel. It was patterned on every other hotel entry foyer he had seen. The commonness of purpose. Not too flashy, not too bland; a long desk with five attentive receptionists, a concierge desk, two luggage trolleys and rotating entry door and chandelier.

He entered the foyer and noted all five receptionists resembled the Plexer Series 18 he had met a few minutes earlier. Even the male receptionist had the same face and hairstyle and wore the same black and grey power suit.

"Cameliel Cameron," he said to the first receptionist.

"Assistant Librarian Cameron. We have been expecting you. You are booked into cell 35 for the duration of your interrogation."

"Cell 35?"

"Our little joke. We know the outcome of your trial and just wanted to make you feel at home."

Cam looked into the eyes of the bot. "So you're designed with a sense of humour."

"Of course. We're modelled on the Series 17 pleasure bot . . . for men and women who can't find a human partner. We have a sense of humour and can play a musical instrument. We can also gossip, if necessary."

"Haven't I met you before," Cam said.

"I don't think so."

"Made in America?"

"Yes. How can you tell?"

"I've detected a lack of irony." He smirked.

***

Cell 35 turned out to be a two-room suite that would have graced the best hotel in any city in the world. Cam settled onto the bed and looked for the TV remote. There wasn't one. In fact there was no obvious TV. He rifled through a bedside drawer and found an entertainment guide. The pages were blank. He looked at the back cover of the guide and found, written, in very small print. *You are in an entertainment free room. For entertainment ring the entertainment manager or walk down two blocks to the London Gentlemen's Entertainment Club.* There was no number for the entertainment manager and no phone in the room. Cam lay back on the bed, closed his eyes and dreamed of cats.

***

"Josephine Whittlesnake QC," the bearded man with pince-nez glasses perched at the end of his thin nose said, as he introduced himself to Cam at the breakfast table on level 16 of the hotel.

Cam half stood, trying not to smile as he took in the man's coffee coloured wig and red and white pinstripe suit under a floor dragging black cape. A red nose and he would resemble a studious clown, Cam thought, before realising the man might be able to read his mind. "And to what do I owe the pleasure?"

"No pleasure. I am here to represent you at the inquisition."

Cam thought for a moment. "Josephine?"

"Of course. I am descended from a long line of Whittlesnakes. We have been at the bar for more than three centuries."

Cam looked into the man's bloodshot eyes and believed him. He repeated his question. "Josephine?"

"Of course. I am descended from a long line of Whittlesnakes. We have been at the bar for more than three centuries."

Cam felt a cyclic nightmare coming on. The man had to be some form of bot. He tried another angle. "You have a woman's name."

"No, sir. Whittlesnake is gender nonspecific. Every member of the family has it. Both men and women."

Cam felt his life draining away. He gave up. "Okay . . . Josephine . . . what are we up against?"

"You are up against L.I.E.U. The most powerful time travel organisation in the world."

"My understanding is they're the only time travel organisation."

"Correct, but by saying *most powerful* I strike fear into your heart and you will be more pleased when I get you off."

Cam couldn't believe what he had just heard. "So there's a chance you'll get me off?"

"No sir, but I'm part Italian and I like to make people feel good."

"What am I being charged with . . . exactly?"

Whittlesnake removed a buff envelope from a valise. The envelope was bound with a pink ribbon. Some things never change. He read from the single page contained within the envelope.

"You are charged with not stealing and the death of a rock and roll star . . . one Barty Spleen."

"And if I'm found guilty, what is the punishment?"

"This is a serious matter. In the worst case you could have your memory chip privileges removed."

Cam sniggered and held his right hand against the side of his head. "Can I just plead guilty?"

"No, justice must be seen to be served. Having a memory chip is a privilege and its removal would be soul destroying for you."

"Wanna bet."

Whittlesnake looked at Cam as if he had gone mad. "You old men never understand."

A bell rang on the wall. Whittlesnake bid Cam to stand up and pointed him toward the door. "The trial is about to commence."

The two walked along a narrow corridor and stepped onto another stainless-steel plate. This time Cam couldn't tell whether he was going up or down as he was surrounded by glass walls overlooking fields and meadows. A Minotaur grazing in a field appeared in the distance. Two unicorns fought for supremacy in a flower strewn arena. Real or imagined? Cam had no idea.

The plate stopped and Cam and Whittlesnake walked along another corridor until they reached a copper covered door set into a gold-plated frame.

"This is where the inquisition will take place. It's an informal hearing but you must answer the questions asked . . . and you may ask questions."

The copper door slid into the wall, which was quite a feat, considering it was fitted with large hinges. Cam stepped through the opening into a barren room. The walls were concrete grey and the image of the sky on the ceiling displayed stratocumulus clouds. It looked as if the room would soon be inundated with rain. In the centre of the room stood a single plastic chair and to the far side of the chair were a bench table and three straight backed wooden chairs. Against one wall was another high-backed chair.

"Just take a seat, Mr Cameron . . . and good luck." Whittlesnake said, before he disappeared.

Cam strolled to the chair as he took in the sparsity of the room. Surely this wasn't a courtroom. Even in his time, no self-respecting magistrate would work in such a space. And what happened to Whittlesnake?

"All stand. Judges Madeov Ivory, Obese Winifred Whittlesnakeproxy and Alwaysbin Armless presiding." The words came from unseen speakers in the walls and echoed around the empty space. Cam was still standing, so he did nothing.

"The hearing is now in session." The speakers again.

As if on cue, three people appeared on the chairs behind the bench. They were all old men. The one on Cam's left as he faced the table was tall and gaunt, with a long narrow nose and beady eyes. He wore red robes, draped to the ground, and a black three-cornered hat on his head. The one in the centre was short and obese, with grey hair down to his shoulders. He too wore red robes but his head was bare. The third man was bald with a full beard and artificial arms, which gripped onto the front of his red robes for dear life. His head was covered with a red cowl.

The one in the centre spoke. "Sit down, Mr Cameron."

Cam sat on the plastic chair. It flexed under his weight but remained upright.

"Mr Cameron. You are charged with not stealing two books and changing history . . . in relation to the death of one Barty Spleen. How do you plead?" Judge Obese said.

"Insanity."

Obese looked to the man with no arms. "An allowable plea, Alwaysbin?"

Cam watched Armless as his eyes rolled in his head like poker machine wheels. When the eyes stopped rolling, the man nodded toward Obese.

"Do you plead guilty insanity or not guilty insanity?"

"Neither, just insanity."

The three men at the bench began an almost silent conversation. Cam waited until they sounded like they were entering meltdown and interrupted. "My barrister said I could ask questions . . . is that right."

Beady eyes spoke. "You must speak through your barrister,"

Cam looked around. "He isn't here."

Beady eyes scanned the room. "You're right, where is he?"

"How would I know? He just disappeared."

Obese turned his jowled face on Cam. "He was double booked. He went to the Old Bailey. There's a case there he has a chance of winning, so he gave it preference."

"Can I speak for myself," Cam interjected.

The men looked at one another and then to the vacant chair, as if waiting for divine intervention. Then, without saying a word to one another they looked at Cam and together said: "Yes."

"Good. My first question is — could those who are human put a hand up?"

All three men glanced at the empty chair against the wall. After a moment Ivory, the beady eyed one, put his hand up.

"And who is the senior judge on the bench?" Cam asked.

Obese raised his right hand.

"So I'm being judged by one man and two robots and one of the robots is the senior judge?"

Judge Ivory snarled. "I'll have you know, Judge Obese Winifred Whittlesnakeproxy is the most learned judge on the circuit. His decisions are infallible."

Cam leaned forward on his chair. "I take it this is still traditional British justice. There's no jury here, so I assume I'm to be judged by my peers and, from my point of view, a bit of fallibility always comes in handy."

"Are you saying you want a panel of human judges?"

Cam nodded his head.

Armless rolled his eyes again. Once they stopped, he addressed Cam. "There are no all human judging panels available until March 2297."

Cam shrugged. "Can I go home then?"

The three judges disappeared. Cam looked at the ceiling. The clouds appeared to be more ominous. The judges reappeared.

"We can simplify things, Mr Cameron. We want you to answer only three questions. Can you do that?" Obese asked

Cam nodded.

"Then I will start. Question one. Why did you not steal *Traité des Arbres Fruitiers?*"

Cam leaned back on his chair. "Simple. It was the wrong time. If we had stolen it when requested, the copy would have been the one to become famous and valuable and you would have had to steal the copy . . . not in our purview."

Obese spoke again without even a pause to reflect on Cam's answer. "Question two. Why did you not steal the *Tales of Beedle the Bard?*"

Cam leaned forward. "There was no need. Barty gave me his copy. You got what you wanted without theft."

"But you killed Mr Spleen." Ivory stated.

Cam shook his head with vigour. "No . . . I granted him a wish. He wanted to watch himself perform. I gave him the opportunity."

"He died and you transported his corpse through five decades before you let it be found." Armless injected.

"No. he disappeared in 1973. I didn't know what happened to him. I figured it was you guys."

"So you think judges carry dead bodies through time?" Obese snorted

Cam shook his head again. "I didn't say that. I just know it wasn't me."

"Why did you not steal the book? Stealing was common in your time." Armless asked.

Cam shrugged. "I assume it's the same now."

Ivory glared at Cam. "You assume wrong. There is no stealing now . . . or murder, or any other noncorporate crime. Time travel has given the police immense power. They just go back in time to the point of the crime."

"So there was crime?"

"Yes, until the criminals realised what was going on. Since then . . . nothing."

"Then why do you guys exist?"

"It is only criminal law that is no longer needed. All other facets still operate as normal."

"But with bot judges."

Obese ignored the comment. "We will rise to consider our verdict."

The three judges disappeared again.

***

Cam perused the chair against the wall. The judges had looked at it twice. They had to be seeing something he couldn't see. He stood from his chair and walked toward it. He stopped and hit his delay timer. Nothing happened.

"It's been disconnected." The bodiless voice had the timbre of melted honey. It was husky, soft and lilting like a good melody.

"Just trying to see you."

"You're smart, Mr Cameron. I like that. You answered the questions perfectly."

"Why have I been disconnected?"

"So you can't disappear. You're in trouble with the authority and can't be allowed to drift in and out of sight."

The authority? It wasn't a word he expected to hear. "I take it this isn't a real court?" Cam asked, hoping the voice would give him some indication as to what authority had him on trial.

"It is the L.I.E.U. court. It has international jurisdiction over time travel matters."

"Does it hand out *legitimate* sentences if one is found guilty?"

"Why do you sound as if you doubt it?"

"I just want this to be over. I don't care if they remove my memory chip. In fact, most days I'll be pleased."

"Obviously you're ill informed. The memory chip is removed by plucking it from your severed head after decapitation."

Cam collapsed.

***

When he awoke, he was sitting on the plastic chair at the moment the judges disappeared. He glanced at the vacant chair and wondered if he had dreamed the conversation. Surely not. He stood, looked at the vacant chair and hit his delay timer. Nothing happened.

The voice was there again. "Glutton for punishment, huh. Try not to faint again."

"Then you're real?"

"Obviously."

"You scared the shit out of me. I had no idea."

"Of course not."

"Okay . . . I'm in trouble, but why? I don't understand why Holly and I exist in your world. There is nothing we do you can't do for yourselves."

"You don't understand our time. You're where you are because of wages. If an employee goes from here to your time, it is two hundred and fifty odd years each way. That means we have to pay the employee five hundred years salary. We know it only takes about two and a half hours each way but the Miscellaneous Time Travel Employees Union International are great negotiators. Imagine if we had to send someone back to have a chat with Julius Caesar. It would send us broke in no time."

"And Holly and I . . . and the other assistant librarians?"

"You're on the same deal. Every month your salary is put into the L.I.E.U. Trust Bank, Paddington Branch."

"I don't know the bank."

"It didn't open until 2257, but your wages are both safe and guaranteed."

"You're joking . . . right?"

"Not at all."

Cam thought for a moment. The judges hadn't reappeared and he was enjoying the discussion. "But why us . . . in our time?"

"Obvious. We needed to find a time to do our work between the beginning of the digital revolution and 2024. It was in 2024 the UN decided grand theft of valuable antiquities, which included rare books, was getting out of hand and decreed that all valuables should be taken from public view and put into permanent storage. From 2024, only digital reproductions were available to be seen by the public. As you know, reproductions can be copied, and are indistinguishable from the originals, but it no longer mattered as the originals were safe. By the way, the work you put in on *Traité des Arbres Fruitiers* was brilliant. We had no idea that you had returned the copy until your friend Thaddeus blabbed when he was trying to impress Lucy d'Loosy."

"I don't understand."

"She was a plant."

Cam balled his fists. "I'll melt him down."

"Bit drastic. He was in love."

Cam laughed, despite his surroundings. "I can't even imagine it."

"You should try."

Cam wouldn't be side-tracked with Toerag's love life. "Maybe . . . okay, I can understand wanting the originals but why steal them. Surely we could have bought them at auction."

"Too rare an occurrence."

Cam felt as if he was on a roll. "Why only four books?"

"They were Sydney's four. Other librarians and assistant librarians were also on the go. We have the world's twenty most valuable books . . . we even have a copy of *Alice's Adventures Underground* with smiley faces. We know it's the original but we're still not impressed. However, given the book's characters drew the smiley faces themselves we've been forced to accept them as part of the original works."

"So I won't be charged?"

The voice let out a liquid sigh against Cam's ear. His heart beat increased to the point of bursting.

"No," the voice whispered. "Judge Ivory would go spare. It would be apachet. He has enough trouble already. He still grieves for his wife."

Cam shook his head. "You've lost me."

"It was Judge Ivory who insisted we invent the three second delay. His wife died in Roman times, while on holiday."

"I heard something about a woman."

"Everyone has . . . and he's been a pain ever since she failed to return from her journey. I've tried to convince him to go look for her but he likes to wallow in his misery."

"And if he looked for her?"

"He can bring her home. She was killed in Nimes around AD 52. Someone needs to go back and find out what happened . . . and bring her back for burial at home."

Cam turned his back on the chair and headed toward his own plastic contrivance. "I take it your little segue to Judge Ivory's wife was planned well in advance."

The laugh was soft and mellow. "You might say that. Here's the deal."

Nimes

CAM was staring at his computer screen studying ancient history when Holly entered the room and glanced over his shoulder.

"I heard you were found not guilty."

Cam turned his head from the screen and eyeballed her. "Not exactly. It was more of a deal. The judges wanted to punish me but they were overruled."

"By who?"

Cam shrugged and shook his head. "I have no idea. I know it was a woman, and I know she has the sexiest voice in the world of sound, but I have no idea who she was or how she fitted into the system. She didn't appear and I couldn't initiate my delay to see her. All I know is I did a deal to avoid losing my head."

"Losing you head?"

Cam explained the method of removing memory chips. Holly turned up her nose and winced. "I bet that hurts."

"More than I wanted to know."

"And what's the deal?"

"One of the judges, Judge Madeov Ivory, lost a wife in Roman Nimes. I've been given the task of finding her."

Holly scratched her chin with her right thumb. "I've heard of her somewhere. There was a photo of a dead woman from Roman times."

"I've seen it. Just after it happened, a cop went back from the future and found the woman. She was dead, so he left her there. He videoed the scene but nothing else. The invisible woman told me they want the body returned. It shouldn't be left where it is."

"And you took on the task." It was more of a statement than a question.

"In exchange for my head."

"Do you know where to start?"

"I know the where and the time. The woman died in Roman times but not in Rome. She was fascinated by the Pont du Gard in southern France. It was built between AD 20 and AD 60. She went back several times to look at its construction."

"I've heard of it. It still exists doesn't it?"

"Yes. It's between Uzès and Nimes on the Gard river. The waterway ran from the Fontaine d'Eure near Ucetia to Nemausus. They're the Roman names for Uzès and Nimes. That's the easy part. They know she disappeared in the summer of AD 52 but not exactly when. I have a three month window to find one event that occurred within an area of around 100 square kilometres."

"It'll take you months, just to get there."

"The things you do for your head, huh."

Holly closed her eyes for a moment, as an expression of utter sorrow crossed her face. She reopened her eyes and smiled. "They were bluffing. They, of all people, know they can't interfere with history. You won't die from having your head cut off in the twenty-third century."

"That's what I figured, as well. But I don't know how I die. I can't access my own records. I figured, if my fate is to disappear and no one ever sees me again, being beheaded sometime in the future may be possible."

"My guess is you will die at the end of your lifetime. Not in some far-flung time zone."

"It's not what happened to the woman who died somewhere near Nimes, about two thousand years before she was born."

Holly spun on her heels, let out a huge sigh, as if divine inspiration had fired her soul. "Not possible . . . and the reason for you to undertake the journey. The legend of the woman who died says she tried to save a Roman slave and was killed by the slave girl's master. There were no delay timers then . . . but . . . and I mean a hopeful *but* . . . the bloke who killed her didn't kill someone from the future. That would be interfering with his history."

"And?"

"You can go back and correct history. You can find her and save her."

"The cop who went back could have saved her."

"Not if he was sent back just to report on what happened and he had ingrained into him the instruction about not changing history."

Cam stood from his chair, shoved his hands into his pockets and began to do multiple circulations of the small room. It started to make him dizzy but he resisted the temptation to stop. Holly grabbed him by the shoulder and made him sit down. "Sit down; you're making me dizzy just looking at you. And stop reading your memory chip. It makes your eyes go all funny."

Cam looked up at her. "Sorry Holly. It kicks in at the most inopportune moments. I'd turn it off but I don't know how."

"Isn't it in the manual?"

"Yes . . . but I can't remember the volume or page and it isn't in the index, otherwise all assistant librarians would have them switched off."

Holly looked at him. "You could be gone for quite a while."

"At least until the end of this chapter . . . maybe longer."

"You mean no time at all then."

"Of course. Irrespective of how long it takes I'll reset time before I ride the tube back to the present."

Holly leaned toward him and kissed him. "I'm glad they didn't find you guilty."

"You're wrong. I was found guilty. Guilty of not stealing something I was instructed to steal and of carrying a dead body through time and dumping it in another time zone."

"But you didn't, did you?"

"Of course not."

Holly nodded her head. "When are you off then?"

"Tomorrow. I've booked an early flight Sydney to London. The trip back to AD 52 takes twenty something hours. So between that and the flight I've going to be comatose by the time I get there."

"Then tonight we'll go out to dinner, celebrate you not losing your head and you can tell me about the future."

Cam took a very old lady to dinner and told her about everything he had seen and done.

***

The attraction of time travel tourism was obvious. Cam had travelled to France in 2010 and visited Nimes, Orange and Arles. This time he arrived at Nimes' Porte Augustus to find not the ruins he remembered but in-tact walls and ramparts. The Tour Magne stood resplendent with soldiers keeping a lookout far out to sea. The amphitheatre was filling for the day's entertainment and brightly coloured stalls sold the ancient equivalent of fast food to nondiscerning travellers. Young men from the ludus gladiator school mixed with young women in flowing robes. These men were not as yet ready for gladiatorial combat but would take their place in the future, when they would not lose in seconds and be condemned to death by unsatisfied spectators. This day, the theatre would fill with 24,000 spectators and human blood would spill onto the gravel of the main arena. At the end of the day, the trainee gladiators would be glad they were still alive to cōpulāre with the fair maidens of their overt desire.

Cam decided to miss the spectacle and sleep. He had travelled for three months by means of oxen drawn plaustrum, chariot, rheda and carruca when possible but mainly by foot. A carruca could travel as far as 150km per day, but to use vehicular transport he had to travel in realtime. Besides, the seats did his back in and he ached at night on hard straw bedding. After one particularly gruelling day on a carriage rack, his back had become so painful he had to rest up for three days. Obviously Roman backs were tougher than the wimp back of a twenty-first century cartoonist. When walking he could avoid trouble by travelling in delay and thus eluding contact with anyone.

The travelling annoyed him but he used it to learn. And what he learned surprised him. He found he could understand Latin and the other regional dialects of the areas through which he travelled. For a while he wondered why language had become simpler and considered whether he might have been impregnated by a Babel fish of either the Google or *Hitchhikers' Guide to the Galaxy* type. Finally he realised the knowledge must have been written into the memory chip. Of course, when you don't like something and want it out of your head, you have a tendency not to give it credit for anything. After all, even without the memory chip, he would have known a Roman oxen drawn cart was called a plaustrum. Doesn't everyone?

In hindsight he realised auto translation should have occurred to him earlier as he had communicated with people in Venice in 1748 and not even considered the possibility they may not have been speaking English.

He was about to move away from the maddening crowd when he noticed something in his peripheral vision. A building, just down from the amphitheatre was registering on his subconscious. Maybe he had seen it before? He thought for a moment and then realised that where the building stood in ancient Roman territory, a cafe/patisserie had stood in 2010. Not unusual for modern day Nimes but definitely uncommon in AD 52 Nemausus. The penny dropped, and he realised he needed to compare the scene with the photo of the dead woman. If his memory served him at all, the woman had died under outside table number four of La Dolce Patisserie and Cafe.

***

Cam turned on his tablet and scanned through his photos of the crime scene. Two bodies lying in the dust. One he knew to be Poaché Ivory, wife of Judge Ivory but the other he didn't know. He assumed she was the slave girl. When he studied the photo, he concluded the death of the slave girl was a waste. She was tall and thin, with white/blonde hair, high cheek bones, blue eyes, a thin, slightly tilted nose and pouting lips. Her neck was long and sat atop perfectly formed shoulders. At least that was what he envisaged from the crumple of her dead body lying beside a woman in her mid to late fifties with short cropped black hair, a pocked marked red nose, which bore signs of a love of the bottle, and rheumy eyes. If he ever had a choice about who he would try to save the frump would be a distant second.

Eenie meenie miney mo. He drove the thought from his mind. He studied the photo in detail. The older women had had her left breast cleaved and the entire front of her tunic was covered in blood. The other had been luckier. It appeared as if a gladius had penetrated her stomach in a single blow.

He continued to scan his photos until he came to the one showing the bodies, with the reference point of the amphitheatre. He looked around and reassessed his original thoughts. He had been right. Both bodies reposed under table four of the patisserie.

He was returning the tablet to his satchel when a shudder passed through him. Someone had walked straight through him. Not an unusual occurrence when using time delay but this was different. This wasn't a physical thing but he had a psychosomatic sensation of being hit. He remembered Holly telling him that Ben Hall could see her. It didn't make sense then and it made no more sense now, but he felt a need to move out of the path of others and lean against the wall of a building.

He had stood there for only a few minutes when a young man and a woman passed. They stopped and the man spun the woman around and pressed her against the wall. Or it would have been the wall if it wasn't in the exact location where Cam stood. He stood still and held his breath as the woman was pressed into him. Then she pushed the man away and spun around to face the wall. She looked Cam in the eyes.

The young man recoiled. "What's up?"

"I thought someone touched me."

The man stared at the wall and into Cam's eyes. "I can't see anything."

"There was something," the girl said as they both walked away.

Cam shuddered. He couldn't be seen but the girl had sensed he was behind her. He thought for a moment and then took the only course of action available. He panicked.

He took off down the street until he found an alley with a wall at its other end. He ran through the alley to the wall and sat on his haunches. Here, there would be no through traffic and he would see anyone approaching.

He closed his eyes and scanned his memory chip. After what seemed like an aeon, but was only sixteen seconds, he found a reference. It was in Volume 1 of the service manual on page 127,895.

> Time Decay: A time traveller may experience a mild form of time decay when travelling more than one hundred and fifty years from source. The traveller may feel a sense of panic when coming into contact with persons using real-time. The traveller may sense the person can see them or touch them in some way. This is not the case and the feeling is psychosomatic. The phenomenon is caused by a weakening of the satellite signal between traveller and satellite.

> Weakening of the satellite signal; If the satellite signal weakens when travelling through time, the traveller must follow the following instruction:

> HIDE UNTIL THE CORRECT SIGNAL STRENGTH RETURNS.

> Note: If the traveller does not hide then he/she/it may be seen. This is in breach of time travel protocol No. 16,756 and will lead to a loss of time travelling privileges.

Time decay; feel it and panic. No instruction on how to detect a weakening signal. Did the signal weaken with every one hundred and fifty years? Was he in a time zone with twelve times the one hundred and fifty year decay rate? He closed his eyes and sat for a while until an old woman came to the end of the alley and threw food scraps over him. She didn't give off any sense of seeing him; nor did the pack of dogs that attacked the scraps.

He typed a question into the FAQ screen on his tablet.

Q: How do I detect time decay?

A: No idea. Closest answer . . . visit a dentist.

***

Bugger it, was the only response to the answer Cam could muster. He would just have to pray each day for a strong signal. But pray to whom? A question more confusing than ever. He threw his satchel over his shoulder and returned to the street end of the alley. He looked toward the amphitheatre and froze. The white/blonde woman was being led along the boulevard, on a short leash attached to a dog collar, by a fat man in a purple toga purpura. The woman stood tall and elegant and was dressed in a short skirt, under which she wore fishnet stockings and high heeled shoes. He gawped at the shoes. These wouldn't be invented for another fifteen hundred years. This sight was impossible. He caught up with the collared woman and perused her from head to heels. Not only were the heels high but they were stilettos. Change fifteen hundred to two thousand years. The woman had high cheekbones and oval blue eyes. She wore light make and smelled of a perfume to be invented in Grasse in southern France, at some time into the distant future.

Then he spotted something he didn't expect to see. The woman was wearing a time travel bracelet. The man on the other end of the leash pulled a small whip from under one of his folds and flicked it at the woman's bottom. She purred.

Cam leaned in and examined the bracelet. It looked normal but there was something missing. The bracelet bore no serial number.

The fat man stopped and pulled the woman to a halt. "Gather round," he called to all within earshot. "I am presenting an hour with my lady here as the prize to the most successful ludus gladiator in the arena today."

The crowd cheered.

Trainee gladiators moved away from their attendant girls and made their way to surround the old man.

"I am aware these young men are not here to fight on this day but who would not fight for an hour alone with this beauty."

The crowd cheered.

The fat man turned toward the trainees. "Put up your hand if you want a shot at the prize."

Eight trainees shot their hands into the stratosphere.

The fat man looked at them and nodded at a few cronies to lead them away. "To the arena," he shouted.

Cam imagined inexperienced blood being spilled all over the arena. He had to do something. He grabbed the woman's wrist and flicked her delay time to *on*.

"What the f . . ." the woman screamed.

"You can't do it," Cam told her.

The woman glared at him. "Can't do what? And what's it got to do with you."

"Everything, lady. I'm an assistant librarian."

The woman spat from the side of her mouth onto the ground. "This has nothing to do with your type."

"Wrong . . . you're interfering with history." Cam could feel anger boiling within.

The woman smiled at him. "So what . . . you can't do a thing about it."

"You mean someone's authorised this?"

"No." She held the bracelet toward him. "Not registered. You can't trace me or disconnect me."

Cam reached into his jacket pocket to get his black box. It wasn't there. He had decided he wouldn't need it. Nonetheless, he had a need to play time cop. "How'd you get an unregistered bracelet?"

The woman shrugged. "No reason not to tell you, I've had it for years . . . a gift from an admirer."

Had to be someone very high on the food chain but Cam didn't even know if there was a food chain. "Do you have a name?"

The woman laughed at him. "Of course I have a name. Sahara Aquasol, novelist extraordinaire. I've sold two billion copies of each of my books." She held her braceleted arm toward Cam again. "My friend who gave me this made it compulsory for every adult on the planet to have a copy. Surely you've heard of me?"

Cam shook his head. "Never heard of you."

The woman sneered. "Impossible. *The Medieval Mistress. The Baroque Bordello. The Renaissance Rapist. The Millennium Mole.* You must have heard of me. I travel in time and experience things as they really were. I've been molested so many times I've lost count. I take real experiences and turn them into graphic stories of sex and lust."

"You write porn novels then?"

"Of course not. It's high art," she said offended.

Cam ogled her from head to foot. "Obviously. I can tell its high art by the way you dress. I do apologise for my ignorance. I shall make sure to get hold of all of your books."

Sahara smiled with genuine warmth. "I'm sure you'll enjoy them."

Cam remembered the photo in his satchel. "What are you writing now?"

"Ahhh, *Roman Romp*. It's a story about a noble woman who is cast into slavery and ravaged by gladiators."

"Will this be your last novel?"

"I don't expect so. Why do you ask?"

Cam shrugged and took out his tablet. "I have a photo of you dead. Taken just near here. I assume it's not far into the future."

He showed Sahara the photo.

"Oh that photo . . . it's not the future. That was a week and a half ago. My old master thought he stabbed me to death. I just hit the delay and covered myself with fake blood and a bit of gore. Then I reset the time and fell down dead. No forensic pathologists in these times."

"The other woman?"

"I don't know what got into her. She lunged at me and tried to steal my bracelet."

"And?"

Claudius killed her. Then he just looked at me . . . and the bracelet . . . and tried to stab me."

"You know who she was?"

"No."

"She's from your time. Her name's Poaché Ivory. She's the wife of Judge Madeov Ivory."

Sahara's face changed colour and Cam thought of Procol Harum. She began to sob. "It can't be . . . it can't be. Poor, poor, Made."

Made . . . Madeov Ivory, Sahara and Poaché. Small world stuff.

"I'm here to try to get her back home."

Sahara's gaze was soulful, bottom lip trembling. "I'm so sorry."

"Then you have to help me. I need to be there at the exact time she was killed."

"But she *was* killed. I watched the life drain out of her as we lay on the ground."

"Your Claudius couldn't kill a woman from the future. We can reverse everything and history won't be changed."

"But you're wrong. All of you are wrong. I change history all of the time. When I do my research, I communicate with people, even have sex with them and then write about it. You can't remove those things and you can't change my history."

Cam returned his photo to the satchel. "Maybe not, but we can try."

Sahara nodded and stared into the middle distance. After a few minutes, she asked, "What do you want me to do?"

Cam looked at the people three seconds ahead of him. They milled around the space from which Sahara had disappeared. "I guess you had better finish what you started."

Sahara's smile resembled a Cheshire cat after its fill of cream. "No need. Caligula Precious died outside the Nimes amphitheatre in AD 72. He was killed by trainee gladiators after promising them something and then reneging. There's no record of what he reneged on . . . but maybe I can guess."

Cam felt his heart stop again. Sahara didn't make sense. "This is AD 52."

Sahara shook her head. "No it isn't."

"Yes it is."

"I could say 'no it isn't' but that would be too much like a panto. It really is AD 72." Sahara stopped talking and rolled her eyes. "Wait a minute . . . Mrs Ivory was screaming at me when she tried to grab the bracelet. I thought she was saying 'gimme it you'. Maybe she was saying 'fifty-two'. If you're in the wrong time, maybe she was as well."

Cam had never thought to look. He closed his eyes and read from the encyclopedia of his mind. *Time travel* error. *+/- 2"*. It made sense. Pissed him off, but it made sense.

"So you don't have to make another appearance here?"

"He's just too fat. I thought Claudius was a pig but Caligula flattens my sternum."

***

It was just after 6:00am, on the Wednesday of Poaché Ivory's demise. Sahara knew Claudius would awaken at just before 6:10am and she had to be there to greet him. From then, the day would advance until the time she was attacked by Poaché Ivory.

Cam followed her through the morning, as she tried to emulate what she had done the last time she travelled through this date. Cam didn't really see why. She was trailing along with her master Claudius but for him everything was happening for the first time, so he had no idea whether or not Sahara was repeating something she had done before.

As they wandered through the day, Cam scanned the faces of the women they passed, hoping the facial recognition software in his memory chip would signal him when Poaché Ivory came into view. Watches weren't worn as part of normal Roman attire, so Sahara didn't know the exact time she had been set upon by the Ivory woman but she knew where they had been and Cam could feel the hairs on the back of his neck rising as they approached the spot.

Then he saw Ivory. She was hanging back in shadows against the wall of a building. Her face was set with grim determination, as if she was about to do something with more than a modicum of planning. For Ivory, going after Sahara wasn't a random act. He had imagined that Ivory may have intended to save the girl from Claudius but now he saw his imagination had been wasting its time. There was something deeper going on. He walked across to Ivory and stood beside her. She was muttering something under her breath. Cam had trouble deciphering what it was until he heard her speak in a whisper.

"I'll kill you, you bitch."

Cam was surprised

The woman took a few tentative steps toward Claudius and Sahara. "I'll get you, you slag," she muttered.

Cam was less surprised. This act wasn't to save Sahara, or even something to do with being in AD 72 instead of AD 52. This was the green-eyed monster of jealousy. This was a twenty-third century domestic drama being played out by time travellers. Ivory hadn't ended up in the wrong year. She was where she intended to be. Cam had to stop it.

He appeared in front of Poaché Ivory. "You can't do it."

She was, momentarily, startled by his appearance but it was only a fleeting setback to her. "You can't stop me," she told him coldly.

Cam grabbed her by the arms. "It doesn't work out for you. The man kills you."

Ivory spat in his face. "You have no idea."

Cam increased his hold. "It's you who has no idea. I'm here to take you home."

Ivory began to cry, "To what?"

"Your husband. He's been miserable since you disappeared. He sent search parties for you . . . and a cop came back here and recorded your death. But I can prevent it. All you have to do is hold back until Sahara is out of sight. Then we'll go home."

Ivory stopped breathing for a minute and glared at Sahara as if she was distilling all of the venom in the world and giving it a single purpose. Then she relaxed her shoulders and let out a sigh. "I guess you're right. I can handle this at home."

"You ready to go then?"

Ivory nodded.

Cam let go of her arms.

She stood for a moment, looking at the ground. Then, not giving Cam a chance to recover she sprinted toward Sahara with all the pace she could muster. As she ran, she produced a long knife from under her off-white stola. Upon reaching Sahara — she lunged,

Cam detected Sahara disappearing and then reappearing in a split second. At the same instant, Claudius wheeled his gladius and split Ivory's chest in two, cleaving her breastbone.

Claudius looked down at the woman with a complete lack of understanding. Then he dropped to his knees beside Sahara and lifted her head, dropping tears onto her face.

Cam kneeled beside him and sniffed the air. Sahara had lied to him. The blood wasn't fake. Ivory's knife had found its way home.

Claudius picked Sahara up and carried her toward the amphitheatre. He rested her on a stool and called for help. People rushed forth but there were none who seemed interested in getting involved. Claudius cursed and waddled off. Cam assumed he was going for help.

The crowd dispersed and Sahara hit her delay.

Cam waited for her. "You lied to me,"

"It's nothing . . . and you know I survived."

Cam smiled. "I found out what she said as she reached you. It wasn't 'gimme it you' or 'fifty-two'. It was 'I'll kill you'."

Sahara nodded. "I know . . . leave me now and we'll meet up where we left off previously. I feel like going home."

Dilemma

THE H.G.Wells inspired time machine took its toll on Cam's desire to take Poaché Ivory's body back to her husband. It went off in the sun during the three-month journey back to Paddington. Refrigeration wasn't big in Roman times and constant ice baths needed ice and there was none available due to ice dispensers not having been invented at the time. The best he could do was remove her bracelet and watch her disappear. He assumed she would be reborn at her birth date but wasn't sure about rebirth if you died in another time zone. Maybe it was one of the joys of time travel; the ability to die *elsewhere*. The possibility had to be considered. He still bore a scar on his chest from being stabbed in Venice in 1748, and Sahara Aquasol wore stitches just below her rib cage from a stabbing in AD 72. Not that she would ever acknowledge the stitches. They had been done by the best Roman doctor available but the differences between her stitches and those at the top of a grain bag were almost indiscernible. He figured there would be more time travel incidents and people *would* die in strange times. Maybe he was just excusing himself for failing to save Poaché Ivory. But did she want to be saved? He had told her she would die but she didn't listen. Perhaps he should have shown her the photo of her dead body? She knew what photos were. He could have stuck the evidence in her face, or stapled it to her forehead. He considered going back in time and having a third attempt at the incident but decided against it. Or, more correctly, Sahara was a little sick of getting stabbed and wanted nothing to do with an action replay.

***

Cam was still thinking of the range of consequences when he finagled from the time machine in Paddington (London) in his own time zone.

Sahara continued onto her time zone and promised she would clear the air with Judge Ivory. She would argue that Mrs Ivory was now twice dead and the Judge could move on with life . . . with a very experienced and beautiful author at his side for as long as he desired . . . or until she got sick of him and sucked away the last of his money. It could take some time as he was extraordinarily rich, but then she was extraordinarily good at sucking money from men.

The plane journey from London to Sydney went without incident. Cam spotted Barty Spleens favourite air attendant. She failed to remember him, but that's the way of things in the noncelebrity universe in which most people exist.

***

He arrived in Paddington and found Holly sitting with her feet up on a desk leaning back and reading the news on her tablet. She stood up when he entered the room.

"Welcome back, Cam. I was beginning to doubt you would return in the same year you left."

Cam looked at her. "I don't understand. I've only been gone for a few days."

"I thought so too, but I've noticed it doesn't always work as intended. I thought you would have picked it up. We don't age when we are in the machine itself but we do when we're on business outside of the machine. I estimate you've been away for six months and, when you return to real-time, it will show."

"You mean I'll be older than I think I am?"

"Yes. While you were away I travelled to Arimathia to look for Godwin Godwell. I told him to give up on his problem, because he can't change anything. He agreed but decided to stay there. He's now an old man. He hasn't nipped back here for a quick visit because he's too old to travel to London Mews. He left here in 1958. He was twenty-one at the time. Now he's eighty-two and looks it."

"You knew about this?" Cam asked.

"Not until I spoke to him. He'd read it in his manual . . . I think he said page 1,682 of Volume 12."

She shook her head. "He's had a lot of time to fill. He told me, in the early days of his mission, he used to flit from place to place studying the people and the times. But on one visit he met a woman and fell in love.

He'd already inured himself to not fixing his 'Son of God' problem but saw no reason to come back to real-time."

"So he gets old there?"

"Yes . . . and it suits him. He and his wife age at the same rate."

"But he's still connected to the satellite?"

"Of course . . . if he removes his bracelet he'll disappear until he's born last century. He told me he'll wear it until he dies."

Cam unhooked his overnight bag from his shoulder and dropped it to the floor. For some unknown reason he felt something was wrong. There was an unwelcome heaviness in the atmosphere. Holly had no desire to chew the fat with him over his trip to Nimes. In fact, she hadn't even asked how the trip had gone and he had been back for almost four minutes.

"You okay?" he asked.

"Just a little tired. I've only been back five minutes. I left just after you did and arrived back just before you. Good timing huh?"

"You sure you're okay?"

"Yeah . . . but I saw three men on crosses."

Cam nodded his head. He imagined the scene and understood the significance. He wondered how close Holly had got to the crucifixion. "Did you get close enough to hear any of them talk?"

"Yes . . . and it was very moving."

"What did he say?"

"I don't remember exactly but it was something about the bright side of life."

Cam dropped to his knees, made a sign of the cross, stared into Holly's eyes and held her hand. "You got to worship at the feet of Eric Idle. I've always wanted to do that."

"Very thin man."

"No alpha male there."

Holly finally laughed at something. Not a laugh with any ranking in the world of great laughs. It was more a subdued titter and acknowledgment that Cam had appreciated her attempt at humour.

Cam stood but kept hold of Holly's hand. "There's something wrong . . . I can tell. You haven't even asked me about how my trip went."

Holly smiled at him. "How did your trip go?"

"Don't ask."

"I take it you couldn't save Mrs Ivory."

Cam reiterated the tale in detail. By the end of it, Holly pondered Cam's recall to the twenty-third century.

"It depends on Sahara's relationship with the Judge. I guess if they're on . . . I'm off the hook."

"What about Miss Sexy voice. She may not be pleased, and she has to be powerful if she sits in with the judges and they look to her for advice."

Cam shrugged. "My feeling was she wanted to make Ivory happy. Like I said, it's up to Sahara . . . I'm off to bed. You going home?"

Holly shook her head. "Not for a while. I have a report to write."

***

Cam woke in the morning to the sound of an alarm he hadn't heard before. He jumped out of bed and wrapped his Joseph coat around his shoulders. He almost sprinted to the control room. He found Holly sitting before **The Book of Fictional Grievances.**

"What's up?" he asked

"This thing alarmed. There's nothing on the screen now but there was a message stating for us to standby for an important announcement."

"We've been connected to parliament then?"

"Droll."

A message began to scroll down the monitor screen. It was marked as *extremely urgent,* which outweighed any other sense of urgency, because of its accompanying adverb. There was a problem on its way down the tube. A woman by the name of Mrs Blindaza Batt was travelling to Australia in 1982 to attend a faith healing service conducted by the Reverend Allan Waysa Scamm of the Fundamentally Self-righteous Church of California. The Reverend All had brought his huge tent show for a once only performance in the showground at Castle Hill. There would be singing, praying, rock and roll bands, and miracles. Mrs Batt was travelling for the miracles. Faith healing was outlawed by the end of the twenty-second century and Mrs Batt had taken to reading about the great faith healers through time, in order to have her affliction healed. Her best friend and doctor, Mrs Irving Schism, told her that her they may not be able to help but Batt was a determined woman and when time travel became a tourist venture, she saved her money and purchased a ticket, in order to have her sight restored. This wasn't possible, as Batt had been born without eyes, but she was determined to try. However, *trying* raised an alarm within L.I.E.U's dodgy traveller system because of Mrs Batt's constant companion, a Plexer 17 Series pleasurebot, which had been converted to a seeing-eye robot when it grew old and could no longer self-lubricate.

Holly read on as the message scrolled past. "Says here she takes the bot everywhere and she intends to have the bot take her to the service."

"I've seen a few Plexer17's and they look like real women. They even talk and have a sense of humour."

"This one plays mandolin and sniffs cocaine as well . . . but we can't let it appear in 1982. Robots were basic at best then. If anyone gets wind of a developed robot all hell will break loose."

"Then we have a problem. In order to tempt a miracle, Mrs Batt needs to appear in real-time."

"Unless we give the Reverend All a bracelet and let him meet her in delay."

Cam's eyes rolled. "It would give him too much power. He's already so far up himself he looks like the letter '6'. He'd end up thinking he's omnipotent . . . which is a problem for him anyway."

"Is he still around?"

"No . . . died in 1987. By then, he believed so much in himself he was convinced his scams were real. At a service in Las Vegas he claimed he would rise from the dead. His last words, as he stood open armed before his audience, wearing a pure gold suit, were 'Give me a chance to prove myself. Kill me and I will rise from the dead.' One of his audience members took him at his word and shot him between the eyes . . . there was no second coming."

"I see."

"When does Mrs Batt get to 1982?"

"She left 2274 around two and half hours ago. She should pass here any minute."

"And we will . . .?"

"We have to stop the bot from being seen. We need to pick her up in reception."

***

Cam and Holly waited in the 1982 reception area. This was the usual reception area but every year it updated its own décor. The only two people who finagled themselves from the time machine were a woman in her fifties and a small child of around twelve. The woman was tall and elegant but seemed tired from the travelling. The child had an urchin quality and wore huge sunglasses.

Holly approached the woman. "Could I ask why you're here?"

"Of course. The fourth Sydney biennale. This is our first but we intend to see every one until their funding dries up."

"And the child?"

"My daughter Capstan. Named after a cigarette brand one of my ancestors smoked."

"Capstan?"

"We have no idea what smoking was but, apparently, advertising made it sound exotic."

Holly nodded and the mother and daughter moved into the street and hailed a cab.

Cam watched them go and returned to the monitor. He'd never heard the word Capstan used as a name, so he typed it into the search engine. The result terrified him.

Capstan. Derived from the name of a one-time cigarette brand. Standard name for people with the genetic eye disease 'lackofeyesblinditis'

"Shit!"

"What's up Cam?" Holly yelled at him as she flew through the door.

"That was them. Mrs Batt must have morphed before she left her time. The woman was the bot. We have to catch that cab."

"We know where they're going. We'll take my car."

Cam looked at her with his head cocked sideways. "I didn't know you had a car."

"In 1982 I lived in the burbs with my husband. I used to drive to work every day. The car's parked in the next street."

"We don't know which way they're going."

"Doesn't matter. This is 1982. The cab driver will take them to Castle Hill via either Wollongong or Newcastle. We'll be there first."

And they were.

***

Cam spotted the pair as they got out of the taxi. It was quite dark and the Reverend All's concert was already into its stride. With luck, no one would see anything. "I'll take the woman and you grab the kid. We'll drive them into the delay zone."

Holly nodded and moved in behind the girl. She wrapped her arms around her and flicked her delay switch. For a moment they were alone but then Cam and the bot joined them.

For an instant Cam thought the plan was going to work, but the next five seconds were more telling. The bot flung him aside and punched Holly square in the face, knocking her to the ground and away from the girl.

"You recognised us then?" the bot asked.

Cam was first to react. "Of course. No one in their right mind ever smoked Capstan. You had to be lying."

The bot stood with hands on hips, like a colossus dominating a couple of field mice. Cam scratched his nose with his paw.

The bot spoke with quiet determination. "We're here on a mission. We won't be stopped."

"It won't matter," Holly mumbled, as she tried to regain her feet and dab a handkerchief to her bloodied nose.

"The Reverend All does good works. He's in all the history books. He was great."

"Which books?" Cam asked.

The bot's eyes rotated and whirled. "The greatest book of all."

"Bible, Koran, Torah, Tripitaka maybe . . . which do you believe in?"

"*The Greatest Deceptions of the 17th to 21st Centuries*. It contains all of the great historic events and those who were responsible for them."

Cam looked at the ground, at the bot's feet. He couldn't afford to let her see him laugh. "And why do you think these events are historical."

"Because deception is a synonym of truthfulness and we all seek truth."

"Antonym," Holly said, before Cam's memory chip had a chance to kick in and regurgitate all of the synonyms of deception.

"What does antonym mean?" the bot asked.

"The opposite."

"My memory doesn't have antonyms."

"There's no reason for it to be there. You were designed as a pleasure bot and adapted later on. I guess pleasure bots have no need to discern between the truth and lies."

"Have I done something wrong?"

"Not at all. You're doing the right thing. The only problem is . . . the Reverend All can't help Mrs Batt. The main prerequisite for seeing is to have eyes and Mrs Batt doesn't have those."

"Don't talk about me as if I'm not here," the child said. "I'm morphed and blind . . . not deaf. And what's this about my not having eyes."

Holly looked down at the child. "You don't have eyes. Simple."

"No one ever told me — no, that's wrong. My father once told me but I didn't believe him . . . so he told me to go look for myself. I couldn't so I didn't bother. No one has told me ever since."

Cam noticed a lead hanging from the coat Mrs Batt was wearing. The plug on its end seemed to match a socket in the bot's side, which could be seen through a split in her dress. "Mrs Batt . . . can you see when you plug into the bot?"

Batt smiled. "Of course. I have 20/20 botvision. I see through her eyes. I just wanted to see for myself."

"Unfortunately Reverend All can't help you."

"Doesn't matter," Batt said. "The main reason we came was because he is purported to carry around a box of gold with him. We thought we might relieve him of it."

Holly felt blood trickle from her nose again.

"I don't know if I can let you."

The bot retrieved a worn sheet of paper from her purse. She handed it to Holly. It was a tabloid report saying the Reverend All Waysa Scamm reported to police that his trailer was robbed while he was giving a sermon at Castle Hill. He refused to tell police what was stolen but the items are believed to have been of great value.

Holly turned to Cam. "I'm getting tired. I thought we might head back."

"And leave these two here?"

Holly stared into the middle distance. "What two are those?"

***

Cam was having a late-night coffee hit when he noticed Holly was still doing her report. "You should go home."

"It's okay . . . I'll finish this."

"You do know you're acting strangely . . . don't you?"

"You mean?"

"You've never let anyone off the hook since I've known you. What you did for Batt and Bot made no sense."

"Didn't matter. They didn't get the gold. I read up on the robbery and the perps were caught the next day. The robbery took place half an hour before we met up with Mrs Batt."

"You didn't know that at the time."

"Still doesn't matter."

"What's up Holly? You can tell me. We've been working together for either three-quarters of a century or ten minutes. I know you. You're never here this late and you can work on reports at any time you like. You just readjust time after you do them."

Holly thought for a moment and then smiled at Cam. "Okay . . . I have a problem. Last night I was halfway through taking off my bracelet and all I could see was nothing. I think I may be dead."

The New Librarian

"DEAD? You're joking," Cam said. "Poor joke at that."

Holly shook her head and smiled wanly. "I'm ninety-three years old, Cam. My time has come. No big deal. I thought it would impact me a lot more but it just seems to feel like the end of a road."

Cam looked at his thirty-four year-old friend. She was beautiful and full of life, albeit looking a bit bedraggled and tired at the moment . . . but tired would pass. "Just stay here."

"I've had a full life. I've had a fabulous job, married a wonderful man, raised children and baby-sat grandchildren. It's time to join my husband. Actually, I've missed him since he went."

"But that's no reason for you to go. You have a choice," Cam realised he sounded as if he was pleading . . . and he was. He had no idea how he would handle things without Holly. "You can stay within L.I.E.U's protection and stay as you are."

Holly nodded slowly. She moved her right forefinger and thumb to her chin and rested them against it, like a Rodin sculpture. "That's an idea, of course, but I've known this has been coming for some time. When we went to London to steal Alice it almost killed me. Being my age is bloody hard work. Nothing works as it used to and you're always uncomfortable. You feel like you're living in some sort of incontinence advert."

"Then stay thirty-four."

"You can't. You will choose to leave here one day and go back to the beginning. I chose not to and this is the end game. You may not have noticed but there are only ever you and I here. Godwin is going the same way as me. He chose to run out of life in a different time zone. Lucian . . . well as you explained it to me, scrambled his brain trying to remove his memory chip. Why do you think he hangs around with clowns like Barty

Spleen? He takes guys on joy rides down the tube. He knows it isn't allowed but he does it so someone will notice and throw him out of the system. Unfortunately, it appears no one gives a shit, and he's too scared to do it himself. I mean, look at him. His job is to recruit librarians. I've been here since 1960 and he's already got Petra to replace me . . . for him because she's my granddaughter and Lucian was told who to recruit. So in reality, he doesn't do much except take drugs and get sozzled."

"We can get Cherry Polenta to finish her case and come back."

Holly laughed. "I guess you weren't told she's a construct. She morphed into a cartoon, so she could handle the Donald Duck nephew case and some cartoonist drew over her and then spilled water on her. She became smudged and can't regain human form. She's lost her third dimension."

"You just made that up."

"Of course . . . reality is, I've never met her and only heard of her when you told me she existed. It's the same with Filipa Mutherbord. He can't come back either. He got his wish and became an avatar. From what I read, he acquired a computer virus and was picked up in a security scan and deleted. Hasn't been heard from since."

Cam ran his fingers through his hair. "So if you go . . . I'll be the only one here."

"No . . . Petra will join you as your new boss."

Cam reset to an earlier thought. "I don't understand. Unlike most people you have a choice between life and death . . . and death has a kind of permanency."

"Nothing is permanent, even in the future, people will die. You think having your head cut off to remove a memory chip because you didn't steal three books does the wearer any good? Things and people will always wear out. I'm just worn out . . . despite looking like I do in this controlled environment."

"Think about it."

"I am, I'm just trying to make up my mind which way to go. Take off the bracelet or leave it on, it's just choice."

Cam decided to relieve the stress he was feeling at Holly's pending demise. He changed subject. "Tell me about your husband."

To his surprise, Holly shook her head. "Not relevant and private."

"Is Petra your son's daughter or daughter's daughter?"

"Good try . . . but the answer is the same."

Cam was miffed. "Is there a reason . . . other than it's none of my business."

"Yes, I promised my husband I would keep things secret. I intend to stay with that."

Cam nodded his head to indicate questions were finished. He didn't want to finish. He was too afraid that Holly would just take off her bracelet and die. He may have to go to her apartment and find her dead. He dreaded the thought. Tears suddenly welled in his eyes. "Promise you won't go until you tell me."

Holly smiled. "Wouldn't dream off it. After all . . . we've been together for either three-quarters of a century or ten minutes. Either way, I won't just leave you. After all, I created Thaddeus for you . . . or do you want to dispute that?"

"It was just his nose."

"But the key to the puzzle."

Cam fell silent. He had run out of things to say. He dropped his gaze and headed from the room. Holly spun on her chair and began to type.

***

"Big decision, huh?" The melodic lilt of the voice sounded like poetry being read by an artistic craftswoman.

Holly didn't recognise the voice, nor could she see its owner. However, the voice met the description of the one Cam had heard in the future courtroom. "Huge," she replied, looking around and trying to locate the source of the sound.

"It's not your choice. The choice belongs to others."

"Like who?"

"Like those who allowed you to change your history."

Holly was puzzled. "I don't understand."

"You remember Agarle?"

"When I first came in contact with the library?"

"Yes. That day changed your history." The voice went silent for a moment but then continued. "You were saved by pure chance. We were still trying to decide on the final location for our European site. We tried Agarle in Kent and probed until 50,000BCE then worked our way forward. Everything was fine until 2031, when a new highway pushes through the village and the chosen site is destroyed. By pure luck we were in Cock Lane when we saw a German plane heading for a crash. It hit the house and you were killed. We had an idea and backed up a bit, putting the doorway of the library within your reach. It worked and we've kept an eye on you ever since. You are an experiment into what can happen if we *do* interfere with history."

"My aunt and uncle were killed . . . why didn't you help them if you were there?"

"It wasn't the same time. They came home to find their house burning. They were putting out the fire when a bomb hit. Coincidence, I guess."

Holly continued to look around. "Who are you and why don't you show yourself?"

"It's simple really. You can't be in two places at once. In a few minutes, Aiko Kirabati will arrive and take you into the future. You will become what you were destined to be and what Lucian Helldale recruited you to do. You will be *the* Librarian. What you have done to date was just an appetiser. Our scientists are on the verge of bending time and allowing inter-time links to be made."

Holly stood and removed her bracelet. "A question. Why is it we can't travel more than about a hundred years into the future. You are two hundred and fifty years away."

"To prevent contact. The line is located at the life expectancy of those in the time zone. It is nominally 100 years, but varies according to future developments. It's an automatic thing."

"And what of Cam?"

"For the moment, he will wake up in the morning with a new boss. Petra starts at midnight. He will be pissed off but he will get over it. Men do."

Holly lifted her right leg to the desk and retied a shoelace. "In that case, I'll grab a coffee and wait for Aiko."

ARTEL

THE voice was almost right. If she had added 'unrelentingly' to her statement she would have been closer to the truth. Cam was enraged. So much so that his teeth began to chatter and his chip went into overdrive and started deleting random information. Then, his blue jeans shrunk in the wash. He couldn't believe that Holly would leave without saying goodbye. They had been through so much together. Surely she should have invited him to be there when Aiko arrived.

He pondered for what seemed an aeon, but probably wasn't. But after a very elongated hour he read from his little book of calm and decided that Holly had been right. Some things are better done alone. Would he have said goodbye to her if the positions were reversed? Probably not.

He tried to control his annoyance, but it lingered until he realised that there was a new Librarian in place and Petra needed his help. She sat at a console, trying to speed-read the knowledge that she would need to make her an effective Librarian. Cam's raving was the least of her problems.

He smiled at her as her entered the control room. "I heard you had started. Welcome aboard." He looked at the multiple screens of documents that Petra was trying to read. "You don't need to do it that way. Let me get my head around Holly leaving and I run you through what you need to know. But not now. I'm really, really, to the power of ten, pissed off. You know Holly had no right to . . ."

Petra ignored the rest of what Cam was saying and went for a walk. When she returned, he was still raving. She let him simmer for while then spoke to him. "What do you know about artificial intelligence?" she asked, as she scanned a page of **The Book of Unresolved Grievances**.

Cam sensed it was back to work time. "My only experience was with the judges when I was on trial in 2263. It was hard to tell who was human. But then, with a bloody chip in my brain I doubt myself sometimes. Why do you ask?"

"There's a delegation of execs and technicians coming down the tube. They're going to visit the first aboriginals in Australia, to see if they can get clear communications back to L.I.E.U. from the beginning of their time. Seems like someone's discovered that aboriginals have been around for 10,000 years longer than thought . . . so minor adjustments have to be made."

"That explains the technicians but why the execs?"

Petra ran her right index finger across the screen. "Bean-counters and water-coolers mostly . . . trying to justify their existence. Travel to the end of the system, patronise some natives, make baseless promises and go home."

"And we fit in where?"

"One of the parties is a Plexer 18 personal security formbot. We're to make sure it doesn't appear anywhere."

"And they're due when."

Petra scanned the screen. "They left two days ago . . . so I guess a couple of months."

Cam felt his chip kick in. "I'm missing Holly already. She wouldn't make this mistake."

Petra spun on her chair and glared at Cam. "And what mistake is this?"

"Elementary."

"Elementary?"

"An extra ten thousand years means around seventy thousand years ago. Translates to seven hundred hours each way. The technobots can do it but humans can't . . . or won't. That's why the reference is in *The Book*. They're not going back seventy thousand years. They're on a far shorter journey. We need to find their destination. You get onto L.I.E.U. and I'll check the recent arrivals. What names am I looking for?"

Petra read from the screen. "The humans are Beige Canephora, Nearan Oasis and Velvety Aquaserve. The bot is Luigi Anasazi."

Cam shook his head slightly. "Ah . . . two coffee-beans and two water-coolers. And I thought you were being metaphoric."

Half an hour later, Cam leaned on the console desk and looked across at the seated Petra. It struck him that she was wearing the same yellow dress with the pleated skirt that she had worn the first time they met. He looked into her eyes. They were the deep green he remembered. At least part of Holly was still around.

"Conclusion?" Petra asked.

Cam bowed like a courtier. "Librarian first."

"Anasazi is more than just your ordinary coffee-bean. Canephor has had to pay fines to cover Anasazi's aggressive behaviour on several occasions. We have a very aggressive piece of artificial intelligence in a time zone where aggression is very closely controlled and in the hands of a regulated few. That isn't the case in this time zone. I found an article in a Robot Fighting magazine and have discovered that there is Robot Gladiator contest being held at the Galaxy Casino tomorrow night. According to the article the climax of the night will be a knock down and destroy competition to determine the best, with twenty robots in the ring at once. One of the robots is called ARTEL. I think that's where we'll find our men . . . your turn."

"Okay, AI is nowhere near as fully developed as it will be. If ARTEL is our coffee-bean he will have a great advantage over the bots that need electronic controllers. Should be interesting."

Petra glared at Cam. "You do understand it's our job is to *stop* ARTEL from fighting?"

Cam smiled at her. She was acting like her grandmother. A good sign. He didn't reply. His mind was too busy running through calculations and permutations of outcomes. He went into the control room, moved forward two days and went for a walk to his nearest local. What he wanted to see appeared on the midday news. The news was as expected. He returned to the control room and reset the time. Petra was looking through a service manual when he approached.

"You're right . . . it's our job to stop ARTEL fighting. Shall we go look for the culprits?"

"No can do. I have too much to learn. Grandma's shoes will be hard to fill."

Cam shrugged. "You'll get there. You have a great fifth assistant."

"Fifth?"

"Actually, I'm now the first but I'd like to remain the fifth . . . I like the distance from the top of the tree — if that's alright with you."

Petra shook her head. "As you wish."

***

His three second delay helped Cam to elude security at the event. Once inside, he was surprised that he was alone. He expected to see his quarry but they weren't visible until he returned to real-time and used his overdeveloped fusiform gyrus to scan the crowd of around five hundred. In a cordoned off section of the casino's carpark he found the faces he sought. He was again surprised to find that the tall muscular one in the group wasn't Luigi Anasazi but the water-cooler Oasis. Anasazi was shorter than average height with spare proportions. He was easy to spot, as the top of his head was flipped up and a panel had been opened in his back.

Cam joined the crowd of gawpers who crushed against the barrier that separated participants from fans and onlookers. Anasazi was one of only three robots that wasn't squat to the ground and ran on either wheels or tracks. Of the other two, one looked like a pair of legs with an axe dangling between them. It seemed to manoeuvre on rotating balls in the shape of camels' footpads. The other looked like a sawhorse with knees. It travelled on rollerballs. Its weapon was a vertical saw. Of the other seventeen contestants it seemed that saws, pincers, flippers, flame throwers and hammers formed the armoury, mounted on circular or rectangular platforms. The contestants fell into two main groups. Around sixty per cent favoured facial ornaments, piercings, multicoloured hair and sleeves of tattoos. The rest lived on pizza and generally existed in the darkness of laboratories and workshops.

The arena was on the first floor of the casino, in a renovated basketball stadium. A seldom used feature that had allowed the casino developers to gain an operating licence. There was a huge steel and bulletproof glass cage surrounded by tiered seating for a thousand. Metal mesh barriers protected spectators from flying debris. A platform ran around the inside perimeter of the fighting arena.

Cam noted that ARTEL would be able to avoid injury by using the platform to put him above the battling throng. He returned to his time delay and made his way into the centre of the coffee-beans and water-coolers.

"Gentlemen," he said as he appeared before them. "Mr Anasazi here should not be seen. You are all aware of that."

None of the men seemed surprised by Cam's sudden appearance. Beige Canephora looked calmly at the man wearing denim jeans, with one green and one red leg, a rainbow tee shirt and sporting McGuinn madcap rectangular sunglasses. "We were expecting someone more traditional."

"Looks don't matter," Cam quipped. "Even this harlequin can turn off your bracelets."

Canephora looked somewhat worried . . . far more worried than he had been a moment previous. "On what grounds?"

"It may have slipped your attention but I can see Luigi Anasazi. Or should I just call him ARTEL?"

Canephora shrugged. "He doesn't stand out. Everyone thinks he's just another robot. They're all curious, of course, but most think he'll be a pushover." He pointed to the low-slung robots that surrounded his position. "Any of those blades can take his legs off."

"Methinks not . . . but you're right. He won't scare the general populace, and no one will suspect he's from the future. I'll let you continue, on one condition."

"Which is?"

"The public and organisers must always think that ARTEL is controlled via an electronic controller. I see you have several. One of the potential problems with fighting robots is that the aerials get disconnected and the controller signal fails. I see that ARTEL's aerial is on a box on his shoulder. Useless of course, but a good visual. I'll provide the glue to ensure that it doesn't get disconnected."

"We have glue . . . you can check the connection."

"My condition is my glue. Take it or disappear . . . here and now."

Canephora looked around at nodding heads. "We accept."

***

For the first time since he had known Petra, Cam saw the devil in her deep green eyes. Or maybe it was the flames shooting from her nostrils. She was seething and every second expletive had sufficient venom to strip the paint from the control room walls. To say that she disagreed with what Cam had done would be a gross understatement.

"Then I'll take all the blame," he said, calmly.

"Not your choice. You broke the rules. You should have disconnected them from L.I.E.U., sent them back to their time not let them continue what they were doing."

"You don't seem to understand. ARTEL blends in with his surroundings. People think he's just more sophisticated than what the other contestants are doing. He's a star of the show already. He'll be all over the Internet by this. People will ask questions if they suddenly disappear. We were too late to stop them. We needed a heads up before they arrived. Blame the system, not me . . . besides."

"Besides what?" Petra spat.

"For once in our lives, we have an opportunity to do something useful."

Cam was sure he saw flames dart from Petra's ears. "Such as?"

"Rid the future of the potential for artificial intelligence to be used in warfare."

Petra's eyes flashed but then she calmed, as if hit with a serenity stick. Maybe he had a point. After all, the perps were in town long before she was notified and they had been seen and undoubtedly videoed and photographed. She walked to the door. "Don't tell me. I can't risk involvement. It's on your head if you cock up."

***

Cam studied all that he could on the Plexer 18 personal security formbot. Unfortunately there wasn't much in the manuals other than the words LETHAL, and BE VERY VERY SCARED highlighted in uppercase. These bots were the bodyguard of the future and fitted with immense firepower. The unnerving thing, however, was that they looked like short and unobtrusive men [6] and were hard to spot.

He removed his fountain pen from his pocket and squirted Toerag onto his desk. Thaddeus shaped up and looked around the room.

"I'm not getting the scent of my beloved Holly," Toerag said.

"I know you haven't been out for a while but you're still plastic. If you've developed olfactory receptors I'll be very surprised."

"I'm not deaf, dipshit; I've heard your wailing and moaning all day . . . and all because the beautiful Holly decided not to die. I'm on her side."

"Okay, okay, okay. I have a job for you."

For the next few minutes, Cam explained what he wanted Toerag to do the following night.

***

The sports arena was packed to capacity. Vanquished fighting machines were being disassembled and rapidly reassembled. The smell of

---

[6]Or women in the case of female execs. Unfortunately the female formbots were designed by men and their proportions prevented their blending into the general populace.

the crowd was piquant. Sweaty bodies and flannel shirts were the fashion statement of the night. Boos burst forth from the crowd as ARTEL won another preliminary bout. His technique was to run around the elevated platform, jump on his opponent and disconnect the antennae. Other teams had complained but Canephora argued that it was the manipulation skill of the console operator that allowed the bot to prevail. On consideration, ARTEL was allowed to continue on the proviso that he did not rip out any more wiring. He could cut it, burn it, slice it or crush it but not pull it out. Cam sat in the crowd and watched the next few tussles. The sawhorse had two of its legs removed by a bot with a circular saw. The legs were eliminated when one of its pegs was buckled by a pincer and subsequently cut off by its own axe. Both teams would have trouble making the final extravaganza without major bodywork.

Cam initially thought the bouts to be elimination matches but he was told that they were demonstrations of tactics and capabilities so that people had a chance to lose money by betting on the mayhem of the final bout.

A short time later, Cam appeared before the futurists. He squirted Toerag onto the junction of the Bluetooth device and control box, disappeared and then reappeared in the TV control booth. He introduced himself to the producer as a man from the sponsor and asked if he could sit in.

***

There were twenty robots in the arena. A siren wailed. Green lights flashed. Cutting tools whirred like dervishes on speed. Hammers smashed unprotected parts to all quarters of the arena. Metal screamed in anguish as it was torn asunder. Rubber burned from contact with flamethrowers. ARTEL stood on his platform and watched the carnage until half of the contestants were rendered as useless junk. He remained aloof until a robotic battering ram ploughed into the platform, below his feet. He staggered and dropped to one knee. He reached past the platform, with his left arm, to stop himself tumbling. At the moment the arm hit the deck it was sliced off at the elbow by a sawbot.

Cam saw his chance and signalled Toerag. Toerag disconnected the devices he was holding and displayed a flying lead. He rolled into a ball and dropped to the floor.

Cam looked at the producer. "Looks like ARTEL is finished, his control is unplugged."

The producer called for a close up.

ARTEL stood, looked at his partially severed left arm and screamed, turned on the laser resonator in his chest, adjusted the mirror in his right elbow, tweaked the lens to the desired focal length and obliterated the bot that had removed his arm.

"That can't happen," the producer told Cam, shocked.

Cam feigned shock. "Rumour says it's Russian or American military . . . maybe Chinese. Far more advanced than anyone lets on. No human control or intervention required."

As they both watched in horror, ARTEL cut a swathe through the other machinery. Next he blew a hole through the entry door before running out of the arena and disappearing (literally). The other coffee-beans and water-coolers followed suit. Cam found their bracelets in the carpark.

The story hit the Internet within minutes. Social media went ballistic. The Russians denied any knowledge. The US stated that they had the weaponry but would never use it against civilians. The Chinese ignored diplomacy and called the Americans liars. The matter was raised in the United Nations on a Tuesday. It died before Friday. Robot gamers created more powerful bots and weapons. The ones who saw the real damage to their machines quit the sport.

"There's a message for you, Cam," Petra said while reading a screen. "A woman called Aiko Kiribati is on her way to pick you up. She says you know her."

Back to the Future

A DIMINUTIVE figure swept into the room like a wraith. What Petra saw was ghostly pale with straight, pitch-black hair, Rectangular glasses, perched at the end of a tiny but interesting nose. The eyes were large, like those of sketched cuteness. The ghost wore a red leather onesie with matching cowl. It spoke. "You must be Petra, the new Librarian . . . Aiko Kiribati . . . L.I.E.U. Historian."

Petra swung on her chair and faced the woman. "I've heard of you. I was told you're here to see Cam."

"Yes . . . he's in trouble again. But that can wait. You look far more interesting. Same eyes as your grandmother. Same cheekbones. Same mouth. Yes . . . far more interesting. It's been a long trip and I'm famished. Would you like to take me to lunch?"

Petra glanced at the pile of files on her desk. "I'd love to but . . . sorry but I have too much to learn."

"It's Cam job to teach you. Obviously he's still narked by Holly's ascension. It's okay. I'll show you how to learn. You will be up to speed by the time Cam returns . . . or pending a guilty verdict . . . until a new assistant librarian is found. It's simple really. You just check the time when you start to read a file and then reset to that time when you finish. Result, no time wasted in learning. Try it with something small."

Petra did as she was told.

"Wow," she said a split second later. "I'm back at the time I started reading."

"Can we go to lunch now? Cam showed me a place where they have the best overcooked hamburgers."

"Okay . . . we have lunch. Then what?"

"I escort Cameron Cameliel back to the future."

"He can't avoid this? I need him here."

Aiko smiled the grin of the knowing. "He was lucky the last time he was called up. If it hadn't been for the fact that they needed a lowly ranked assistant to find Judge Ivory's wife, he would have been in real trouble. You think he would have learned a lesson by escaping punishment, but no. He seems to have an internal moral code that doesn't necessarily fit in with our master's desires. Mind you, he's not the only one to break ranks . . . but they no longer work for L.I.E.U. It's a shame really. I like Cam."

Tears welled in Petra's eyes as she looked at Aiko. "I really need him here. I'll never cope by myself."

"Yes you will. Women, throughout history, always cope with the onslaught of adversity. It's domestic stuff that tears them apart."

***

The following day, Aiko dropped Cam off at a two storey, granite brick building a block from the L.I.E.U. edifice.

"I hope you do well," she said as she opened the sliding door of her hover car to let him out.

He stepped from the vehicle and smiled at the diminutive woman, who was still wearing a red leather onesie complete with cowl. They had hardly spoken for the entire journey. It had been Aiko's decision, based on the fact that she had a new boyfriend and recent sleep was limited. She claimed the trip to 2019 and back had not been scheduled. Either that or she had an upset stomach from six dodgy burgers and three jugs of ale.

"Holly works in this building?" he asked.

Aiko smiled. "Would I deliver you to a building where she didn't work?"

Cam shook his head and shrugged.

He stood back and studied the beaten copper door that stood inside a narrow Corinthian columned portico. He remembered it from 1940 but this was the first time he had seen it in situ. He read the name above the door *Literary Institute Real-time Administration.*

He pushed down on the handle. It moved with a sonorous click and opened. He walked through the entry foyer and tried the handle on the Library door. It opened on well-greased hinges. Through the doorway was a large glass-panelled bookcase against one wall. Beyond the bookcase was an ornate archway leading to an oval room. In the oval room there were three tiers of book shelves running the length of the curved walls. Polished brass rails ran the circumference of the oval and redwood ladders (attached to the rails) slid sideways to allow the ladders to move horizontally. There were reading desks and seating. Each desk had a green lamp shade on a brass base. Plush pile black carpet covered the floor. He remembered trying to open the door on the day he first met Holly. The door was locked to him but had opened for Holly. The difference between being Librarian and Fifth Assistant?

He walked down a flight of stairs before heading for a stainless steel doorway at the far end of the bookshelves. He pushed against the door and it slid open to reveal a vast room, the size of an aircraft manufacturing hanger. He had never encountered such size, especially when he saw that the ceiling floated above the walls with no signs of supporting columns. There were hundreds of what he first assumed to be humans but which turned out to be formbots. Floating forklifts manoeuvred through the space moving boxes from location to location. Stacked conveyors crisscrossed the space and Plexer 18 security formbots with winged feet flew slowly around the various bays, laser weapons at the ready. He wondered if Luigi Anasazi among them.

"Incalculable, huh?"

Cam spun on his heels. Holly stood there with her hands clasped behind her back. She had changed. Gone were the jeans and tee shirts. She now wore a stylish mid-length navy blue dress with matching mid-heeled shoes. Her hair was shoulder length but currently held with a bun. A pair of pince-nez glasses rested on the end of her nose. She was no longer thirty-four.

Cam was tempted to move forward and hug her, but he couldn't remember when that had ever happened. He resisted the urge but overtly took in every detail of her presence.

Holly smiled at the look on his face as he tried to take in the changes. "Easy . . . I've been here for two years. Courts aren't held in real-time. They're held in the past, to avoid any current events interfering with the trial. Real-time is two years from now. I came back to see you."

He looked at her, closely. "You seem older somehow."

Holly returned his gaze. "I am. I'm no longer static. My time clock has restarted. Whether I go backward or forward in time, I age at the normal rate. I'll live here until I return to dust."

Concern skittered across Cam's face. "Your choice?"

"Of course. I was dead before I came here so any time is a bonus."

"You didn't say goodbye," he protested.

Holly shrugged. "When I arrived here, I looked at your actions for the next few days. I was impressed at what you did to make sure you were called back for another trial. Risky but impressive. But then I couldn't say goodbye. It wasn't in me. Besides I've known for some time what happens to you and Petra . . . so there was no need to end a relationship that wasn't about to end."

"So you just left."

"Yes."

"No regrets?"

"None. I avoided death and now do a job I love."

Cam saw no advantage in continuing the thrust of the conversation so changed the topic. "You run this place?"

"I'm the Librarian. I control everything that goes on here and I'm in charge of the entirety of what is stored. We have every important document from world history . . . visual, oral, aural and documented. If there any political issues to be resolved, we can take world politicians to any point in their respective country's history and find the root cause of issues. Very handy but fraught with problems. Trying to change history is a modern political game. Truth is still an alternate commodity."

"L.I.E.U. runs the planet then?"

Holly shook her head. "No, no, no . . . not at all. We're like a think tank. All we control is the time machine. Everything else is an extension of what happened in your time."

Your time. Cam felt his heart sink. Where once they had been separated by decades, they were now separated by hundreds of years. There was no possibility of return to his preferred normality.

An alarm buzzed on Holly's wrist.

Cam was pleased with the distraction. He could feel depression seeping into his socks. He wanted to be elsewhere. There was only one more thing he needed to know. "You never did tell me who you were married to."

"Ahh . . . that old chestnut. Just for the record, his name was Kenneth Formby. He followed me from England. Arrived in Australia just after I joined L.I.E.U. Only male companion I ever had. I told him everything. He knew where I worked and we even went for holidays down the tube. I tried to get him to become an assistant librarian once, but he couldn't get his head around having conversations with inanimate objects. He declined the job."

Cam's smile was broad. "Whew, I'm really pleased."

Holly seemed taken aback. "Why is that?"

"We're near the end of the novel. There's no time to add a new character,"

Holly's laugh was subtle. She nodded her head in agreement.

The alarm on her wrist buzzed again.

She looked Cam directly in the eyes. "Have to go I'm afraid." Her expression was forlorn, but she said no more.

***

London Mews hadn't changed. It was still dominated by the *Light Interrupting Educational Unit*. He maintained his dislike for its architecture. He entered the building through the door that was fitted into a corner and had egress to two streets. The same formbot sat at the desk, reading a magazine. He crossed to it and introduced himself to the woman. She glanced up from her page and looked him up and down. "You're good for your age," she said.

"I am?"

"Yes. You're 274 years of age. You carry it well."

Cam considered mimicking what she had said. Her words were those from his previous visit. He decided against it. "Thank you."

"You may proceed to level 2. You're booked in for the duration of the inquest. Do you know how to get to the hotel?"

"Descent-well three. It's over that way. I stand on the stainless steel disc and it will take me to the hotel."

On a remembered impulse, he leaned over the desk and smelled the bot. Her scent was as remembered. "Intimate nights. I love that perfume."

The bot looked at him. "I know. Ms Petra Petitfille wears it. That is why I generated the scent for you."

Cam smiled, shook his head. "How am I going with her?"

"She may not wait for you if you do not survive your trial."

***

The disc at descent-well three took Cam down an unknown series of levels until it stopped at the hotel level. He entered the foyer and counted the reception bots. They were the same as on his previous visit. Same clothes, hairstyles, mannerisms. He wondered if anything ever changed. There was no requirement for shift changes in bot world.

"Cameliel Cameron," he said to the first receptionist.

"Assistant Librarian Cameron. We have been expecting you. You are booked into room 35 for the duration of your stay."

"What happened to cell 35?"

"We decided not to repeat our little joke."

Cam looked into the eyes of the bot. he remembered something previously said and repeated it. "So you're designed with a sense of humour."

"Of course. We are modelled on the Series 17 pleasure bot . . . for men and women who can't find a human partner. We have a sense of humour and can play a musical instrument. We can also gossip, if necessary."

***

Cam found his room, settled onto the bed and looked for the TV remote. This time it was on a bedside table. He pressed a button marked M and a hologram butler appeared in the centre of the room.

"May I help you, sir?" it said.

Cam pressed the button marked F. The virtual butler turned into a maid.

"How may I serve you, sir," it said, with a coquettish grin.

Maybe some things never change.

As he would have to be prepared to defend himself the next day, he turned off the remote, lay back on the bed, closed his eyes and dreamed of the new Librarian.

Eloise

AT BREAKFAST, the following morning, Cam looked at the bizarre looking man, who was casting a shadow over his plate, and had a déjà vu experience.

"Josephine Whittlesnake QC. I've been appointed as your barrister for the trial. I have organised a wheelchair to enable you to move around freely," said the man wearing a red and white pinstriped wig and coffee coloured suit under a red cape.

"I need a wheelchair?" Cam groaned.

"Your age of course. Mind you, for a man pushing toward three hundred, you don't look to be as decrepit as I imagined. Have you been coated with elastagel?"

"Elastagel?"

"The skin tightening gel. Everyone uses it. Lasts for hours. Just coat yourself every five hours. Surely you've seen the ads? Anyway, we can't have you falling down, so use the wheelchair."

Cam stared at Whittlesnake. "Last time we met, your wig was coffee coloured and the suit was pinstripe."

Whittlesnake furrowed his brow, as if searching his memory. "Have we met before?"

"I was on trial for not stealing, and dragging a dead body through time."

Whittlesnake expanded his chest and drew back his shoulders in a gesture of narcissism. "I don't remember . . . but you're here, so we must have won the case. That would be why you hired me again."

"Not quite as I remember it. My memory says you didn't think you would win so you flitted off to the Old Bailey."

"Ahh . . . then we've not met. Josephine Whittlesnake QC. I am descended from a long line of Whittlesnakes. We have been at the bar for more than three centuries and have never lost a case."

Cam remembered his last discussion with Whittlesnake. Just like then, he felt a cyclic nightmare coming on. "I know your family history."

Whittlesnake smiled benignly. "Of course, the most lauded family in the history of the British bar. I take it you have read the tomes that honour the family."

Cam chuckled. "Not quite . . . I try to avoid comics." He let out a deep breath. "What are the charges then?"

Whittlesnake opened a ubiquitous buff folder. "You are charged with not preventing a change in history. A very serious charge indeed."

"Penalty?"

"Let me see. Ah, that's it. Loss of three per cent of your salary and removal of executive bathroom privileges . . . no . . . sorry. That's the penalty for executive fraud or corruption. Let me look again . . . your penalty will be loss of employment and return to whence you came."

"Better than chip removal."

Whittlesnake read the charge sheet again. "No . . . it's on top of chip removal."

Cam began to feel a little queasy. Was it Whittlesnake's presence, or the thought of having the top of his head ripped off? "When does the trial start?"

"Five minutes in Court 2."

"You'll disappear again, I take it?"

Whittlesnake glared at Cam. "What do you take me for? Whittle-snakes have never lost a case."

A bell rang on the kitchen wall. Whittlesnake bid Cam to stand up and pointed him toward the exit. "We're being called."

They left the restaurant, walked along a narrow corridor and stepped onto a stainless steel plate. Same routine as his previous visit. Only change, the Minotaur was bright pink.

The plate stopped. Cam and Whittlesnake walked along another corridor until they reached the copper covered door set into a gold-plated frame.

"This is where the inquisition will take place. It's an informal hearing so you will answer the questions that are asked and you may ask questions."

Cam smiled as he realised that Whittlesnake had repeated the words from their previous outing. He was still on script.

Cam stepped into a barren room. The walls were concrete grey and the image of the sky on the ceiling displayed stratocumulus clouds. It looked as if the room would soon be inundated with rain. In the centre of the room stood a single plastic chair. To the far side of the chair was a bench table and behind the table three straight backed wooden chairs. Against one wall was another high-backed chair. Same courtroom, same layout.

"Just take a seat, Mr Cameron . . . and good luck," Whittlesnake said, just before he disappeared.

Cam laughed at Whittlesnake's predictability as he strolled to the chair in the middle of the courtroom.

"All stand." The words came from unseen speakers in the walls. The sound echoed around the empty space. Cam remained seated.

"The hearing is now in session." the speakers again.

Cam waited for the judges to appear but no one entered the room. The artificial sky, that had threatened rain, cleared to a blue sky. Seconds crept to hours. The clock on the wall ran backward. Cam pressed on the sides of his head to clear his thoughts. He closed his eyes.

***

"Whittlesnakes never lose a case because they disappear when they are in a losing position. Josephine's grandfather left it, one time, until the jury were about to make their pronouncements." The voice had the texture of warm honey.

Cam opened his eyes.

Before him stood a tall elegant woman in a knee length grey dress. She looked to be in her late middle age, with a grey swept back hairstyle. Grey shoes with silver spiked heels adorned her feet.

Cam looked into her pale blue eyes as she smiled at him. Her full lips slid across her perfect white teeth as she spoke. "Eloise Manuka. Some know me as Professor Itzall Bovincrap."

Explained the honeyed voice, if nothing else. Cam rose from his chair and lightly clasped a proffered hand. "I'm in more trouble than usual then?"

Eloise shook her head slightly. "On the contrary. You showed us a flaw in our system. There has been no weaponization of artificial intelligence machines since it was outlawed by the UN in 2027. Your antics were partially responsible for the expedition of that ruling. Since that time, humans have not been able to hide behind robots in warfare."

"I'm off the hook then?"

Eloise smiled with her eyes. "Hardly. Despite the outcome, the end doesn't justify the means. You are charged with not preventing a change in history. You should not have interfered. Methinks it was your intention to be hauled before the court again."

"Not really. I knew the result before I interfered. ARTEL was all over the net before I was on the scene. His antics simply focused attention on a problem."

"You blamed the Russians."

"I planted a seed. Dogs of war and the media did the rest."

"'Cry havoc and let slip the dogs of war . . .' Mark Antony's words no longer hold resonance in this time. While there are problems aplenty we no longer have odious narcissists with power. What you did was merely a futile gesture that gave minor amplification to the work of others. You failed to do your duty . . . and there are inevitable consequences."

"I'm not off the hook then?"

"No . . . you broke one of the cardinal rules. You allowed someone to change history."

Cam knew his position had no strength but flogged the dead horse anyway. "I take it, you saving Holly didn't change history. A child should have died but, instead, grew up, married, helped to populate the world. She lived in society and lives three hundred years past her time. Then, of course there's Sahara Aquasol and her bawdy adventures . . . or do we not mention her." He waited for Eloise to say something, but she remained quiet. He continued. "All I did was help make a point about something that was going to happen anyway."

"Any more flaws in our system you'd like to point out?" Eloise quipped.

"Maybe, but I'm unsure of my ground when I'm here. I'm in a place I don't fully understand. Nobody's ever explained it to me and my chip has nothing to give. After all, you prevent us from coming this far into our future."

Eloise nodded. "You're right. Why don't I take you for brunch and show you what happens outside of the time travel world. My guess is, other than technological advances, you'll find it isn't much different to your time. Take my hand . . . we'll look in on the locals in time delay mode."

Cam took the extended hand and, for the next two hours, travelled in the world of the future. He removed the extraneous from his mind and concentrated on the differences. He searched for the *Fifth Element* and/or *Blade Runner* experiences but they weren't to be found. There were no layered traffic jams or flying cars capable of tight right-angled turns or vertical flight. There were no *Witches of Chiswick* and no *Discworld* stories to be lived. Eloise was right. This was 2019 with another quarter of a millennium of technology. High rise buildings were lower and transport vehicles were driverless tubes in traffic lanes marked TRANSPORT CORRIDOR. Maglev was the dominant form of public transport for short distances with Vactrains the preference for long distances. Both men's and women's fashion looked to encompass comfort more than any other he'd seen and pets on leashes were automated. There wasn't a real animal in sight. Maybe it was an animal rights issue. Soho provided its expected share of alternate arrangements for all sorts of things. The main difference here was that the night ladies changed image every minute or so. Some so quickly that they created a strobe effect that damaged the eyeballs of potential customers.

"Formbots?" Cam queried.

"Real women don't need the degradation. Pleasurebots can guarantee satisfaction." Eloise replied.

"You're right, it's only the technology."

Eloise smiled. "We humans think that we change from generation to generation. We have evolved over hundreds of thousands of years but have hardly changed since we became intelligent. Even then it's only the genii who make difference. This is around three hundred years from your time and you can see that changes on the human level are insignificant. People still love and hate, and testosterone still makes for belligerent young males."

"Lucky you're one of the genii."

Eloise was matter of fact. "Not really. I was the one at the end of a long line of developers. I like to think that I slotted the last pieces of the jigsaw into place . . . if you ignore the fact that my father was able to finance the physical development of the system. . . . time for brunch."

Brunch was taken at the themed *Whitechapel Murder Restaurant* on the north bank of the Thames in Wapping High Street. The menu had delicacies with names like 'Liver of Dead Prostitute' and 'Heart of Victim with Slit Throat Dressing'. Cam stuck with water. This could be ordered with or without impurities.

"I brought you here to show that bad taste still prevails in some places. Take my hand again."

Cam did as he was told. There didn't appear to be any movement but Cam found himself in a French brasserie on the South Banks of the Seine. Eloise looked at him as if her magic act was too dull to discuss.

Over grilled quail and watercress with a light Pouilly-Fuissé, Cam decided to enquire about his future. "Am I in a bind or are we both?"

Eloise's smile was disarming. She leaned forward at the table, placed her elbows on the table and steepled intertwined fingers. "You're a man with choices to make. You're 274 at the moment. In your time, you died in your mid-eighties. You reached the general life expectancy for your time. Your first choice is that you can remove your L.I.E.U. bracelet. This won't do you any good. You'll simply disappear with no life to go on with."

Cam raised his eyebrows. A quizzical expression flitted across his face.

"I can tell that you're thinking about people like the panhandler who Holly sent back to the future. In cases like that, they aren't born until the date of their birth in the future. What changes for them is that they live their life until they apply for a time travel permit. Their application is rejected and they go on with their life without ever having travelled through time. You're already dead so can't be born in the future."

Cam had never considered that outcome. Mind you, he had never considered removing his bracelet.

"Your second choice is to do nothing and we can return to the court. This is your second time before the court so little, if any, leniency will be granted to you. You will be found guilty of dereliction of duty and sentenced to have your chip removed and returned to your own time . . . to go on with your life before L.I.E.U."

Cam shuddered.

"Don't worry. We'll return you to 2078 and you will decide not to have the chip implant done. The operation won't proceed."

Cam looked Eloise directly in the eyes. He was mesmerised by them. "I'm done either way."

"There is a third choice. Why don't I tell you about it over dessert? They have great Bruges chocolates here, served with strawberries and gelato."

Cam pondered his future after chocolate.

The Other Side of Midnight

NOT many Paddington residents knew of the quaint little shop that had been open in their midst for longer than many had been alive. They passed it daily without registering the shop's existence. What passers-by see is a sun yellowed terrace with a rusty gold wrought iron balustrade and under-watered pot plants. There is a small wrought iron gate and a metal fence topped by ornate fleur-de-lis balustrade spears. The shingle on a hanger outside the small shop says 'Penworthy Rare Books' and it was the books that garnered the customers. It is said to be the second-best source for rare books in the world.

Cameliel Cameron stood on the footpath and stared at the building. While L.I.E.U. changed its décor from time to time, he swore this building had once been two storeys. Maybe it was his latest scotch-soaked all-nighter that was clouding his memory. Must have been. Now, he had a dry mouth and thumping headache; always a reminder that he should cut down on his drinking. He walked to the beaten copper entry door and placed his hand on the entry pad. The electronic reader picked up his palm print and immediately opened the door. He reeled back in shock. There was dust everywhere, spiders' webs hanging from the ceiling and traces of rat on the floor.

It suddenly struck him that while the L.I.E.U. portal whirred away in the background, the shop at the front of house hadn't been operated for years. But now he had time. He would clean up and open for business again. He went to the control console and ordered up a battalion of micro-cleaning bots. They would have it sparkling in no time.

***

Petra Petitfille looked inside the small bookshop and spotted a man up a ladder. He was attempting to reach a weighty hardback that appeared to be moving further and further out of reach. She stared at the man in the bright yellow shirt, tucked into blue denims. Off-white canvas shoes with bright designs of multicoloured strips adorned his feet. His dark hair was brushed back across his ears and reached his shirt collar. The rectangular McGuinn madcap glasses he wore just covered his eyes. She knew the glasses from her studies on the music of the Byrds.

She realised it wasn't the book moving but the ladder sliding sideways on a brass rail that ran the length of the small shop. She rushed through the door and shoved her foot against the bottom of the ladder. The man looked down and Petra was mesmerised by grey eyes.

Cam smiled as he looked past her face to her right foot. "Great brake," he said.

He stepped down from the ladder, moved it along its rail until it was under the book he had been trying to grab. He stepped onto the ladder and looked down at her. "Can you hold the ladder for a few seconds . . . while I grab the book?"

"Sure." Petra's eyes wandered to the floor of the shop. White marble tiles, worn with age. A black tiled border and four letters set into the floor in onyx. "What does L.I.E.U. mean?" she asked.

Cam stepped down from the ladder and placed his book on a low shelf. "You're very lucky to see the letters. They're usually covered by a Persian rug. They only come out when I have time to clean. Are you a Douglas Adams fan?"

"I don't believe so."

"Doctor Who?"

"Occasionally."

"In that case, the letters mean *Live In Eternal Unity*. The shop was started as a small chapel."

Petra shook her head. "No it wasn't. It has always been a rare book shop. I know . . . I'm a Penworthy."

Cam was stunned. "A Penworthy . . . huh?"

"Yes . . . Petra Petitfille. I'm related on my mother's side."

"Girl or Granddaughter? Your name . . . it's not quite right but could be adapted to French to mean Girl or Granddaughter."

"I'm named after my grandmother."

"Petra?"

"Her name was Holly. Old English for *dwelling by*. Petra is *rock*. Dwelling by the rock."

"I'm so pleased the connection isn't obscure," Cam chided. He picked up the Persian rug and replaced it over the onyx letters.

Petra stepped back to avoid being flicked by the rug. "You're closing?" she asked.

"Not open. I've just been doing some cleaning. I've been away for a while."

"That's disappointing. I came a long way to see the old family shop. I knew Gran had sold it but didn't know it was closed. I was hoping to look around."

Cam observed the young woman as she spoke. Her hair was black, cut in pageboy style. She wore a yellow dress with pleated skirt. Her eyes were deep green and lively. She emitted the scent of the perfume 'Intimate nights'. His favourite . . . although he didn't know why. There was something familiar about it but he couldn't remember any context. But then, he was having trouble remembering lots of things lately. The most important being that he had no idea how he came to be travelling in time with a company called L.I.E.U. He had been told that he needed an adjustment to update his memory chip. He was warned about side effects and told that useless knowledge from his own memory would be scarified. After the operation, he had run a spot check on himself and everything seemed to be there except for how he was recruited into the organisation. But then, it didn't matter. The important thing was that he had been given the task of inducting a new Librarian and a very attractive woman with a beautiful smile and lively green eyes had walked into the shop. Best thing was that she bore the name he had been told to expect.

"I was just about to go get some lunch. If you'd like to eat with me, I can reopen after and you can look around then."

Petra looked him over. Right age, handsome enough, ridiculous clothes sense. A pass . . . but only just. For a moment, she hesitated for effect. "That would be nice."

***

Lunch went well. They left the rare book shop with the intention of going to Paddington for a quick bite. They ended up in an Italian family restaurant, off Oxford Street, for a long lunch. This led to a cab ride into the city and a late evening meal at Quayside They arrived back at the bookshop just after midnight.

Cam was pumped, Petra was mellow.

"I guess I should take you home," Cam said.

Petra pointed toward the copper door of the shop. "Not until you show me around."

"You've had too much to drink."

"I'm a country girl. We never have enough."

Cam knew his job but felt he couldn't continue with Petra more than half stoned. "I'll pick you up in the morning. This is a very special shop. You need to have your wits about you."

"It's only a pissant little bookshop. You promised. It will only take you a minute. Then you can take me home. I don't live far from here."

Cam was curious. "Where do you live?"

"Just a couple of blocks away. Nice apartment . . . belongs to a cartoonist. He's away. Real estate bloke doesn't know for how long."

Of the more than one and a half million dwellings in Sydney, Petra had rented his apartment. A coincidence? Not likely. "It's nice around here. Close to everything."

Petra shrugged. "I think I'll like it. I just hope I get a trace on Grandma."

"Grandma?"

"Yes . . . my grandma Holly. She disappeared after grandpa Ken died. We used to be close but after he died, she sold her house and went to live near where she worked. I have no idea where that was and she didn't let anyone in the family know. I didn't even know what she did for work . . . but she didn't retire at the normal age. Grandpa wanted her to retire when he did but she just kept putting it off. I hope she's still alive somewhere . . . but I don't know. Anyway, you promised to show me the shop."

Cam reassessed Petra's drunken state. In the past few minutes the effects of a long drinking session seemed to have disappeared like an alcoholic haze on a crisp day. Maybe she was ready. "Okay . . . let's look at the shop."

Cam opened the door with a palm press. Petra furrowed her brow but said nothing. They entered the small shop and Cam held his arms out, open handed. "Take your time to look around." He hit a switch and the room lighting burst into life.

Petra moved the ladder from place to place, studying the books as if looking for something in particular. From high on the shelving she looked down at Cam. "Gran brought me to the shop a long time ago. She showed me a book called *The Book of Fictional Grievances*. She said it wasn't for sale. Did you sell it?"

"No . . . it's still here."

"I can't find it, where is it?"

The time had come. "To see that book takes a leap of faith. It's on the other side of that door at the back of the bookshop."

"A leap of faith. I don't understand."

"You said you're only an occasional Dr Who fan and you don't know Douglas Adams. That lack of knowledge may make it harder for you suspend your sense of reality."

Petra smiled benignly. "Now I understand even less."

"Do you understand the concept of the TARDIS?"

"Everyone knows that."

"Then take my hand and prepare to begin an adventure. That is if you don't mind holding my hand."

"We passed that point hours ago."

Cam took Petra's hand and he led her through the rear door into the control room.

Adrenaline kicked in but Petra couldn't move. She closed her eyes and listened to her heartbeat. Her heart had stopped. She breathed deeply and listened for her heart to restart. When she opened her eyes again, she saw that Cam was smiling at her. His head was tilted slightly to one side, as if he was contemplating her in some way.

"This is an alternate reality. You'll soon find it is as real as what you consider to be reality. The only change is time and an ability to transfer to different time zones." Cam said. He remembered the same words being spoken to him . . . but couldn't place them in context. "Or maybe it's an optical illusion."

Petra looked across the room and spotted ***The Book of Fictional Grievances***. "This is the one. You still have it." She looked around the room. "This is where Gran brought me to when I was little. She played a game with me. She told me it was a time travel machine. She said she would take me on a trip one day."

Petra smiled and grabbed Cam by the shoulders, looking him in the eyes. "Gran always told me she would never lie to me. She said I would travel through time with a man who I fell in love with at first glance. She said he would wear funny shaped small glasses and dress like a rainbow." She hesitated for an aeon, as if not wanting to know the answer to her next question. "Was she lying to me?"

Cam was disarmed. "Your gran wouldn't lie to you."

Petra began to giggle and dance around the room like a small child. She slumped into a chair, in front of a monitor. Cam hit her mouse and the screen burst into life. On the top left corner of the monitor was a photo of a woman of about thirty-four. Petra zoomed in on the photo, turned to Cam. This is Gran when she was young. Did you know her?"

Cam studied the photo closely. He racked his brain, scanned his chip, but there was no recognition. "I don't know her." He looked at his watch and smiled. "But, in real-time, I only started here five minutes before I met you."

Post-ramble

HOLLY Penworthy got to be a woman of destiny. She died in 2309 at the age of 382. It was claimed, at her funeral, that she was the oldest person to ever live on Earth. There is, of course, the tale of Methuselah who, supposedly, lived to be 969. However, this lifespan calculation was contentious. In his early days with L.I.E.U., Godwin Godwell tried to find Methuselah, for a chat, but the words 'myth' and 'legend' were too readily used by old Meth's peers, so not a lot of faith was placed on the voracity of the lifespan claim. In Holly's case, a platinum plaque attached to her grave with golden rivets allows passers-by to read her legend. I would give you the location of her grave but it has not, as yet, been determined.

At the time of her retirement in 2300, Holly was the most respected Librarian in the world. This was mainly due to the fact that she was in charge of the world's largest and most valuable collection of books. This should not, however, diminish any of her other achievements. She was the first librarian to introduce a lunch break for her robots. She was also the first person to introduce retirement facilities for ageing characters from fiction novels.

On the downside, she was lucky to avoid jail time for historic theft. When investigated by the organisation in charge of historic corruption (Commission for the Reduction of Antique Predicaments), it was found that she had been instrumental in allowing for the installation of emojis into historically significant works. She was found guilty but deemed too old to incarcerate.

She never did get to see the Great Attractor but was closer to it than any of her friends from school.

***

If you're wondering what happened to Cam and Petra, wonder no more.

In 2020 they were made redundant as time cops, due to an algorithm that allowed time travel bracelets to predict aberrant behaviour and cut off automatically.

Some future librarians and assistants were kept on to oversee travellers and give a human context to the operation. One of the lucky few was Lucian Helldale, who specialised in adventure tourism for extreme sports enthusiasts. Lucian was also instrumental in covering for Cam when he went to 2078 and had the adjustments to his chip reversed. His agreement with Eloise Manuka was that he have all memory relating to his adventures with Holly removed, as if he was leaving L.I.E.U. and returning to his normal life. He told nobody about his memory reinstatement.

The time machine portal in Paddington remained operational but 'front of house' reverted to being a rare book shop.

In 2266, Eloise Manuka perfected the forward movement of her time machine. In theory, this allowed the time machine to travel into the future's future. Cam and Petra were engaged as test pilots and closed their bookshop. In January 2267 they left for a journey into the unknown. It was quite an adventure . . . but that's another story.

Thank you for reading IN L.I.E.U. We hope you enjoyed it.

If you would like to be kept informed of further releases from Hague Publishing, why not subscribe to our newsletter at:

www.HaguePublishing.com/subscribe.php

And if you loved the book and have a moment to spare we would really appreciate a short review. Your help in spreading the word is gratefully received.

About The Author

BARRY Dean is a mid-century relic. A fossilised remnant of a young boy born in 1949 in Lithgow.

From his early days as a long-haired muso with attitude, Barry worked as a technician, construction inspector, engineer and engineering consultant before a stint as an expert witness for barristers sparked an interest in writing fiction.

Inspired by the likes of Douglas Adams, Roald Dahl and Terry Pratchett, writing fiction that sits just to the left of reality appeals to Barry's quirkier tendencies.

In his writing, Barry has created a world of his own making, inspired by the music of life, global travel, a love of history and old ruins, and observation. In fact, his first novel The Garden of Emily Washburn (Hague Publishing, 2012) was inspired by watching the Cannes Film Festival and the incongruous sight of a beautiful woman on the arm of a man "with a head like a Picasso painting".

Barry splits his time between the home he shares with wife Theresa on the shores of the River Tamar and indulging a love of travel. At any given time, you can find him immersed in fiction writing, photography, curating a vintage guitar collection, or jamming with other ancient musos.

Hague

Publishing

www.HaguePublishing.com

PO Box 451 Bassendean
Western Australia 6934

www.ingramcontent.com/pod-product-compliance
Lightning Source LLC
Chambersburg PA
CBHW071109100726
47908CB00008B/2319